When the World Wept

Copyright © 2013 Juniper Independent Books
All rights reserved.
ISBN: 1491068108
ISBN 13: 9781491068106

When the World Wept

by Carol Albrecht Dare

Acknowledgments

I owe a great deal to my sisters, Helen Carucci, Joyce Bauermeister, and Audrey Albrecht.

I owe thanks to members of my writers group who gave me many excellent suggestions.

And to Sarge Dare, my husband, who always supported me.

Chapter 1: Juniper, Oregon. 1932

Alice felt a gnawing in the pit of her stomach after the noon break. Though she'd had water and slices of windfall apples that dropped on the road, it was not enough to quiet her hunger pangs. The younger children and her mother, expecting another child, needed milk in the house. Alice refused it; she hungered for the smooth drink. There was nothing else to eat.

Her mouth watered as she watched June finishing a banana on the playground right before the school bell rang.

All afternoon she dreaded her errand. It was up to her. Mother had the youngsters to look after. Dad was off looking for work in California. He'd told his family, "If I can't find work in California, I'll ride the rails to Washington and I'll march with the Bonus Army."

"What's the Bonus Army, Dad?" Emma asked, looking up from the worn copy of *Heidi* that she read to little Jennie.

"They're veterans promised extra cash for their service in the Great War. We need the money now." John Bauer polished and buffed his shoes as he talked.

It was up to Alice. The family depended on her.

With a worried look on her face, her mother had explained to Alice what she must do. At age twelve, Alice felt the family's deep shame as she listened to her mother. She had heard about poverty.

"Her family's dirt poor," June had said to her classmates as they talked about a girl they all knew, dismissing her from further discussion.

After the dismissal bell rang, Alice lingered behind the other children, shuffling papers, pretending to straighten her desk. If she waited until they all went home, no one would see where she went.

When she finally arrived at the building, she cringed to see some classmates from school hanging around nearby, chatting and laughing. The boys jostled and punched each other. Alice stopped and gazed in a store window.

Time dragged. When the children noticed her, they walked her way.

"What are all those dirty spots on your face, Alice?" one boy asked, referring to her freckles.

June, her blond curls swinging, smiled. "Hi, Alice. I've admired your dress *so often*. Got something to do around here?"

"Are you headed for this building, Alice?" Merle asked.

"My folks say the Bauers are poor as church mice," June said to the others. "Their kids will never amount to anything."

Alice's face burned with shame. Saying nothing, she walked away and continued all around the block. They were still there when she rounded the last corner. Mother would be waiting for her. The office might close.

Shoulders straight, she held her head high and walked past the children as they chided and insulted her. She felt more miserable than she had ever felt in her young life when she entered the relief office to ask for agricultural commodities. They were still there when she came out with her arms full. She heard them snicker behind her back as she walked away.

*　*　*

THE GREAT DEPRESSION. MARCH 1938

Alice decided halfway through high school that she wanted to become a nurse. She wished to help sick people and earn a steady income. Never again did she want to wonder whether there was enough money to pay the rent and buy groceries. She was tired of being laughed at in school for her worn shoes.

She intended to have a steady career, not just some menial job while she waited for Mr. Right. Besides, she wanted to leave Juniper. She had often felt stifled by the small-town mentality and the lack of diversity in the community.

Waiting at home was her carefully polished application for Portland nursing school. Mrs. Johnson, her science teacher, told her that she had mailed in a reference for her that morning.

She needed another reference, but she also needed more money to supplement her savings. With only three months until graduation, she decided to ask about her application for a scholarship and perhaps nudge the process along.

Alice sat stiffly in front of Miss Webb, the head of the Scholarship Committee at Juniper High School. Miss Webb had a reputation for pandering to the most prominent members of the community. Alice had avoided her in the past. She'd only had her for English class. But Miss Webb could not influence her class grade now.

"There's only so much money to go around." Miss Webb pursed her thin lips.

Alice tried to look sympathetic. "I realize that, but my grades are very high."

Miss Webb shuffled some papers on her desk. "You've gotten some Bs."

Alice hadn't expected that. Still, she had an excellent record. "Miss Webb, I'm in the running to be salutatorian of the class."

Miss Webb curled her lips. "The final grades aren't in yet."

"Even so…"

"I see your father is unemployed."

"He's hoping to get on at the mill soon."

"Nevertheless, he's unlikely to give you any financial help."

"Of course. That's why I need the scholarship."

Miss Webb was silent. At last she said, "A scholarship cannot pay the full cost of training for three years to become a nurse."

"I know that. I work after school and on weekends at the Jiffy Café. I've saved some money."

"Perhaps you should have saved enough to pay your own way at nursing school."

"I've saved every penny I possibly could."

"But you still need money. Well, Alice, you have set your sights too high. Your family history doesn't suggest you'd succeed with higher-level training."

Alice gaped. "My mother is a teacher."

"A substitute teacher, which suggests she has not bothered to keep her credentials current."

"She has my two little sisters at home to look after. Anyway, I fail to see what that has to do with it."

"You fail to see." Miss Webb shook her head as if Alice was hopeless. "Your records indicate you've done well in typing class."

"I…don't want to be a typist."

"We sometimes have no choice in these matters." Alice sensed Miss Webb was enjoying her own words.

Alice stood. "Am I getting a scholarship or not?"

"Well, you don't need to be snippy. You could obtain a typing job right here in Juniper."

How dare she tell Alice where to live? "Where I choose to work is none of your business."

Miss Webb raised her eyebrows. "I've always heard that redheads have hot tempers. With that kind of an attitude, you'll not get a scholarship. I'll be urging the committee not to approve your application."

Alice reeled. She'd counted on a scholarship all along. But Miss Webb had taught at the school for years. She had the power to block her scholarship. Now Alice would have to go somewhere else for money with no idea where.

She steeled herself for her next request. "Will you at least write me a letter of reference?"

"I think not. You're unlikely to succeed at nursing school, and your attitude is reprehensible. I intend to mention this to the rest of the staff here at Juniper High School."

Alice's heart sank. As she walked to her after-school job, she tried to think what she should do next. She'd get no scholarship money. Miss Johnson's recommendation was already in the mail. But she needed at least two references. Where could she get her second one if Miss Webb turned the entire staff against her?

She thought about appealing to the principal, but she knew he was unlikely to help. He seemed to have no interest in the students.

Chapter 2

Alice's father landed a steady sawmill job at last. Though he had worked only one week, the knowledge made Alice cheerful, despite her own troubles. She could hold her head high. Her father had a job.

For years he had worked part-time or occasionally, earning meager wages. Recently he had loaded railroad cars and was paid by the car. It was not steady work. When he tried to sell automobiles, he was a dismal failure. Nobody had any money to buy.

She knew his first pay would go toward back rent, utilities, and unmet family needs. Still, they could look forward to better days.

Last night her mother had splurged on tapioca pudding for dessert.

Now her date with Chet, her senior classmate, seemed an added bonus. Looking forward to a rare movie and popcorn supper, she dressed carefully for the day in her best blue-flowered skirt and a white blouse and sweater.

She wished she had pretty shoes. But the brown oxfords were the only pair of shoes that were suitable. She cut out cardboard to reinforce the soles. On payday, she could get them resoled and sewed up on top.

Before she changed into her white uniform that afternoon, Dixie, another waitress, and Brad, the gangly kitchen helper, noticed her bright skirt, different from the usual faded cotton dresses she wore. She told them about her date.

"Oh, the football star?" Dixie asked.

"Do you know about his reputation?" Brad asked, with a slight frown.

Alice ignored his comment. She'd scorned Emma's advice not to date Chet. Just petty small-town gossip, typical of Juniper.

The only thing Alice liked about Juniper was the distant view of snow-capped mountains—Mount Jefferson, the Three Sisters, and even Three-Fingered Jack in some places. Otherwise the town was surrounded by too much sagebrush and too many rocks. She had visited Aunt Kate and Aunt Edith in an intermountain valley town to the west and admired the wealth of evergreens, flowers, and color.

Chet, driving an old truck, often stopped off at the Jiffy Café in the afternoons when he shopped for supplies. When Alice finished her shift on Friday, the two walked around the corner to the Majestic Theater. After the film, they sipped strawberry sodas at the hotel food counter, and she told him about her dream to train as a nurse.

Chet dabbed his mouth with a napkin and set it down carefully on the table. He eyed her suggestively and smirked, "Don't nurses get to see men naked?"

"Well, of course, it's all part of the job. But not the important part."

"Well, what is the important part?"

"Getting them food, changing their beds, tending their wounds, giving them medicine, making them comfortable. It truly is an honorable profession. My aunt Freda is a nurse."

"I'm not sure everybody would agree with you," Chet said, paying their bill on the way out.

"And it provides a better living than most jobs for women."

They chatted about the movie until Alice noticed with irritation that Chet had stopped the truck on a deserted side road some distance from her house. "I have to get home, Chet," she said. "I have a hard day tomorrow."

"We won't be long." He pulled her toward him and held her face in his hands while he kissed her.

"Please take me home." She drew away. "My parents will be worried if I'm out too late." Couldn't he be satisfied with a kiss at her door?

The stop was so transparent. She had petted with Cliff though; they had been steadily dating before his family moved away.

"Well, then, let's hurry up. Maybe you need some training for nursing." He laughed, groping her breast and holding her close with the other arm as he tried to kiss her again. Did he think that because she was poor she'd be easy?

She struggled away. "If you don't take me home now, I'll get out and walk."

His face hardened. "OK, OK," he said and started the engine. "What the hell are you saving it for? If you're going to be a nurse, you'd better get some practice."

"Go to Helena," she said as she slammed the truck door shut at her house. Did everyone believe that all nurses were tramps?

Chet was a handsome athlete. It was a shame he was such a hateful person. She supposed that was the last she would see of him. Well, good riddance. She barely knew him anyway. The only reason she went out with him was because June, who actually had a crush on him, had taunted her, and Dixie, who worked at the café, had urged her to go out more.

Alice fumed as she stomped upstairs past Fred's room. In the girls' room, Jennie, age twelve, slept on a cot next to the double bed. Emma looked up from her homework as Alice entered.

"Bad date?" she asked. "You're scowling. Did you have to walk home?"

"That Chet Southwick is a wolf." Alice undressed, flinging her clothes on the bed. "He thinks all nurses are sluts. Be careful not to ever date him. You were right about him. He wants just one thing." She yanked on her flannel nightgown and slipped into her robe.

"And what would that be?" Emma affected an innocent smile and batted her wide blue eyes. Alice thought it big of her to refrain from mentioning that she had advised against the date with Chet.

"The same as all of them, it seems. I'm going to stop dating entirely."

"That's what all the girls say, but none of them stops."

Still upset about Chet, Alice decided to mail her application for nursing school the next day. She was sick and tired of Juniper and its people. Somehow she'd get the money and the reference that she needed.

* * *

The next afternoon the male customers who always sat with Chet in the café stared at Alice when she walked in. While she put on her apron and hair net in the back, she asked Dixie why.

"That awful Chet." Dixie shook her head. "I heard him telling some of the other guys earlier that you had gone all the way with him."

"What? Why, that's not true. Why would he say something like that?" Alice's eyes flashed with anger. How could he do such a thing? That was the worst thing to say about a girl after a first date. Her eyes filled with tears as she thought of her ruined reputation.

"Honey, he's just trying to get even with you and make himself seem like Mr. Romeo." The older woman put her arm around Alice.

"Dixie, I can't go out there with everybody believing that." It was humiliating. She covered her face with her hands, wanting to run away.

"Look, Alice, it's your word against his. Just hold your head high and pay no attention to the stares. Most people won't believe it anyway. I certainly don't."

As he peeled potatoes, Brad Mayfield piped up, "I wouldn't believe anything Chet Southwick said. I've heard him tell plenty of lies."

"That's right, and even if it were true, he would be a nasty heel to be talking." Dixie patted her shoulder.

Alice stared at Brad and Dixie. Of course Dixie was right. Rumors should be ignored. Her elders had always told her that. She could not go home anyway. She needed the money if she was going to train at nursing school. She would have to do as Dixie said. She had done nothing to be ashamed of.

But it was difficult. As she took orders and served the customers, she tried to ignore the young men who eyed her suggestively. Holding her chin high, she kept a straight face, answered questions tersely, and ran up their checks in the till. Only toward the end of her shift did she relax enough to smile at a couple of female customers.

Even when she got home, she was too humiliated to discuss it with Emma. She decided she would stop dating. She'd become an old maid like Aunt Kate, who seemed to be quite content. A career as a nurse would be fulfilling. Surely not everyone had such a low opinion of nurses as Chet did. But first she had to gain admittance to nursing school.

* * *

At home in his room, Chet nursed his bruised ego. *That little slut. I'll ruin her reputation in this town. Plenty of girls would like to spread their legs for me. Who the hell does she think she is anyway with that red hair and freckles? Poor trash, that's what her family is. Don't own a damn thing. I'll get even sometime.*

* * *

In the school hallway, Alice stared past Chet and swept by him. At work she avoided his table when he came in to eat. He tried to talk to her, but she sailed off as he scowled. Eventually the rude rumor was forgotten by everyone except Alice.

Brad and Dixie were both sympathetic. Dixie always took Chet's table so Alice would not have to wait on him. "He's a jerk," Brad told her, his dark eyes brimming with indignation. "You're wise to ignore him."

Chapter 3

The next weekend, Aunts Kate and Edith Bauer rumbled up to the house in Kate's Model T Ford. The women burst in with laughter and energy, their arms full of gifts—coffee, cans of chocolate, and a sack of bananas. They hugged everyone before settling down for a visit in the kitchen to avoid waking the little girls, asleep in their parents' bedroom downstairs.

Almost as old as their father, Aunt Kate happily chatted with John and Gloria about old friends and relatives. Edith was considerably younger and was finishing her teacher training, living with Kate, and working part-time as a housekeeper in various homes.

Turning serious, Kate said, "John, you're lucky to have the sawmill job. In our area, the mills are laying men off again."

"Yes, but we never know when there might be layoffs at the mill. There are plenty of trees—ponderosa pine and Douglas fir—in the mountains. But not much demand."

"Valley farmers have suffered too. They've lost their land because they couldn't pay their mortgages. And the drought hasn't helped."

"Let's hope President Roosevelt can bring the country further out of the doldrums."

"Edith has lined up jobs with six families for the summer—one house for each day of the week."

"At least more housekeeping will be a change from classes." Edith wore a cheerful but somewhat resigned expression.

"I have your navy dress ready, Kate." Gloria spread out the garment, graced with a white lace collar, a remnant from her own more prosperous days. "I used Alice as a model since she is about the same size as you are. And I'm almost finished with your dress, Edith."

"Oh, you're fast."

"The girls can help me with the hem tomorrow so you can take it with you. You should try it on in case it needs any adjusting."

Kate held the navy garment up in front of her. "This dress might even make me look good."

She was actually an attractive woman with sparkling blue eyes, wavy brown hair, and a willingness to see humor in nearly everything. Since she was in her late thirties, Alice wondered why she had never married.

"And I brought some emerald-green material for you, Alice, for your graduation. It should go well with your red hair."

"Thank you, Kate." Alice caressed the new cotton fabric. "Mother has a plan to use it for another occasion. Because Emma is taller than I am, Mother wants to make the seams larger than normal so she can take them out and redo them for Emma's graduation next year."

"What an ingenious idea. It will complement Emma's blond hair. Gloria is so clever."

John chuckled. "Our girls are the best dressed in town due to Gloria's sewing."

Gloria blushed. "Oh, go on, you two. You exaggerate, John." She pretended modesty, but she saw her dressmaking as her one chance to use her skills creatively, to stand out. None of her other household duties gave her such pleasure.

Alice set the cloth down. "I probably won't wear it much in the meantime, except perhaps to church. It's too good for every day."

"Alice might go to nursing school in Portland," Emma said.

Kate turned to Alice. "I didn't know you were considering that."

"It's not a new idea. I've checked out several nursing schools. But I doubt I can save enough money for some time."

"Money, money, money, always the problem. You might get some help," Edith said, with a knowing smile. "I certainly am."

"When I graduate next year, I'll try for the work-for-tuition program at the college here," Emma said. "Dad found out about it."

"Are you still interested in teaching?" Edith hid a yawn. It had been a long drive. Her eyes were wide with fatigue.

"Oh, yes. I'm going to follow my two favorite aunts into the field."

"Better not let Freda or Gloria's sisters hear you call us favorites." Kate stood up to seek her bedroom for the night. "Hey, wake me up when this Depression is over, will you?"

As Kate headed upstairs, she thought of her youth in Juniper and of the man whose love for her long ago kept her tied to this town over the years. Where was he now? What was he doing? So close but so far away.

* * *

The next day, as the family ate oatmeal and toast, Gloria said, "Alice, take Kate for a walk after we eat. Hike down to the creek. Show her the new houses farther out. You know how she enjoys your company."

Alice and Kate headed away from their house on the edge of town toward the scattered juniper trees and through the sage bushes and bunchgrass. In the distance loomed rugged bluffs. A railroad trestle spanned a deep gorge.

Tumbleweeds rolled in front of them, reminding Alice that in some areas of the West, people were burning it for fuel. At least her family still burned coal in the front room stove.

"I've heard," Kate said, "that ancient people made sandals out of the sagebrush that grows so abundantly here."

"I wish I knew how to make them. I could use some for summer."

Kate said, "So you're applying to nursing school."

"Yes, I am, but I have no idea how I can actually go. I won't be able to save enough this summer to pay the tuition and other costs."

"I know it seems impossible." Kate plucked a sprig of sagebrush in order to better absorb its pungent odor. "But things have a way of working out. You'll be able to earn your room and board. That's what your Aunt Freda did."

"But I won't have the start-up money for tuition and uniforms."

"When I started my teacher training, it seemed impossible, but I stuck with it. Now I'm able to help my younger brothers and sisters by loaning them money to get the training they want."

"You helped raise Freda and Edith, didn't you?" Alice knew that Grandma Bauer had died young.

"Well, it was mostly John and Gloria. Now if you can't save the money, I'll give you what you need to get started. You can repay me by helping your younger sisters and Fred with schooling if you ever get a chance."

The offer took Alice's breath away. She tilted her head and studied Kate. "That's very generous of you. Are you sure you want to do that?"

Kate nodded. "It's true that some teachers in poorer communities have been paid in produce and anything else the community has to offer, but I've been paid in cash so far. And what else do I have to spend my money on? You and the others are my only nieces, and Fred is my only nephew."

Alice remembered that Kate sometimes bought new shoes for Fred and all her nieces. She'd always been a doting aunt.

"Do you realize that some people think nursing is not a very respectable occupation?" Alice asked. "Iris Reynolds told me nursing was vulgar, that I might see men undressed. And she knows I have a younger brother. I've been babysitting for some time. Who does she think changes the diapers? Of course, she told me that *she* never babysits."

Kate laughed. "Well, Iris wouldn't have. Her family has owned a portion of this town since its beginning. I wouldn't let ignorance bother me. Nursing provides a decent, steady living, and it's an honorable profession. Look at Freda for your role model. She's now teaching student nurses in California."

"Will things ever get better, Kate?" Alice kicked a big rock, stirring up dust. "I know we don't have it as bad as others, but it seems we're always facing an emergency of some kind."

Kate linked her arm through the younger woman's. Of similar size and coloring, they could almost be sisters, except for the difference in hair color and the slight wrinkling around Kate's eyes. "I think that President Roosevelt's policies are working. Things are much better than they were when he took office."

Alice shrugged and grinned. "If you say so, it's got to be true, Kate."

"Thanks, but I'm not quite that brilliant." Kate became pensive. "John and Gloria and I weathered three difficult years in Wyoming. In our second and third years, I taught in an old mining shack.

"I arrived at dawn to sweep the floors and carry water from the well. We used fruit crates for desks and shared books. I sometimes spent the evenings copying out an extra chapter to use the next day."

"It's remarkable that you managed." Alice pictured them in the small shack, working by the light of a kerosene lamp.

"Well, it didn't hurt me. Things got better when I started teaching in the Willamette Valley."

"Shall we invite the others for a walk downtown? Mother needs some green thread from the store, and the kids enjoy a walk with you and Edith. I have to work this afternoon."

"By all means. Let's see the metropolis one more time. Lead on, future Nurse Alice."

* * *

Their town looked much like hundreds of others in the western part of the country. An old but well-kept hotel, a bank, a couple of restaurants, several retail establishments, a seedy tavern, a post office, and the movie theater, featuring a Shirley Temple film, graced its main street.

A friendly housewife, doing her shopping, called out a greeting to the group. Realizing that Kate and Edith were among them, she stopped to talk.

"Kate, how good to see you. How is the teaching going? Haven't seen you in years." They all stopped while Kate and Edith visited.

The two-year college on a nearby hill was the town's most striking feature. The party of children ran up and down the building steps, jogged around the huge brick classroom building, and cavorted in the playing fields.

Alice laughed at their antics. Though she sometimes found them to be obnoxious burdens, she also enjoyed Jennie, Fred, and Linda with their high spirits, exuberance, and boundless energy.

Why had their parents had so many children? Not many of her friends were in families as large as six.

* * *

For days Alice worried about how to get the second reference required by nursing school. With Kate's money, she could manage the expenses of nursing school. Why did the nursing school officials need another reference? They knew she was a good student because she had sent the required transcript of her school grades to the Portland nursing school.

She believed that Miss Webb had ruined her name with the other teachers. Maybe a character reference from somewhere else would suffice.

She went to Mrs. Gillis, who, with her husband, owned the Jiffy Café. "Why, of course, Alice," Mrs. Gillis said, as she checked bubbling pots and sizzling meat cooking on the grill. "I'll write a letter to your nursing school. You're a good worker. But be careful what you wish for. I know for a fact that nursing school is grueling. My sister-in-law dropped out because she couldn't handle the long hours."

"Oh, thank you, Mrs. Gillis." Alice could barely contain her relief. "I know it will be difficult, but I want to be a nurse so badly that I'd do almost anything."

* * *

That spring, Alice heard a customer mention Germany's union with Austria, making Hitler's Germany more powerful than before. She thought of her father, who had more than a passing interest in Germany. His parents had emigrated from there before he was born. He still corresponded with a cousin in the old country, who seemed displeased with fascism.

Besides, John Bauer had fought in the Great War, hoping to right wrongs against Belgium and to end all wars. Mussolini's invasion of Ethiopia, Japan's invasion of China, and Adolf Hitler's takeover of areas in Europe caused him to rant and rave.

Meanwhile, her mother heard from her sister, Pearl, in New York, whose Jewish friends frantically tried to get their desperate relatives out of Germany and Austria because of Hitler's brutal treatment of them.

At her high school graduation, Alice walked to the stage in her new emerald-green dress. Kate, sitting with her family, proudly watched. As chairman of the school board, Grant Hunter handed her the certificate and shook her hand, smiling broadly, until it seemed he reluctantly released it. She thought he was a very pleasant man.

Her first goal had been realized. She had finished high school, unlike many students who were forced to drop out to help on farms and ranches or contribute to the family income in other ways. She now had as much education as her parents. Her mother and Aunt Kate had studied to become teachers in the two-year normal school after ten years of public schooling.

Alice started working full-time at the café with Brad, who had graduated from high school earlier. She saved as much money as she could for the day she started to train as a nurse.

* * *

Summers were always dry. The dust stirred up by wagons and automobiles got into the mouth and eyes and the open windows of homes. The sun beat down on the dusty brown grass and sage, and the few flowers in town drooped.

At dinner around a scratched table covered with a worn oilcloth, Jennie said, "How come the marine air everybody talks about never has any rain in it?"

"Most of the moisture is dumped in the two mountain ranges west of us or in the valley between," Gloria told her. "Yet the valley doesn't get much water in the summer either, according to Kate. Try some cool water on your face and arms. Or better still, go wading in the creek."

Jennie laughed. "Have you been to the creek lately? There's barely any water in it."

Their dad recalled the terrible dust storm in the spring of 1931. "Dust blew everywhere for a day and a night, coming from as far away as Montana. And it blew onto ships in the Pacific Ocean. This is not nearly as bad."

"Remember how your Aunt Pearl's husband asked when they visited from New York, 'Doesn't it ever rain here?'" Gloria said.

Fred laughed. "Yes, and Dad told him that it did once."

"It's a good thing he saw a sprinkle while he visited, or he would have believed your father," Gloria said.

* * *

At the restaurant, the heat made it difficult for Alice and the other waitresses to keep their white uniforms looking fresh and their hair to stay curled. The dry summers affected the grazing areas on the mountain slopes and the crops grown for cattle feed. Ranchers were hurting.

As she waited on customers, Alice heard about their problems. Farmers and ranchers got behind on their mortgages and faced foreclosures.

Men roamed the country looking for work. When they walked by the railroad tracks, the girls and Fred watched the trains zoom by, filled with men riding in empty cars, seeking a better life somewhere else.

Sometimes a man would knock at the back door and ask their mother for a meal. If she had anything to spare, she would give it to him, asking him to chop some wood at the woodpile before he left. She thought the men would feel better if they earned their food. They always left a large pile of chopped wood, stacked up and ready for the kitchen stove.

Alice heard nothing about her application for nursing school during the summer. But she was relieved to hear that she could continue working at the café full time. She saved every penny she earned.

It was an exciting day when John Bauer drove home in an old Model T Ford that he'd bought in halves with Gloria's sister, Dorothy Turner, and her husband. Fred looked it over from top to bottom. John took the whole family for a ride in the country. Now John and Russ could ride together to the sawmill with other workers as paying passengers to help defray the cost of gasoline. The steady pay the men earned at the mill provided both families with some security.

Now Gloria wouldn't have to trudge all over town to do her errands. When she substituted in a school, John could drive her to work before he left for the mill.

All summer Alice waited for word about her application to nursing school. She became concerned. New students would be starting their training, and she would not be among them.

Chapter 4

In September, while interested Americans and most of Europe sighed in relief when Neville Chamberlain claimed that he had secured "peace in our time," Alice worried about nursing school.

Alice's father listened to the radio at the Turner house as H. V. Kaltenborn reported on the crisis in Europe. Hitler had assured European leaders that he would occupy only the German-speaking portion of Czechoslovakia and no more.

At home John said fighting was a brutal, thankless business that settled nothing. He moaned to his family that it seemed to him that Europe was heading for a gigantic disaster all over again, despite the paper agreement the British prime minister reportedly waved in the air.

Alice thought about the millions of young men in Europe who might die in a war. The Great War had been a terrible tragedy for the world.

"Thank God for Mr. Chamberlain," Russ said when he and Aunt Dorothy visited the next day.

"I wonder." John stroked his chin. "Hitler's been very aggressive. Do you really think this will satisfy him?"

John kept a map of the world spread out on a small table in his living room and consulted it every time Hitler made a move in Europe. In addition, he kept a notebook handy to keep track of events going on in the world.

Passing by on her way upstairs, Alice observed him poring over the map or scribbling in his little notebook. He sometimes called everyone over after the evening meal to show his family where all the countries with the strange-sounding names were located.

"You know, Dad, we study geography in school," Fred said. "My history teacher read Hitler's *Mein Kampf* in German, in which Hitler outlined his plans for expansion. He borrowed the book from a friend who got a copy when he visited Germany, since the book was not available anywhere else."

John's cousin in Germany wrote that hundreds of Jewish shops were wrecked and looted by Nazi thugs. When the owners protested, they were beaten by the troops. Some were killed. Synagogues were burned in the tragedy called *Kristallnacht*.

Cousin Helmut and his colleagues were greatly disturbed by the attacks, but the German government claimed it knew nothing about them.

And now Jewish property was being confiscated. Cousin Helmut, a university professor, had worked with Jewish professors. Not anymore. They had all left the country after Germany passed laws in 1933 barring Jews from the universities, government service, the professions, and the arts.

Aunt Pearl wrote that New York newspapers had earlier commented on the large number of Jewish refugees in Paris, many of them artists from the movie industry.

* * *

One day John came home with a pleasant distraction. An Italian friend, Antonio, was driving him, Russ, and others to Portland in his truck to buy grapes for wine.

"Apparently," John told the family, "we need to go to the railroad yards and look for boxcars from California that drip juice from the bottom. That will show that the grapes are overripe, just perfect for making wine. We want to buy our grapes from those cars. Russ and I plan to make some wine in his barn."

"How very European," Gloria said. "I haven't tasted wine in years."

"Of course, we can hardly compete with French wine." Suddenly Dad laughed. "Remember Tod who served in France during the Great War? He did a little work, such as he could manage, for my father on the farm. He says he left one arm in France, and that it's now enriching the soil where the wine grapes grow."

"Well, if that's true, there could be thousands of limbs left in France enriching the soil," his wife commented with a touch of irony, remembering the battles in that ravaged land.

* * *

One warm evening Alice sauntered home after dark. It was well past the dinner hour. Radios were tuned to dance music that drifted out the windows (now that Kaltenborn had finished reporting on the crisis). She smiled at a cat slinking away as she crossed a street. She heard a dog barking in the distance.

She was wending her way beyond the blocks of houses, on the path through the sagebrush, when she sensed someone behind her. Turning, she found Chet standing there. Her eyes narrowed. "Why are you going this way?"

"Oh, I just thought I'd get what I had coming to me." Suddenly he grabbed her, pinning her arms. He covered her mouth with a huge hand and pulled her to the ground with him.

Chapter 5

Squirming sideways, Alice clawed the dirt. Chet lost his grip on her mouth. As he struggled to overpower her, she cried out.

"Stop it! What are you doing?" She shoved him off, pushing her fist into his face. He recoiled. She tried to scramble away, but he grabbed her skirt. Breaking away from his grasp, she darted off. But she stumbled on a sage bush and fell to the ground screaming.

"What is wrong with you? Are you crazy? Help! Help!"

He fell on top of her. "Shut up!" Chet began to grope at her clothes.

She kicked and pushed, trying to escape his clutches. "Get your hands off of me!"

"Hold still, you little bitch."

Terrified, she scratched at his face and eyes, and his grasp loosened for a second. In that second, she shoved him away and sprinted off. It seemed her only chance to get away from his clutches.

Chet jumped up and started after her. But Brad suddenly appeared, blocking Chet's way. "What do you think you're doing?"

Chet stumbled backward. "Leave us alone, for Christ's sake. We're on a date, you skinny jerk."

Alice stopped and pulled her blouse straight. "He attacked me!"

Brad stepped threateningly toward Chet. "You liar," he thundered. "Get out of here. And don't come near her again."

Chet gave Brad a shove and then disappeared into the darkness before he could recover. They heard him snarling. "Damn jerk, stupid bitch."

Brad turned toward Alice. "Are you all right?"

"Yes, yes, I'm so glad you came along." She brushed dirt off her skirt.

"I saw him take off after you and thought I'd see what he had in mind. Let me walk you home. I'd like to walk you home every night, if you'll let me."

"Thanks, Brad." Alice straightened her hair. "Yes, please walk home with me." She didn't like to impose on Brad, but she didn't want to walk alone. "I had no idea he could be so obnoxious."

"He's more dangerous than he looks. We should report him to the police."

"Oh no, Brad. It's my word against his." Alice knew that accusations of rape were rarely prosecuted because there was no way to prove who was telling the truth. And attempted assaults were even less likely to be taken seriously. People assumed that the woman was at fault by putting herself in a vulnerable position. Besides, her family would be embarrassed if she were the subject of a controversy.

"They'll just think I did something to bring this on. I want to forget about it."

Brad's face was grave. "All right. We'll let it go if you're sure you don't want to go to the police."

At home that night Alice told Emma about the attack. "You were right about Chet. Your instincts are better than mine. I was foolish to ever go out with him in the first place. He's good-looking but so shallow, and violent too."

"It sounds as though he has many faults. Be careful not to let him get anywhere near you again."

"The worst part is that he has sullied my name with all his friends by telling them outrageous lies. He's made up things that never happened between us."

"Oh, Alice, I'm so sorry. Don't think about it. It will pass. The sun will come up tomorrow just the same."

* * *

In late fall Alice came home to find Jennie greeting her at the door. "You've got a letter."

"A letter? Where?"

"On the kitchen table. What could it be? It's in a big envelope."

Alice read the return address. The nursing school. Hands trembling, she ripped the envelope open.

Jennie waited. "What does it say?"

It was Alice's acceptance to nursing school for the winter term. She was elated and began to dance and sing about the room. "I'm going. I'm going."

Jennie danced and sang with her. "Where? Where?"

"I'm going to nursing school." With funds from Aunt Kate, she could manage. She would leave in January, and she eagerly began to make her preparations.

Then, just weeks before Christmas, John Bauer was laid off. What would the family live on? Maybe she should stay and give them her meager salary. Plenty of young people were forced to do that. With a heavy heart, she talked to her mother.

Chapter 6

"What a ridiculous idea," Gloria said when Alice suggested staying to support the family. "We'll get by somehow. It's very good of you, Alice, but Mrs. Walker asked me to make her daughter a dress, and she'll pay me. Don't worry. We'll manage."

When John was out of work, an anonymous donor left bags of groceries on the porch during the night along with a ten-dollar bill. The first time she found the bag, a note was included: "A gift for your family from a well-wisher."

Gloria had cried in relief. The money had paid the rent and the food fed the family for two weeks. Though she wondered who had left the presents, she was in no position not to use them.

* * *

Alice considered what her mother had said. Aunt Kate had urged Alice to get her training at all costs. Kate wanted her to go. The folks wanted her to go. She yearned to go.

Sometimes when Alice heard the train whistle blowing, she felt a great longing to be somewhere, anywhere, else. She felt soiled in Juniper since Chet had spread false rumors about her.

Besides, to help her younger sisters and brother, she had to train as a nurse.

* * *

"I wonder if Fred is too old to get a slingshot this year." Emma consulted her Christmas list before bedtime. "It would be easy to make one from a Y-shaped tree branch with a piece of rubber stretched between."

Alice brushed her long hair, working on the one hundred strokes as their mother had recommended. Jennie slept on her cot, her dampened brown locks of hair rolled over strips of rags to curl it for Sunday school the next day. They were the poor girl's substitute for expensive curlers or permanents.

"Let's go in together and get him a model airplane kit so he can build another plane. He loves to do that."

"Like his room isn't already filled with sticks and tissue paper. Cleaning that room is like working around raw eggs. Well, we might as well *surprise* him."

"I'm thinking of getting Jennie a puzzle."

"Jennie gets to work plenty of puzzles at Cecelia's house, Alice. And she reads comic books over there too. Why don't we go together and get her a real book—say, *Little Women*."

"Fine. As it happens, Iris offered me a few of her books that she's already read. Maybe one of them would be suitable for Jennie."

"What would you like?"

Alice sat down on the bed beside Emma. "I have an idea. Why don't we skip gifts for each other and get the folks a radio for Christmas. You know how Dad likes to know what's going on. We'd all benefit from it. We could listen to music and news."

"A good idea. Together, we just might be able to afford it."

"For the little girls, we can make some doll clothes. I can start by using this old blouse that I'm wearing." Alice pointed to a rip under the arm, too large to repair.

"And, since I'll be wearing a nurse's uniform most of the time, I'll leave the green graduation dress for you to keep until you need it."

* * *

As they walked to church the next day through falling snow, Emma and Alice watched the younger children picking it up and trying to make snowballs. If it continued, they would be able to play in the snow and make snowmen later.

Brad fell into step with them as he often did on Sundays. Today Alice, Emma, and Brad stayed for the church service, letting the other children go home to their mother and daddy.

Gloria seldom went to church, claiming she had no clothes to wear, and it was true that she possessed only a few faded housedresses and some worn shoes.

She owned an old hat and gloves but had not worn them for years. All of her jewelry had been sold before they left for Wyoming, and her fancy clothes had been redone for her daughters.

When the three young people started home, Brad scooped up some snow and pelted the girls with snowballs. They returned the fire, and before long Naomi and her friend, Roy, and other young people had joined in. Missiles flew in all directions, and everyone ducked to avoid being hit.

"Naomi can't hit the broad side of a barn," Roy shouted.

Naomi gathered up snowballs. "We'll see about that." Several snowballs smashed against him as the rest of them all laughed.

Brad chased Alice until she stumbled and fell to the ground, laughing. He playfully rubbed snow on her cheeks. When his face leaned into hers, she noticed that his pimples were disappearing and that his strong features were becoming more pronounced.

For a moment they stared at each other. Then Brad scrambled to his feet and offered her a hand up. As she and Emma left the others, Alice realized it was the first time she had laughed in days.

* * *

As the time for her departure approached, Dixie and Brad at the Jiffy Café teased Alice about moving to Portland. "You'll probably become a snob with all that training," Dixie said. "You'll work for rich families and never talk to us again."

Brad looked pensive. "I'll miss walking you home, Alice. Watch out for the city slickers. Portland's not like Juniper, you know. Keep your money hidden in your clothes or they'll steal you blind."

"Listen to you two. Anybody would think that I was going to New York City. It's only Portland. I'll be visiting my family here sometimes, and I'll see both of you now and then. I'll never forget you."

Dixie touched her shoulder. "Honey, we both wish you the very best."

"I may be moving to Portland soon myself," Brad announced. "I've been saving for it a long time."

Chapter 7

Before Alice went to Portland, her father said to her, "You've always done well in school, Alice. I don't suppose I have to tell you to study hard."

"No, Dad. I wouldn't want to disappoint you and Mother and Aunt Kate. I'll do my best."

"I want you to know you can always come home to stay if you want."

"I know." She kissed his cheek. He had a hard time saying goodbye. She would miss him too.

She remembered their younger days when he had taken Emma and her for walks and read *Heidi* to them at bedtime. Later he read it to Fred and Jennie. He was reading it now to Linda and Marie.

John and Gloria decided to drive Alice to Portland and spend the night with Dad's younger brother and his wife while they were there. They took the other children along and planned to leave them with Uncle Ernst and Tess while they drove Alice to Marquam Hill. The hospital and dormitory stood at the top, high above Portland.

They all piled into the old jalopy and left the sage and canyons behind. They plodded through winter roads, tire chains thudding, over Mt. Hood, and through the town of Government Camp, marveling at the amount of snow piled against the sides of the road and up the cliffs.

Dad took them to have a look at Timberline Lodge on Mount Hood, situated at six thousand feet on the south sloop. Built by the Work Projects Administration, a program started by the Roosevelt administration to put people to work on needed public projects, President

Franklin D. Roosevelt had dedicated it in 1937. In his speech, Roosevelt had visualized thousands and thousands of visitors in the years to come, looking east to livestock-raising areas, and west to wood-using industries.

"I wanted to work on the building," John said, "but it was just too far away from my family." He winked at his wife, who rewarded him with a smile.

It was early in January when Alice and her parents presented themselves at the nurses' dormitory behind the Multnomah County Hospital. A small building, it included a basement and three floors of rooms. A fourth level, called a penthouse, was in the middle of a black-topped roof. Only senior students could live in the penthouse.

The dormitory supervisor, Mrs. Watson, showed them the room that had been assigned to Alice on the second floor. Three narrow beds would hold the occupants, and they were to share a bathroom with three more student nurses.

"This is the only time the students will be permitted to have men in their rooms," the woman told John. "Bed check is at ten thirty p.m."

The rooms all had doors with frosted glass panels. Besides the three beds, there was a desk and chair and a tall chest of drawers, two drawers to a student.

After the director of nursing welcomed them, uniforms for the students were brought into their rooms. Although each girl had sent in her measurements, few of the garments fit the person who had ordered them.

"Golly, I'll never be able to wear this." A tall girl named Rose held up one of the dark gray dresses, which hit her above the knees.

"It might do for me," Alice said. "But what can you do? Mine won't fit you even though it is too long for me."

"She can have this one," another tall girl said. "I'll have to find something from someone else."

So by switching around and by shortening and lengthening the hems, the students were outfitted in their three dresses to go with the other basics of their uniforms: four collars, three cuff sets, twelve aprons, and twelve bibs.

The uniforms cost $33.50, and students paid a matriculation fee of five dollars, tuition of forty-five dollars, building fee of one dollar, room and board (for the first three months only) of forty dollars, and ten dollars for books. Without the money that Aunt Kate had given her, Alice would not have been able to afford it.

Alice quickly discovered that the other students came from more affluent families than she did, but she determined to work harder than anybody to prove her ability to make the grade.

The next morning the students started their eight-hour workdays and the sixteen hours of classes they would take each week. They were sent to the wards immediately and assigned to carry food trays and to feed the most helpless patients. They were recognized as students by their lack of caps.

Next they learned to make beds and give bed baths. After breakfast they worked a couple of hours, took a morning class, had a short meal break, worked a few more hours, took an afternoon class, got another meal break, and spent two hours in patient care in the evenings.

Dana LaRue and Alice often worked in the same ward. "I'm so tired," Alice said to her roommate one evening after the end of their shift. "When are we supposed to get our studying done? Mrs. Watson will be around soon for bed check, and we don't dare have any lights on."

"Do what Rose and I do." Dana pulled a flashlight out from under her pillow. "Get yourself one of these and use it to read under the covers."

"What if someone sees the light outside?"

"What if we don't make the probationary period because of poor grades?"

Alice bought a flashlight and studied every night as long as she could stay awake. She had to adjust to the grueling routine if she wanted to become a nurse.

Mornings were busy, as the rooms had to be left neat with beds made and clothes hung up in case of room checks. In the evenings, the girls took turns washing their hair, their cotton stockings, and their undergarments in the bathroom sink.

The rooms were cleaned for the students once a week when they were given fresh linen. And once a week their uniforms were laundered and returned.

Besides nursing procedures, the students took anatomy, physiology, chemistry, and elementary *materia medica* (medical drugs). Everyone studied hard, but at the end of the probationary period, nearly a third of the class was weeded out by poor grades, instability, and unsuitability, determined by the personal judgment of the supervisors.

Alice, Rose, and Dana passed the three-month probationary period, and they and others were capped in a small ceremony. They would now wear the caps the remaining months of their first year.

They were also allowed to buy the blue-gray capes with scarlet lining that cost $14.50. Aunt Kate wanted Alice to have one and paid for it as a gift.

From now on the girls would earn ten dollars a month, and they would not have to pay room and board. From the earnings, most of them would have to save as much as they could manage for tuition and clothing.

Alice, relieved at overcoming the first hurdle, celebrated the capping by reading *All Quiet on the Western Front*, a serious book about the Great War. Someone had given it to her dad, and he suggested she take it with her to read.

Too exhilarated to sleep, Rose and Dana wandered in and out of the bathroom, talking and giggling.

Suddenly they heard the elevator ascending. Alice turned off her flashlight and tucked it with her book under her pillow. Rose and Dana jumped into bed. They heard a gentle rap on the door, and the housemother stuck her head in.

"I saw the light on," she said. "I wondered if anyone is ill."

They assured her they were fine, and she went away. But the young women felt chastised. They had a long way to go, hard work, and many rules to follow before they became nurses.

* * *

In Juniper that spring, John Bauer finally got work on a new highway for the Works Project Administration. It was a relief to have the work, and he found it extremely interesting and challenging. But he complained to his family that the WPA work felt like charity. He disliked it for that reason.

Meanwhile Emma prepared for high school graduation. She would start the work-for-tuition program at the local two-year college in the fall in preparation to teach school.

The Bauer family was chagrined to learn that Hitler's Germany had taken over the rest of Czechoslovakia, marching into Prague on March 15, 1939. Appeasement had failed. Hitler's actions were very warlike and the goose-stepping soldiers anything but friendly.

"That crazy Hitler has snatched more territory," John said, frowning, as he read the newspaper after dinner.

Emma felt her dad's deep disappointment. Since the Great War to end all wars, there had been a civil war in Spain and fighting in Asia. Now hopes for peace in Europe were dimming as Hitler expanded.

Cousin Helmut wrote that he was now in the German army. With his country conscripting men, he had no choice.

Despite the war worries, for Emma the year was golden. Unlike Alice, she loved their home in Juniper. She savored the crisp, dry air on her morning walks to school and inhaled the snappy smell of sagebrush with zest.

Voted a cheerleader in her last two years, she happily juggled her work, studies, and game activities. Cheerleading required practice, which the girls managed during lunch period or in the evenings, meeting at one of their houses.

After school she hurried downtown to work a few hours at the hotel. Sometimes she missed the evening meal at home and made do with food she saved from lunch, or she took a free meal that Grant Hunter offered all his employees at the hotel food counter.

She rarely had time to even date boys, but her best friend, David Walker, had played in all the sports and still showed up at the Friday night games even after he graduated. A large, pleasant young man, he worked on his father's ranch.

Emma remembered when she had first noticed him. He'd driven his mother out one Saturday afternoon to talk to Gloria Bauer about making a special coat for her. Not more than sixteen at the time, he had just started to drive.

While his mother discussed fashion with Gloria, he had waited outside, watching Emma play drop the handkerchief with Jennie, Linda, and some visiting neighbor children.

After a few minutes, Emma had asked mischievously, "Want to play?" Even at fifteen, she knew that no teenage boy would be caught dead playing a children's game.

To her surprise, he had joined the circle, thereby winning her everlasting admiration. "Sure. I think I can run as fast as all of you."

Excited by the new entry, the children had laughed. For a short time, they had basked in the attention from a big boy, to them almost a man.

They had all coveted the opportunity to drop the handkerchief behind him and then outrun him around the circle of players back to his empty place. The cheers and laughter rang through the sage.

These days David usually drove Emma and other cheerleaders home from the game before he and another cheerleader, Odette Glass, began the ten-mile drive to their small community of Springdale.

Odette's family owned one of the largest ranches in the area as well as immense tracts of forestland to the west. She planned to study at an exclusive school for girls after graduation.

She smirked at Emma. "Do you really want to teach a bunch of runny-nosed kids?"

"I like kids," Emma said. "My mother taught before she got married. My aunt Kate is a teacher and she likes it fine. She says teaching kids is touching the future."

"So make sure you never have to touch the kids." Odette swung her black curls around her heart-shaped face and marched off, laughing.

Emma watched her. Odette would never have to think about what to do with her life. With all her family's wealth, she could choose to do nothing at all. She could spend her time reading books, picking roses, and traveling to exotic places.

She had heard that Odette had been dating David recently. In the past he had dated girls his own age, but Odette was as young as Emma. She sighed as she made up beds at the Juniper Hotel.

When Emma finished that evening, Grant Hunter asked, "Is there a game tonight at the high school, Emma?"

"Yes, we're playing Madras. Did you play football in high school?"

"I wasn't big enough or talented enough for football." He gave her a wry smile. "Besides, I worked at the hotel after school. I didn't really have time to practice. In the winter, though, I played basketball. Dad saw to that because he liked the game."

Grant was a distinguished-looking, genial man with hair turning white in streaks among rich russet locks. His sharp, friendly eyes were usually smiling. When the rooms were all made up, he had her scrubbing the kitchen floor, dusting the banister, or cleaning the cupboards.

She hoped it was not make-work. Nobody wanted that.

* * *

Grant found Emma to be a competent worker, gracious to the guests, and pleasant in her dealings with the rest of the staff. The family, while poor, had a good reputation. Still, it was just as well that the older Bauer girl, Alice, with her uncanny resemblance to Kate, never came looking for work. Could he have handled it? The curiosity?

At one time or another, he saw all the comely Bauer children and their parents from the windows of the hotel: John and his brother-in-law, Russ Turner, on their way to work; Gloria, the formerly pampered daughter of a rich rancher, doing her meager shopping with the youngest children; the auburn-haired Alice going to the Jiffy Café; and all the children heading to and from school.

Their life was hard, but he envied them anyway. His own wife had divorced him early in their marriage and had moved away. He had no children. Emma, his youngest employee, was a breath of fresh air in his solitary life.

He remembered when John, Gloria, and Kate Bauer left for Wyoming to homestead. The land turned out to be dry, almost desert. They'd stuck it out three years, just long enough to prove up their claim.

Grant could only imagine the hardships they must have gone through, sixty miles from the nearest town, before they sold out. He had heard that Kate taught the children of other homesteaders and that John worked in coal mining operations in nearby Casper.

Eventually John and Gloria came back to Juniper with two little girls, and Kate went off somewhere to teach school. There was little for John to come back to. His mother was dead. His father was on his deathbed. They left John very little except for the small house they lived in and underage siblings to look after. Ernst and Louis were teenagers and soon out on their own, but Freda and Edith were young children.

John and his family moved in there for a time, caring for the old man, raising the girls with Kate's help during the summers, until their own family got too large and the brothers were gone. By that time the old man was dead.

And Kate? What was her life like? What were her regrets?

Chapter 8

Naomi and Roy were dating steadily. Emma knew they were getting very intimate, but she refrained from asking how intimate, though she had her suspicions from comments that Naomi made. The young couple talked of a life together, but Naomi's parents felt she was too young yet to be planning marriage, and they did not approve of Roy. They wanted her to wait.

One Friday after the ball game, Emma noticed Naomi looking unwell, her usually rosy cheeks white. She seemed to be in pain.

Emma hurried over to her where she sat on the bleachers. "What's wrong?"

"I've got the cramps bad. I think I'm having a miscarriage."

Horrified, Emma asked, "Can you walk home? You're pale. Shall I go with you?" She thought Naomi might faint on the way home.

"No, I'm fine. I'm so relieved. I caused it by rubbing turpentine on my stomach, like the girls at school said. My parents would kill me if they knew about this."

Temporarily dumbfounded, Emma said, "You should see a doctor."

"Are you kidding? We got no money for doctors."

They left the game together. Despite Naomi's protests, Emma decided to walk home with her.

David called to her from the parking lot. "We're waiting for you, Emma. All the cheerleaders are here."

"Go on without me. I'm walking tonight." She stayed close to Naomi until they reached her house, Naomi clutching her abdomen and keeping her head down.

"You must think I'm awful."

"No…I'm worried about you."

"Roy and I are going to get married, you know—as soon as I'm old enough. My folks won't let us get married now. Don't tell anybody, please."

Emma promised not to say anything. Then she hurried through the dark to her own house on the opposite side of town, wondering why Naomi didn't insist on one birth control method the girls talked about: rubbers.

The following Monday at school Naomi seemed to be back to normal. She smiled nervously at Emma and never mentioned the incident again.

When he saw Emma downtown, David said, "I'm glad to see you got home safely Friday night. Sorry you couldn't ride with us. We stopped for sodas."

"Naomi wasn't feeling well, so I thought I should walk home with her."

"That was good of you, but I could have driven her home."

"Thanks. It was nothing serious, but I didn't know that."

David smiled as Emma left him. She was such a thoughtful person. It was two miles or more from Naomi's house to hers.

* * *

One afternoon Grant asked Emma to help out at the food counter. Her first customers were David and Odette. They came for a sandwich in town, as there was a game that night at Juniper High School.

Happy to see her friends, Emma smiled at them, ready to take their order.

"Why, Emma," Odette said. "I didn't know you were a waitress. I thought you were a *maid* here."

"Just for today. The waitress is sick. What would you like?"

Odette said to David in a low voice, but loudly enough for Emma to hear, "I suppose this means our order will take forever. Best order something simple."

Emma flushed, and David looked uncomfortable. "I'm sure Emma will be a fine waitress. She's good at everything else."

Odette looked annoyed. "In that case I'll have a beef sandwich with coffee."

When David ordered, Emma rushed to deliver the order to the kitchen. She felt heartsick. Why had Odette insulted her? They were cheerleaders together. She had admired the pretty brunette and thought they were friends.

Despite Odette's insensitive remarks, David left a large tip for her.

* * *

At home Emma now shared a bed with Jennie, while Linda slept on the cot in their room. Jennie was becoming very quiet and serious. When the family talked of going to spend Decoration Day with Uncle Ernst and Aunt Tess in Portland, where they would have a chance to see Alice, Jennie balked and said she would not go. She would stay overnight with her friend, Cecelia.

Surprised, the family tried to coax her out of her mood. Unable to get her approval, Gloria and John dropped the subject for the time being.

Emma wondered. Perhaps Jennie had a difficult time adjusting to the seventh grade. At twelve, she was younger than most of her classmates. Alone in their bedroom, Emma pressed Jennie. "Why in the world don't you want to see Uncle Ernst and Aunt Tess?"

Finally Jennie blurted out, "He bought us candy, but I still don't like him. When we visited last year, he kissed me on the lips and stuck his tongue in my mouth and wiggled it. It was awful."

Emma could hardly believe what she heard. Jennie did not lie. She was much too confident and bold, and she apparently had never heard of French kissing. "When did this happen?"

"When Aunt Tess took Fred and Linda and Marie to the store."

"But I was there." Emma sank onto the bed.

Jennie picked up a blouse and rummaged through the sewing box for a button. "You were washing the dishes in the kitchen. Mother and Dad were with Alice at the nursing school."

"Tell me what happened."

Jennie threaded her needle. "He got out the candy and gave me some. I was reading a book. Then he kissed me. I don't know why he did that. I felt awful. What would Aunt Tess say?"

Emma remembered the occasion. Everything rang true. She felt a little stab in her heart. She had always liked Uncle Ernst. But right now she wanted to help Jennie understand.

"Jennie, it wasn't your fault. Uncle Ernst shouldn't have done that. I'll talk to Mother, and you won't have to go to their house. You did right to tell me. If something like this happens again, please let me know. Or try to avoid it if you can, as you're doing. You're wise not to go."

"I was afraid to tell Mother and Dad. I thought I had done something wrong, but I didn't know what."

"No, you didn't. It was not your fault at all. There was nothing you could have done."

Emma felt furious at Uncle Ernst. How could he have treated her little sister like that? And Jennie used to love him, more than the others did. Perhaps that was why he had chosen her to violate.

Would their mother believe it? She tended to block out unpleasant thoughts and facts.

"It must be some mistake." Gloria stared in distress when Emma told her about Uncle Ernst kissing Jennie. "Surely he meant nothing by it. We kiss in our family all the time."

"Not like that. Why don't you and Dad go up for Decoration Day, and the rest of us will stay home. I'll look after the others."

"But you're too young for that, and what would your father think? You're certainly not going to mention it to him, his own brother." Gloria's eyes filled with tears.

"I won't mention it, if you let us stay home. It will be a nice weekend for you and Dad."

"But you won't get to see Alice."

"Alice will be coming to see us in a few weeks anyway. We'll enjoy her visit when we're all here. And in the future, you can't leave the girls alone with Uncle Ernst."

Gloria agreed to the bargain but tentatively, it seemed to Emma. She had to accept the responsibility. Emma couldn't mention it to her dad. How could she possibly tell *him*?

She spoke to Alice about it when she saw her. "Why, that old pervert. How could he?" Alice asked. Disturbed, she agreed that they must keep their younger sisters away from Uncle Ernst.

* * *

In Portland, Alice looked forward to her one day off from the Multnomah County Hospital. If she and a friend were free the same day, they would hop a trolley or hike to downtown Portland and take in a movie or window-shop at the glamorous stores.

Once they stopped at the lunch counter at the Woolworth Department Store for a soft drink. Dana chatted about joining the Red Cross as a nurse if she met the requirements.

"What are the requirements?" It sounded interesting to Alice.

"Graduation from an approved nursing school, which ours is, state registration as a nurse, membership in district and state associations of nurses, US citizenship, and twenty-one to forty years of age."

Alice's eyes lit up. "We meet some of those already, and as soon as we graduate, we'll meet the rest."

"Why not join up with me? We'll travel and see the world. They might send us anywhere." Dana's boyfriend was about to join the air corps. "Alan will be gone anyway. I might as well be off on my own."

"Maybe I will." Alice remembered reading about Clara Barton and seeing pictures of her leaning over sick soldiers. Would it be dangerous?

"Alice Bauer." She heard a surprised male voice behind her. When she turned, she looked into the face of a sturdier Brad than she remembered.

"I never hoped to run into you," he said. *She gets prettier all the time. And the few freckles on her face just enhance her clear complexion.* "How is the training going?"

"Brad Mayfield. What a surprise. Nursing school is exciting, thank you. What are you doing here?"

The lanky youth had filled out considerably. He even appeared taller.

"Taking college classes, and trying to find enough work to pay for them. Do you have time off very often?"

"One day a week. We usually come downtown. Dana, this is my high school friend and coworker from Juniper, Brad Mayfield. My nursing friend, Dana LaRue."

"Can I buy you two a pop?" Brad sat down beside Alice.

"We've just had one, thanks. Do you get home much?"

"Hey, I'm going to Juniper in a few weeks in the car my dad loaned me. Want to ride down for a weekend? I can't stay more than one Saturday night. I have to head back the next day."

"I'd love to. Let me have your phone number and an address where I can send you a note. I'll let you know when I next have a Sunday off." They exchanged addresses and talked a bit more before Brad left them.

"Well, he's nice looking," Dana commented as they lingered in front of the fashionable store windows. "Did you date him in high school?"

"No, and this isn't a date. I don't date anymore. We worked together in the Jiffy Café. He washed dishes and peeled potatoes. I waited tables. He used to walk me home after work. He was very skinny and not quite as tall, and had pimples."

"He certainly doesn't have them now." Dana rolled her eyes. "The pimples must have changed into dimples and the skinny into solid. I hope you have fun on your nondate to Juniper."

They did have fun. Brad called for her late Saturday afternoon. They stopped to eat at a little park. "I thought you'd like to eat here at the Ritz," Brad said, as he spread out a clean cloth on a picnic table and then set out lunch meat, bread, pop, and two apples.

Alice looked around at the trees and grass. "The Ritz is delightful," she said, and they both laughed.

He regaled her with droll anecdotes of his experiences on odd jobs he had taken to support himself. He'd stocked shelves at a grocery store at night, filled in at Chinese restaurants for sick workers, chopped wood, and even graded papers for professors in exchange for a free meal now and then. Once or twice he sold apples on the street.

He told Alice that his mother's cousin had a large family of her own and could not give him space in their house, but she had offered to let him live in a little room in the back of their garage. A small coal-burning stove heated the area, but he seldom used the heater. He busied himself with work and classes, and usually returned only to sleep.

Brad and Alice crossed the mountain pass in the dark and, since it was almost summertime, saw very little snow on the roads, although some covered the verge. Her parents were waiting up for her when they pulled into Juniper.

The family news was good. John worked now as foreman at the WPA, building roads and clearing areas for parks around the county. Emma kept her job at the hotel for the summer.

Fred scrounged around and found a few odd jobs now and then. And he and Jennie earned money from the grocery store by turning in bottles they scooped up. In the fall, when Peter's father had offered to drive young people to the forests of the state park so they could pick walnuts and huckleberries to sell, they grabbed their gunnysacks and joined the group. And the two planned to raise extra vegetables in the summer and market them at the grocery.

Aunt Kate and Edith had motored over to visit while Alice was home. Since they slept in the girls' room upstairs, Alice crawled in with Emma on the living room couch, eager to visit with everyone the next day.

She was proud that she could report to Kate that she was not one of the students to fail the three-month probationary period at the nursing school. She would have hated to betray all of Kate's faith in her and the waste of the money her aunt had spent.

She awoke to the smell of frying bacon. Gloria made pancakes with maple syrup and the aunts fussed over Alice. As Alice discussed her plans to become a Red Cross nurse, they all listened wide-eyed, enchanted.

* * *

Kate and Edith walked to Sunday services with the young people. As they promenaded past the hotel, Emma called out a greeting to Grant, who was sweeping the front walk. He smiled, returned her greeting, and stopped to watch the group curiously.

A fixture in the community, Grant had lived in Juniper all his life and now served on the city council as well as the school board. Sooner or later everyone stopped by his hotel food counter for coffee or a sandwich, and he knew and greeted each customer.

Grant asked Kate where she was living and how she was doing. She answered that she was doing fine, thank you, but didn't say where she was living. She spoke quietly, without stopping, hurrying the others on their way.

"Did you know him well when you lived here?" Alice asked, curious as to the quick departure.

"Yes. I even dated him. He married a classmate of mine."

"He's divorced now," Emma said. "I heard a maid and the cook talking about it. His wife left for California."

"I believe I did hear that," Kate said. "Poor man." She spoke casually, then seemingly dismissed him from her mind and gave all the youngsters a little extra money to put in the collection plate.

Alice invited Brad to their house for a meat loaf dinner before they returned to Portland, and he happily accepted. He seemed at ease in the houseful of females, teasing the little girls, flirting with the aunts, and praising Gloria for the tasty meal. Fred managed to talk airplanes with Brad, who knew a lot about them, it turned out.

Dad brought up events in Europe and remarked, "Hitler's like a small boy who wants all the toys for himself."

Brad sipped coffee along with a piece of apple pie he was savoring. "Seems he lusts for an empire like the other countries of Europe have in Africa and Asia."

The visitors left in the early evening, and Alice barely met the 10:30 p.m. deadline at the nurses' quarters.

* * *

In late summer Emma gave Grant her notice. He congratulated her on her acceptance into the teaching program at the college.

"Are you going to be a teacher like Katherine and Edith?"

"Yes, I want to teach. I'll be working in the college library between classes and in the late afternoon, but if you can use me to fill in on weekends or holidays, I'll be glad to do it."

"I'll remember that. Good luck to you. How's Alice?"

"She's happy, starting her second year of nursing school soon. She's thinking of becoming a Red Cross nurse."

Grant frowned slightly. "Is she now? What will that mean?"

"I think she will be working anywhere they send her, maybe even overseas."

"That's quite a life. And your aunts, how are they?"

"We're expecting Kate and Edith for Christmas this year. They're both teaching now. Freda is nursing in San Francisco."

"It'll be good for your folks to have them all for the holidays."

"It will. Thanks, Grant, for all your help."

"I'm sorry to lose you, Emma, but it's good that you're going to college." He smiled benignly, almost like a favorite uncle, she thought.

* * *

Emma had not even started her college classes yet, when Fred burst into the house one late afternoon and announced, "Hitler's invaded Poland."

John stood up. "That madman. He can't get away with that. Britain and France have vowed to defend Poland's borders."

Edward R. Murrow reported on the invasion from England. On the radio they heard that the attack, called the blitzkrieg (lightning war), caught Poland completely by surprise.

Germany claimed that Poland had attacked their forces, an attack that later proved to have been staged by Hitler. In response to the German offensive, France issued an ultimatum for Germany to withdraw, which was ignored. So two days after the attack, Britain and France declared war on Germany.

Poland appealed for immediate assistance from Britain, France, even the United States. Nothing happened in response. They were all woefully unprepared to fight Germany.

In three weeks, virtually all of western Poland had been overrun. Startled by the German attack, the Russians attacked from the east to get in on some of the bounty, or perhaps to create a buffer zone, or to buy time before an attack on their own country by Germany.

Dad received his last letter from Cousin Helmut Bauer. To be sure it arrived, Helmut had given it to a visiting British acquaintance who mailed it after he left Germany.

When we heard our country was at war, we felt a sense of gloom. Of course the Nazis and the young people who are trained in the Hitler Youth camps are applauding.

But for those of us who remember the other failed war, it is a time of dread. I was just a boy, but I remember feeling the hunger and the suffering. Some predict complete disaster.

Rationing of gasoline and food is to start right away. Blackouts go into immediate effect.

People in the United States were appalled to hear about all the territory being gobbled up by Hitler, and now about the war in Europe that the world had been dreading.

"How could this happen?" Gloria asked, as she sewed buttons on Marie's new dress.

"Well, see"—Fred moved a model airplane about in the air—"the Germans have these fighter planes and Stuka dive bombers, so they were probably able to do a lot of damage by air. The next war will be fought in the air."

"As I understand it," Dad said, "the Germans have been mobilizing for years with modern armor and tanks."

"Didn't the Poles fight back?" Jennie asked.

"Yes, but they used outdated weapons and horses for transportation. Yet I don't think the next war will be fought in the air."

"I guess the Germans and the Russians are friends now." Jennie was somewhat perplexed at the swings of European politics. It was difficult to keep things straight. And it all seemed a bit foolish, rather like children on the school ground.

Gloria heard from Aunt Pearl in New York that some of her Jewish friends were trying to get their relatives out of Poland. A few succeeded by unorthodox means or by political connections. Most did not.

The country watched nervously. Though much of the population was oblivious of events in the rest of the world, nearly everyone who paid attention hoped and prayed that the war would be confined to

Europe, and that the United States would stay out of the fighting this time.

John opined to the family that he feared the United States might be pulled into the fighting, while Russ and Aunt Dorothy argued that President Roosevelt would not take America into war again.

"Why should we get into another war?" Russ asked as they sat around the dinner table on Sunday. "Did the last one settle anything? Did the lot of the poor improve? Who's going to fight it? The workingman's sons against young people of Germany. Who's going to benefit? The racketeers and industrial giants, that's who."

"You're right about that. I just think Roosevelt will want to protect US interests. It's all about territory and markets." John leaned back in his chair.

"Remember what happened after the last spat among the Europeans," Aunt Dorothy said. "President Wilson promised not to take the country to war. When he did, many people felt betrayed. And Congress refused to join Wilson's League of Nations afterward, even though he had campaigned for it."

"It's different now," John said. "Hitler wants a lot of territory. Eventually we'll have to get in to stop him."

Later he told the family, "Every time Russell's Socialist brother visits from Seattle, he gains new insight on things. He's absolutely right. The last war didn't settle anything. And another one probably won't either."

* * *

During the winter, while Alice studied and worked at the hospital, and Emma pursued her teaching career, a phony war prevailed in Western Europe. It was assumed that both sides were planning strategy.

To everyone's dismay, in April 1940, Nazi troops overran Denmark and Norway. Feeble attempts by the British to invade Norway and drive the Germans out failed badly. In June, Norway surrendered.

"Why attack Norway?" Fred looked up from studying the directions for assembling a new model airplane. "Norway didn't attack Germany. Hitler can't claim that."

"Probably to prevent a British blockade in the seas up there," John said. "The Allied blockade has pretty much collapsed with this action. Germany now controls thousands of miles of harbor."

"Thank goodness it doesn't affect us," Jennie said. "We've got the Depression to deal with."

Hitler's troops next invaded the Low Countries and France, and forced the British Expeditionary Force out at Dunkirk. France was defeated by June.

"It's too bad for France and England, but surely there is no risk to the United States," Russ said. "Hitler's planes can't even get over here, let alone attack this huge country."

President Roosevelt, in an emergency address to a joint session of Congress, asked for fifty thousand planes a year, but Congress balked. Even with the attack on France, the United States Congress was in an isolationist mood. Besides, it was thought to be a ridiculously high estimate of need.

"We can't stay out now," John said, thinking of the resources that Hitler now controlled: oil, food, factories, and labor. "We'll need to give the Allies aid of some kind."

"It's not our concern," Russ said. Jennie and the rest of the family knew he was thinking of his two sons, seventeen and nineteen. "I think Roosevelt knows that. Thank God Congress passed the Neutrality Act."

Chapter 9

"Maybe I'll go over and fight Nazis for the British when I graduate," Fred said as he and Jennie walked home on Saturday.

Their light brown hair matched, and they might easily have been taken for twins. Jennie was tall for her age.

"Why would you want to do that? You might be killed."

"I wouldn't be. I'd like to be in the Royal Air Force and bomb some Nazi bases and ships. They have to be defeated or they'll take over the whole world. Our history teacher says Hitler is a mad dictator."

"Mother and Dad wouldn't let you. They're already worried about Alice joining the Red Cross in case we get into the war."

"I don't think she'd be in any danger. For your information, the hospitals are behind the lines. I read about the Great War. The one Dad was in."

"Don't be such a smart aleck. If he thinks it's dangerous for her, then it is."

"What do you know? Do you study it at school?"

"We study it sometimes."

"Not like we do. My teacher knows all about it. Look, I'm going to stop by Peter's house. Tell them that I'll be home soon." With that, he left Jennie to walk alone.

Jennie sighed, wishing she had some answers from grown-ups. Why were boys so different? What were the true differences between men and women? What were they not saying about that? Why did men have the important jobs when any fool could see that women could handle them as well or better?

What was really going on in the world grab for land? What was it about Jews that her parents talked about all the time? Weren't they just a religious group like Catholics? Not that there were any in Juniper. Even the few Catholics in town went to church somewhere else. Why did people tell you to relax when you were about to get a vaccination shot?

When she got home, she found her parents listening to news about the Battle of Britain on the radio. German planes were bombing their country. Was there ever any other news? What did all that fighting have to do with them?

She'd rather listen to comedians: Jack Benny, Red Skelton, or George Burns and Gracie Allen.

She hoped for an early meal. She had promised Linda and Marie that she would take them to see *Snow White and the Seven Dwarfs* in the afternoon.

Now that her dad was working for the WPA, they had more money to spend on movies and other fun things. Gloria even bought some fabric and made a new dress for herself recently.

Still it was hard to be so young. If she were older, she could get a job and wouldn't have to spend so much time at home. She longed to hear from Alice about her exciting life in Portland. Emma, busy with education classes and work, seldom had time for her these days.

Yet, maybe the older girls didn't have it so good either. One time when Alice visited, Jennie had said at the dinner table, "It must be wonderful to work in a smart outfit, make good money, doing something you love to do."

Alice had looked at her in bewilderment. "Who are you talking to, Jennie?"

By the end of September, Sunday dinner conversations between the Bauer and Turner families continued to revolve around the world situation. While John's family thrilled to Churchill's vow that the British would never surrender, Russ called Churchill a fool.

"The British can never hold out against the German military machine," Russ said. "Their planes, airfields, and cities are being destroyed by the superior Luftwaffe. And their RAF pilots are dying right and left. Churchill would be wise to agree to an armistice."

"How can the British keep taking the bombing?" asked Aunt Dorothy, the hostess, as she brought out pumpkin pies, still warm from the oven. "They slink underground into shelters during the bombings. They've sent the children away to the country and overseas. Almost everything is rationed. Life must be horrible."

"Hitler would probably attack us if the British gave in," Emma said.

"I wouldn't worry about an air attack," Fred told them with his newfound knowledge. "German attack planes can't carry enough fuel to cross the ocean."

Agitated, Russ stood up to serve coffee. "This pact that Germany has signed with Italy and Japan will make it even harder for Britain," he said.

Jennie, with her usual sarcasm, said, "The Germans bomb London. The British bomb Berlin. Mussolini attacked Greece and British holdings in North Africa. Tit for tat."

"Maybe when Wilkie gets elected in November, he can do something to keep us out. Roosevelt and his Lend-Lease Act." Russ, a longtime Democrat, snorted. "An illegal arrangement just so he can defy the neutrality law and give Britain some ships. He shouldn't be running for a third term anyway. None of our presidents has had a third term. Two terms were long enough for George Washington."

"We'd probably go back into a depression with Wilkie," said Gloria as she stood and began to clear the table. "Roosevelt's policies have helped this country."

"Roosevelt told us 'again, again, and again' that our boys wouldn't be sent into a foreign war." Russ pronounced the word to rhyme with "gain," imitating the president's speech.

"Say," Mark said, "you should all see this film *The Great Dictator*. Charlie Chaplin plays Adolf Hitler and makes him look so silly, wearing a short mustache, pounding his fist in the air. Fred and I went yesterday, but it's still on next week."

"Let's go together, Jennie," her cousin Doris Turner said. "Everyone says it's very funny."

Jennie agreed. A few laughs would do them all good, even the adults.

John grinned. "Maybe we should see the movie, Mother."

"By all means," Gloria said. "Whenever you're ready."

* * *

Emma and her classmates spent their second year of college practice teaching and observing classes at the local schools. In November, while the first young men of the peacetime draft were designated for induction in the army, the students were trying out their newly learned skills.

Emma sometimes visited the classrooms of her younger siblings. Once she noticed Linda slipping into a broom closet as she came down the hall. She opened the closet door. "What are you doing in here, Linda?"

The younger girl looked as though she were about to break into tears.

"The teacher made me sit in the hall. Please don't tell the folks. I didn't do anything real bad. I just got sent out here for talking. I told the class that the war was stupid. Jennie said so."

Emma hid her amusement. "Listen to your teacher, Linda. If I catch you in the hall again, I'll have to tell."

"Oh, you won't, you won't. I'll be quiet. I promise."

Saturday afternoon during the Christmas holidays, Emma worked in the hotel food counter as the jukebox played "I Don't Want to Set the World on Fire."

When Odette, home for the holidays, swished in with David, she asked, "Have you seen Naomi around lately, Emma?"

Emma, still hurt by Odette's rude remark, said, "Not often. She's having a hard time finding work, though she did pick potatoes this fall on a farm."

"She's rather plump, isn't she?" The black-haired beauty smoothed her pleated woolen skirt and slipped onto a stool. "Perhaps that's why she can't find anything."

Emma frowned. "She's not that heavy. Just hard luck, I think."

"My parents say anybody who wants work can find it."

Emma stiffened. "Well, I don't know about that. May I take your order?"

David seemed chagrined by Odette's callous remarks. He smiled at Emma. "I hope Naomi finds something."

Emma took their order and escaped, flushed with anger. How could Odette be so insensitive, and why would a fellow as humane as David spend time with her?

While the couple ate, a slim boy about fourteen or fifteen walked up to the counter where Emma stood, wiping it clean. "Got any leftover food?" he asked in a low voice. Emma looked at him carefully. He was not from Juniper, she guessed. Probably passing through, looking for work. Dark, haunted eyes peered out from his thin face, pleading.

"Wait here," Emma told him, as she headed for the kitchen. Odette and David were close enough to have heard the conversation. After a time Emma reappeared with a brown paper sack and handed it to the boy.

"Thanks, miss. I'm joining the forces as soon as I'm old enough for them to take me, but young as I am, I can't find much work."

"Where are your parents?"

"Back home, hungry, most likely. I send them a little money when I can. They ain't got nothin' back there. And my dad ain't good. He's ailin'."

When the boy was gone, Odette said, "Does Mr. Hunter know that you're giving away his food?" Emma noticed the hint of threat in her question.

"Odette—" David said.

Emma held up her chin. "He probably wouldn't mind since he's a very compassionate man, but it doesn't matter because I intend to pay for the food myself out of my salary." That quieted Odette. The couple left soon afterward.

* * *

Emma spoke to Grant at the first opportunity. "I gave away some food to a hungry kid who came by. He looked like he hadn't eaten in days."

She handed him a slip of paper. "Here's what I took. I tried to take stuff that might've been left over anyway. Cook watched as I wrote it down. I want you to take it out of my salary."

Grant glanced at the list. "Emma, I'm glad you fed somebody who needed it. But you don't have to pay for it. I'm happy to do that." And he tore up the list and threw it away.

But Odette hadn't finished with her. Emma met up with her in the dime store. "I hear you're taking training at the college," Odette said. "My aunt is on the staff over there. Have you met her? Mrs. Mosher?"

Emma's heart sank. Mrs. Mosher headed the Education Department and taught one of her classes. "Yes, I've met Mrs. Mosher," she said.

"Poor Aunt Gladys. She has to reject students when they are not suited for teaching." Odette smiled—viciously, it seemed to Emma—and walked off, her ebony curls swinging around her shoulders.

Disturbed, Emma wondered why Odette had mentioned her relationship to Mrs. Mosher. Did she intend to speak ill of her to Mrs. Mosher? Could Odette keep her from her life's dream of school teaching?

Chapter 10

Jennie Bauer heard her parents talk about new air bases and army camps around the country. They said that Roosevelt was urging industry to produce more planes. Foreign orders for military aircraft rose, and, as a result, the economy picked up.

She figured that things must be going badly for the Allies when Winston Churchill brought in conscription for women. Young unmarried women were to serve in the armed forces, police, and fire services. Older women were to register to work in factories for the war effort.

Jennie listened to the talk on the radio and at the dinner table. By spring, all the world news was fighting, fighting, fighting—in North Africa, Asia, the Mediterranean, the Balkans, and the Middle East. She imagined a huge alien looking down on the earth and seeing the shooting, the bombing, and the fires all over the globe as people hustled, hammered, and banged about to defeat others like themselves.

How much land does a dictator need anyway? How much land does a country need? Why not just do the best they can with what they have?

Why couldn't Hitler be satisfied being chancellor of Germany? Wasn't that glory enough? Why bother to ask? Nobody seemed to know.

One afternoon she came home to find eight-year-old Linda and six-year-old Marie playing Red Cross. They used part of an old sheet and pinned red strips of cloth on it.

"We're nursing people who are hurt and displaced," they told her, arranging their rag dolls on the bed and covering them with scraps of material for blankets.

* * *

In her final year of nurse's training in Portland, Alice wrote letters to Brad, who had joined the air corps. He knew that sooner or later he would be called for military service anyway.

He and Alice had made one last jaunt to Juniper before he left. He had kissed her for the first time on the lips—a slow, sensuous kiss that left her breathless. She had never imagined a kiss could be so fascinating or that a close body could feel so…exciting.

She remembered their last conversation: Brad wanted to see something of the world, but he had vowed that he would return someday. Oregon was where he wanted to live.

Alice had no idea where she would be going. Her main goal was to make her own way, succeed in her career, and help her family as well as her patients. Her work as a nurse was taxing, but she knew it was important.

Many of the patients were destitute, and their pride was hurt. One little elderly schoolteacher told Alice how she had worked and paid her own way all her life. When her meager life savings were finally used up by her long illness, she'd been sent to the county hospital. The proud woman looked so distressed that Alice feared it would affect her recovery.

Her heart went out to her patients as she worked to relieve their suffering and help them forget their miseries. Still, she hoped she and Brad would see each other again sometime.

* * *

Up at the college in Juniper, Emma Bauer needed to see Mrs. Mosher for approval of her final program. The situation made her nervous. Odette might have said something derogatory about her to her aunt. Well, Emma was prepared to defend herself against any ridiculous charges. She would become a teacher despite Odette.

"Your schedule is light this term." Mrs. Mosher shuffled some papers on her desk.

"Yes, Mrs. Mosher." Emma sat straight in Mrs. Mosher's office. "That's because I've completed most of the heavy classes. I wanted to get the hard courses finished at the beginning of my training."

"Very wise, Emma."

"I've gotten good grades."

"Indeed you have." Mrs. Mosher gave her a sharp look. "My niece knows you. Her name is Odette."

Emma waited. Finally, she said, "We were in the same class in high school. And we were cheerleaders together."

"That's what she says."

Emma tried again. "If you have any trouble with my record, you could talk to my other instructors. Or my high school teachers. Or Mr. Grant at the hotel where I worked. Or the librarian where I work here."

"I'll do that, Emma. Odette claims you took food from the hotel restaurant."

How could she? I told her I was going to pay for it.

"I offered to pay for it from my salary. If you talk to Mr. Grant, he'll tell you that I did."

"Yes, well, Emma, I'll have to wait to approve your program while I investigate this." Mrs. Mosher stood up.

In despair, Emma left the room. What could she do? She would talk to Grant. He knew she had not stolen food. Then she'd have to wait patiently for Mrs. Mosher to decide whether or not she could become a teacher. Meanwhile, she'd have to be extremely careful not to make any mistakes that would give Mrs. Mosher ammunition to keep her from teaching.

* * *

"Grant, I have to talk to you." Emma stood at the hotel counter.

"Hello, Emma. It's good to see you. Come into my office where we can talk."

When she was seated across from him, Emma said, "Do you remember me taking food for a hungry boy and offering to pay for it from my salary?"

"Of course. It was very generous of you."

"Odette Glass has told the head of the Education Department that I stole the food. Mrs. Mosher will be asking you about it. She could keep me from becoming a teacher."

"Gladys Mosher? The widow?"

"Yes, I believe that is her name. She's Odette's aunt."

Grant smiled. "I know her. Don't worry, Emma. I'll tell her the truth about you. And it's all good."

"Oh, thank you, Grant. This is very important to me. I told Odette that I planned to pay for the food. I can't imagine why she said such a thing about me."

"The Glass family has had a prosperous life here. She probably can't imagine that you would spend your money on a starving boy. Maybe she didn't believe you. But I'll get it straightened out. Don't give it another thought."

Emma stood up to leave. "I owe you so much, Grant."

"Not at all. I'm rooting for you."

* * *

Gladys had become a widow early in her marriage. Grant had taken her out for dinner a couple of times, but their relationship had gone no further. He considered them friends, though it was obvious that she would like something more.

Before he had decided exactly how to proceed, she telephoned him.

"Grant, I need to talk to you about one of our students who worked for you. Could we get together somewhere?"

"Of course, Gladys. I'd love to see you. How about meeting at the Pilot Butte Inn in Bend? Could I treat you to dinner?"

Gladys seemed pleased to accept his invitation.

Grant saw right away that Gladys had dressed carefully for their meeting in a form-fitting black dress adorned with a pearl necklace and matching earrings. He decided to let her bring up the subject of Emma. They discussed local gossip, the widening war in Europe, and their personal lives.

"How's your brother Howard getting along? I hear that prices for beef are up. He should be doing fine."

"He is, yes. Farmers and ranchers often prosper during periods of war. That brings up the subject I wanted to talk to you about, Grant. His daughter, Odette, tells me she observed Emma Bauer taking food from your restaurant for a handout."

Grant put on a surprised look. "She did?"

"What can you tell me about that?"

"Gladys, Emma told me about giving food to the boy right away and wanted to reimburse me for the food she took. She said to take it out of her salary. She's such a generous girl. Well, of course, I wouldn't let her pay for it. But the fact is, she would never steal anything."

"I see. Was she a good worker?"

"The best. I can't praise her enough. I'm sure she'll be a credit to the college when she starts teaching. The Education Department deserves credit for selecting her for the teacher program. Was that your work?"

"Her record is good, except for Odette's accusation. Why would Odette accuse her of taking food?"

"Oh, who knows? Jealously about a boyfriend? Some minor spat? Could be that Odette really believed the worst of Emma."

Gladys said nothing for a time. At last she spoke. "She's been a difficult child. I love my niece, but I recognize she is sometimes petty when she thinks she is threatened. Perhaps she sees Emma as a rival for David Walker's attentions."

Grant laughed. "I wouldn't know about that. Isn't it great to be beyond all those young concerns? As for you, Gladys, I hear many good things about the Education Department—from Emma and others."

Gladys beamed with pleasure. Emma certainly deserved to graduate from the teaching program. She would let the girl know about it right away.

* * *

When Germany invaded the USSR, a recent friend with whom Hitler had signed a nonaggression pact, the whole world realized that signatures and promises meant nothing to Hitler.

"I thought Stalin and Hitler just signed some kind of agreement," Jennie said in puzzlement at the Bauer dinner table.

"That was a few months back," Fred said. "Some people say the Russians have underground factories producing bombs in the Urals. They might be hard to beat."

"A two-front war," John mused. "Maybe the British are off the hook for the time being."

"But aren't the Russians Communists? Can they be allies with the British?" Fred asked.

"When Russia was friends with the Germans, it was friendship between extreme left and extreme right. It doesn't seem to make much difference in wartime," Jennie said with a sneer. They were fighting in Russia now, fighting in Europe and Asia and Africa and all over the Pacific. She watched newsreels of the fighting at the movies. The world was crashing in fury and horror. When would it all end?

By October, German tanks were within forty miles of Moscow. All the experts said it looked like another victory for Hitler. But amateur historians, Jennie's father among them, predicted that the Russian winter would engulf the German army, as it had Napoleon's. Those vast forests would defeat the Germans.

"The man is surely a maniac," John said at the family meal. "Does he want to control the world so badly that he will destroy his army?"

"Well, Hitler's willing to let Italy and Japan control some of the world." Fred waited for dessert.

"Napoleon was defeated in Russia because of the harsh winters and the difficulty supplying his army over all that territory." John got up to consult his world map.

"Our teacher says Hitler wants to contain communism. What do you hear from your cousin in Germany?"

"Helmut?" John looked glum. "Not a thing, Fred. He could be on his way to Russia for all I know."

* * *

That summer Emma looked forward to her first teaching job in Springdale, ten miles from Juniper. The Springdale students came from farming and ranching families, and Emma knew many of them. Mr. Walker, the capable school board chairman, suggested that she board with the Andersons.

All her life she had dreamed of a classroom of her own. When she had completed the necessary county forms, she put up charts, planned educational bulletin boards, and prepared her grade book, inhaling the pleasant scent of the freshly waxed floors.

And when she had finished all that, she cleaned chalkboards, filled her lesson plan book for several days, and sketched out a half-year outline for each of the four upper grades. Miss Shafer, the much older primary teacher, was helpful and pleasant.

During the week, Emma walked to school from the Anderson home, two miles away, unless Miss Shafer or a passerby gave her a lift.

On Friday evenings or on Saturdays she usually got a ride into Juniper so she could visit her family. If she had no way back to Springdale, John drove her to her boarding house on Sunday evening.

As the students were headed home one Friday afternoon, David Walker stopped by. They all greeted him loudly.

One older boy asked, "Are you going back to school?"

"I guess I'll have to if I want to keep up with you geniuses."

They laughed as they set off for home. "Geniuses, he calls us," the older boy said.

Inside the schoolhouse, David greeted Emma, who was checking papers at her desk. Fingering his hat in his hand, the broad-shouldered rancher asked her if she'd like to run into Juniper for the evening and see a movie.

"We could have a sandwich or something at the hotel counter before the film."

Emma hesitated. "What about Odette?"

David's eyes met hers. "We've decided to call it quits. We have different ideas. She's gone back to college."

Emma's heart jumped. "Well then, I'd like that. I haven't seen Grant Hunter for some time. What's playing?"

"I think it's a western." David wore a sardonic grin. "You know, where the rancher always wins over the bad guys in the end. I always like the endings."

Emma laughed. "Are you working hard on the ranch these days?"

"We always work hard." He spoke wryly. "Prices are up some, but the uncertainty in Europe is difficult to deal with. I'll pick you up at your boarding house at five."

"That would be fine. I'll just stay in town for the weekend with my family."

Late that afternoon Emma pinned her blond curls back with bobby pins and chose an emerald-green summer dress, the graduation dress, for the evening. She almost concealed the birthmark on her jaw with the first makeup she had ever bought.

When David arrived, she failed to notice his sharp intake of breath when he saw her. "You look wonderful," he breathed.

At the hotel counter, Grant, pleased to see Emma, sat down with the young couple for a few minutes. "We miss you here, Emma. But I know you're doing what you want to do. What do you hear from Alice?"

"She'll finish her training in January." Emma sipped a chocolate milkshake. "David says beef and farm prices are up some. The community must be recovering."

"I'm glad to hear that." Grant nodded to David. "I've seen evidence of a turnaround myself. Are you working with your folks?"

"Yes." David set his ham sandwich down. "I like the work, and there still aren't all that many jobs ready and waiting out there. If I left, Dad would just have to hire someone else, probably at higher pay." He grinned. "So there's not much sense in my leaving a ready-made job, even if I do get on Dad's nerves now and then."

Grant chuckled. "That's probably a generational thing. My father didn't believe, even on the day he died, that I was capable of running the hotel." He sobered. "Some young fellows around town are joining the armed services before they're drafted."

"Yes, and that's a possibility if we ever get into the conflict."

As usual Grant asked about Emma's parents and about Kate, Freda, Edith, Ernst, Louis, and about her mother's family. But Emma noticed that he always seemed most interested in Kate, who was closer to his age, about forty, she decided.

At her door that night, David put his arms around her small waist cinched in with a green belt, slowly drew her to him, and leaned down to meet her lips with his. She had a firm body with enticing breasts, but she was yielding against him.

With her arms around his neck, she found his soft brown hair at the back of his head smooth and silky.

When he finally drew back, he suggested that they picnic on Sunday before returning to Springdale, and she readily agreed.

* * *

He picked her up at her parents' house in the afternoon. They found a picnic spot beside the sparkling Deschutes River not far from the highway. It was a sunny autumn day, and the air felt fresh and clean from a recent sprinkle. As a shy deer raised its head from behind a juniper tree and then leaped away, David helped Emma spread out food and cool pop on a blanket.

"You know I might not have any choice about going into the service if we have to go to war," he said as he held a roast beef sandwich.

"Surely Roosevelt will keep us out of war. Things are just beginning to get better in this country." She chose a carrot stick.

"I hope he can keep us out, but some of the things I read indicate that we will not be able to stay out long. We're mobilizing for war now. I read about a shipyard built by Henry Kaiser in the Portland area. They're expecting to build lots of ships in the Pacific states."

"How ironic that our fathers just recently fought in the Great War," Emma said, with a touch of melancholy. "If you have to go, will you write to me?"

David stared at her in disbelief. "Of course I'll write to you. You're one of my best friends. You'd write back, wouldn't you?"

"Yes." She touched his hand. "You're one of my best friends too." She looked away quickly.

They watched red-winged blackbirds sitting in the trees beside the rustling river. Magpies flew overhead as they lounged on the blanket. David noticed the curling lashes above her brilliant blue eyes, her full lips. He leaned over and put his hands on her shoulders, then slowly caressed her, moving his large hands across her shoulders, down her arms and around her slim waist, studying her trim body as he did so.

This was extremely erotic, and when he pulled her to him for a slow, sensual kiss, she felt almost weak with passion.

"You're lovely, you know." He ran a hand over her blond curls, his large, friendly face filled with admiration.

A car drove by on the nearby road, and they decided it was time to get back to Springdale. It would not do for rumors to fly about the local schoolteacher, who was expected to be a model of decorum.

* * *

The next day David stopped by to see Emma after school was dismissed. The older students raised their eyebrows as they started down the road toward home.

"Do you have to take a test now?" asked one, looking sideways at the other children with a knowing grin on his face.

"If I do, I'll get better grades than any of you."

They hooted and laughed.

He found her grading papers at her desk and invited her for dinner with his family. She knew his younger sister, Sarah, who was still in school, about Jennie's age, so she looked forward to the dinner.

The Walkers lived in a large rambling ranch house surrounded by a few trees and outbuildings. She had expected to be nervous around Mr. Walker. But he was a large, jovial man, much like his handsome son. He inquired how things were going at the school and invited Emma to let him know if she needed any supplies or had any trouble at the school.

As the three women were cleaning up in the kitchen, Sarah asked, "How long have you and David been dating?"

"Why, not long at all. We've only been out together once."

"That's strange. I gathered he was very interested in you. When he was in high school, he talked about you often." Sarah washed a tall pitcher and swished it in the rinse water.

"Well, of course, we were both involved in sports." Emma took the pitcher and dried it. "I was a cheerleader, and he played every sport and always came to the games, even after he graduated. I wonder if he misses all those practices and games."

"He's too busy to miss much." Mrs. Walker put the dishes away as Emma dried them. "He works very hard on the ranch."

"He was dating Odette Glass, but now that you're here in Springdale, he'll probably be dating you." Sarah was an energetic girl, tall like the men in the family, with long brown hair and soft brown eyes.

Emma blushed, causing Mrs. Walker to laugh. "Sarah's outspoken. You'll have to get used to her."

Sarah wrung out the dishrag and plopped it over the faucet. "Odette is a self-centered snob anyway. I'm glad she's gone off again."

When the women joined the men in the living room, they found the conversation, as usual, on the world political situation. "Things are getting better for farmers and ranchers," Mr. Walker said for Emma's benefit, "but I don't think things are going well for the rest of the world. I hate this talk of a second world war. Still, I imagine we'll be in the conflict before long. They're increasing aircraft production in plants down in California—Los Angeles, San Diego."

Mrs. Walker settled into a soft chair. "And they're mass-producing houses near the plants to house the workers," she said.

"I read that they're producing munitions and tanks in the East," Emma said and sighed.

"How many times do we have to fight wars in Europe? It's ironic," Mrs. Walker said. "Still we have to help the British with munitions and supplies."

Everyone felt an air of expectancy in the country. Something was going to happen.

Later David drove Emma back to her boarding house. When they parted, he said, "I think my family likes you. Sarah was actually polite. She can sometimes be downright rude."

"Was she rude to Odette Glass?"

David grinned ruefully. "Sarah never did like her. But I won't be seeing Odette again."

During the next few weeks, Emma saw David regularly. He drove her to Juniper every Friday afternoon and then drove her back to Springdale on Sunday.

They saw the movie *Gone with the Wind* and explored country roads. David took her to a farm where the owner had built child-sized castles, bridges, and walkways out of rocks he had gathered.

They collected their own agates, pebbles, and stones on their long walks through the sage-covered hills. They meandered through the graveyard on the edge of town, reading the gravestones, pondering unknown lives.

On the Indian reservation, they swam in the warm-water pool, naturally heated by hot springs. David caressed her and kissed her until she shivered and flushed with excitement each time she saw him. Later she would remember those warm, peaceful, autumn months of 1941 as some of the happiest of her life.

She invited him for Thanksgiving at her Juniper home. Gloria served a huge golden-brown turkey along with sweet potatoes and pumpkin pie from their garden harvest. John Bauer showed David his map of Europe, and they discussed the likelihood of another world war.

After dinner David asked Emma to go for a walk. Unusually serious as they strolled down the road, he said, "Look here, Emma, we like the same things, the same people."

"We do, don't we? I always enjoy myself no matter what we do."

He hesitated and finally burst out, "Emma, when you fed that boy out of your salary, I knew what a generous nature you have, what a good heart. I've loved you ever since high school, I think. I didn't know if I had a chance with you then."

She beamed with delight. "I've loved you since you played games with all the children at our house."

He stopped. "Will you marry me?"

Emma gasped and rushed into his arms. "Of course I'll marry you."

He breathed a sigh of relief, kissed her, and held her close. "You realize I might have to go into the service. I thought we could marry soon, maybe early spring. I want us to be together while we can, to be husband and wife." His words sent a potent thrill through her.

"Dad says we can live in the old foreman's house," David continued. "We haven't had a foreman in years, so we'll have to fix up the house, but it's snug and we can be together. If you want to finish the year at the school, that's fine. But you can quit if you want. Our spread isn't large, but we get by."

"Oh, David, it'll be wonderful to live together. I'll finish the school year. We can use the money, and I enjoy it. Let's talk about a wedding date next week."

"Meanwhile"—David gave her a huge smile—"I've got a ring for you." He slipped a small diamond ring on her finger and kissed her again between the fields of sagebrush. The following week they decided to marry in March 1942. They began to make their plans.

* * *

On December 7, 1941, the Bauer family, preparing for a church social, was too busy in the morning to listen to the radio. Cecelia was to join Jennie at the afternoon potluck.

When Jennie stopped by Cecelia's house, she found the whole family in an uproar: Cecelia's mother crying and the others trying to console her between their own tears. The family had heard on the radio about an attack on Pearl Harbor by Japanese warplanes.

The harbor had been bombed, destroying many American ships. The number of casualties was enormous. They were frantic to hear from Cecelia's older brother, Arnold, stationed in Hawaii with the navy. Consequently, Cecelia would not be going to the potluck.

Chapter 11

At the church, Gloria helped to prepare for the evening event. Jennie would never forget the horror and desolation on her mother's face when she told her about the attack. The bombing was particularly shocking since they had recently heard on the radio that Japanese envoys were in Washington, DC, for peaceful discussions with the United States government.

Gloria thought of James and Mark Turner, Russ and Dorothy's sons. Both were likely to be called up for service. Their parents had worried about that possibility. Then she thought of Fred, her own son, who was about to graduate from high school. Her shoulders sagged as she flopped down on a chair in the church kitchen.

The other bewildered women spoke in low voices of the calamity. Where was Pearl Harbor? What did it mean? Was it war? Would they be attacked? Would their husbands and sons be called for military service? Jennie sat by her mother, unsure of what she might say to reassure her.

John Bauer and the rest of the congregation joined the group as the time came for the meal. John put his arms around his wife and daughter and held them close.

What could he say to console them? He closed his eyes and saw again, as he did over twenty years ago, hundreds of young men marching off, their faces fixed. He heard the bombs and the explosions and the screams of the wounded. He smelled the stinking trenches and the putrid wounds. Now he hid his face in his wife's hair.

Several people went home, others felt bound to stay and eat the carefully prepared fried chicken and potato salad. The children, called inside, hastened to join the adults. Unaware of the morning disaster, they chatted and laughed. Halfway through the meal, someone turned the radio on, and they listened to further news of an event described as "treachery."

As soon as the church was tidied up, everyone left to discuss the developments with their families and their neighbors, some to pray and some to cry.

* * *

David and Emma heard the news at Grant's counter where they drank lime-flavored carbonated water in drinks called "green rivers." Other shocked customers stared dully at each other.

People immediately thought of the young men they knew who would be called upon to fight. The young men thought about their plans. Those might be changed. The draft might be stepped up. They might be killed.

That night David drove Emma back to her boarding house in Springdale. "Why should we wait, Emma? I could be called up any day. Why not get married over the holidays while some of the relatives are here? We can be together that much sooner."

Emma agreed to the change. They would be married two days before Christmas.

* * *

The day after the attack on Pearl Harbor, the Bauer family, along with the rest of the nation, listened to President Roosevelt's speech to Congress.

"The Japanese probably used that scrap metal we sent them for war materials to destroy our navy," John said.

"Our teacher says they need a supply of petroleum that they don't have," Fred said. "Do they think they can get it from us?"

"Probably. I imagine the Brits, the French, the Russians, and the rest of the Allies will be pleased to have us in the war on their side. We can supply them with more ammunition and supplies."

"And men too." Gloria could barely keep from crying, as she imagined Fred, James, Mark, and other young men leaving to fight, and possibly die, in some foreign country. It was happening all over again.

When they dropped by that afternoon, Aunt Dorothy and Russ Turner agreed the attack left Roosevelt no alternative. Sick at the possibility of their sons going to war, they agreed, nevertheless, that Roosevelt had to declare war on Japan.

"But how will we ever catch up with the enemy?" Jennie asked. "They've been mobilizing for years, and now they have all the war materials they need in German-occupied Europe and Japanese-occupied Asia. What if we lose?" No one responded to her question.

Later that day, as Jennie walked downtown to pick up buttons for Gloria, she noticed a long line of about twenty boys in front of the courthouse, some who were still in high school. As she strolled by, she stopped to talk to Peter, who stood in the line. "We're waiting to sign up for the service," he said.

For teenage boys, they were unusually subdued. They spoke quietly, laughed a little—no shoving, playful hitting, or loud laughing. Suddenly they acted like serious young men, boys no longer.

* * *

In Portland, Alice anticipated her January graduation, with eleven other students, and a career as a Red Cross nurse. They had nursed in every ward in the hospital by now. Soon they would qualify for jobs as full-time registered nurses in hospitals and clinics anywhere in the country.

A sober nation was still absorbing the news of the Japanese attack. Coming off her shift at the hospital the next day, Alice found her roommates listening to a radio broadcast of President Roosevelt's speech announcing his decision to ask Congress for a declaration of war against Japan.

Rose said, with an air of finality, "Girls, I guess we know what we'll be doing after graduation."

"Our country has a right to our services," Dana said. "We're trained and ready. We owe a few months to our country." The others nodded in agreement.

Alice's dreams of working in a hospital were shattered. She'd have to give up those dreams for whatever service the country needed.

Within days after the attack on Pearl Harbor, the United States was at war with Germany and Italy, as well as Japan. The Axis, the enemy was called, as opposed to the Allies—Britain, France, the United States, and over twenty other countries eventually.

The majority of the graduating nurses wanted to enter the navy or the US Army Nurse Corps. Alice and Dana LaRue hoped to become army nurses and to be sent to camp together. They mailed their application papers to headquarters in the same envelope.

* * *

Shortly after the start of the war, Alice received a letter from Emma asking her to be bridesmaid at her wedding. They would both wear teal-blue day-length dresses with white collars and cuffs, dresses that would be useful for many years.

Gloria was sewing them up already, with Emma and Jennie doing the hand stitching and Jennie serving as a model for Alice's dress, since the two were close to the same size. The wedding would take place in the Bauer home with a small reception following the ceremony.

Gloria worked late into the evenings on the dresses. When she saw Emma's guest list, she raised her eyebrows. Grant Hunter and Kate Bauer would both be at the wedding. What a fascinating situation. The two had barely seen each other in years.

Since Uncle Ernst had signed up with the army several months ago and was off in training, Alice rode to Juniper with Aunt Tess. Forty guests crowded into the living-dining area of the Bauer house, spilling out into the foyer.

Edith and Kate drove over from the valley. Aunt Dorothy baked the wedding cake. Mark Turner and Fred confiscated large caches of rice to test their aim when the bridal couple left the premises for their ranch home. With that in readiness, they decorated David's car with trailing tin cans and old cloth streamers of various colors and patterns.

Pleased to be invited to the wedding and reception, Grant visited with neighbors and friends as he munched on small sandwiches and cake. Seizing the opportunity, he approached Alice. "It was a beautiful wedding, Alice. Those gowns you and Emma are wearing are very attractive."

"Why, thank you, Mr. Hunter. Mother made them with some help from Emma and Jennie. I'm so glad you could come. Emma thinks a great deal of you. She always tells us how fine it was to work at the hotel."

Grant flushed with pleasure. "I'm sure she exaggerated. How good of you to come down from Portland. Did this wedding interfere with your training in any way?"

"No, I got special permission. But we graduate from nursing school in January anyway. I don't think anyone wants to hold us back now. The country is going to need nurses."

"I'm afraid you're right. What are your plans after graduation?" He longed to keep her talking so he could observe her facial expressions, her profile, and her eyes.

"My friend and I have applied to become army nurses. We want to help the war effort."

"Very commendable." Grant stared at her soft complexion and the familiar, clear blue eyes enhanced by the teal dress. His breath caught. He knew those eyes.

"The news about Cecelia's brother is so sad. He was killed at Pearl Harbor, you know. Were you in the Great War, Mr. Hunter?"

"Yes, I volunteered in the navy. We thought it would be the last one," he said, with a wistful smile.

"My cousin James Turner had just signed up with the Civilian Conservation Corps. He needed the work, but he was promised that, by being in the CCC, he wouldn't have to go in the service as early as others did. And do you know, his complete group has been called up already."

"It seems all bets are off now that we're at war, Alice. I'm sorry about the death of Arnold White. It must be very hard on Cecelia and her parents."

"Yes, it is." Then Alice confided, "I just heard that Naomi Landrey and Roy Davis were secretly married last week. He's planning to join the army. They've been dating for years, but her parents kept delaying the wedding."

A friend called to Alice. She smiled at Grant, excused herself, and walked away, leaving him slightly dazed. He shook his head and surveyed the room.

He yearned to talk to Kate alone. He had tried for years to discreetly discover where she lived. He wanted to write to her and see her. He seldom ran into John and Gloria. On the few occasions when he talked to them, they always managed to evade his questions. And Emma, bright as she was, would wonder if he asked her.

Finally he spotted Kate in the kitchen making more coffee and he joined her there. For a moment, he feasted his eyes on her. Still beautiful, she wore a lavender dress, one of her favorite colors. She turned toward him.

"Lovely nieces you have, Kate. They are almost as beautiful as you are." He walked toward her and took one of her hands in both of his.

She drew her hand away. "Aren't we a bit old for that type of flattery?"

"It's not flattery, and we're not too old for anything," he said impatiently.

She rolled her eyes. "Would you like to leave now?"

"No, I wouldn't. Look, I've wanted to talk to you. Couldn't I come see you sometime, take you out for dinner or something? It would be easy for me to get away."

Kate stared at him. "But not so easy for me to do," she said, her voice hard. "That's all over, Grant." She looked away. *A date? After all these years?* She wouldn't dare.

"Why does it have to be? There are things that I want to know. I need to talk to you. Let me come see you."

She picked up a platter of sandwiches. "You had your chance, Grant." She sailed out of the kitchen, her pulse racing. She had to get away.

"How could I defy my mother's deathbed wishes?" he asked, not sure that she even heard him. She didn't turn around, and he realized he'd lost possibly his last clear chance to see her alone. What could a man do?

Chapter 12

For several months after bombing Pearl Harbor, Japan was in complete control of the Pacific. With the US Pacific Fleet's battleships destroyed, Japan quickly overtook Guam and Wake Island. Hong Kong, Singapore, Thailand, Burma, the Netherlands East Indies—all were lost to the Japanese. They even attacked Australia and took the Philippines from the United States.

Fred informed the Bauer family, however, about a remarkable raid led by General James H. Doolittle on April 8, 1942. "A small group of planes took off from an American aircraft carrier in the Pacific and flew hundreds of miles to bomb Tokyo. Of course, they did little damage, but they must have startled the Japanese."

"They certainly raised American spirits," John said. "I understand three of the boys were from Pendleton."

* * *

Despite the fact that they could make more money in private positions, Alice and Dana joined the Red Cross Nursing Service, thereby making themselves available for the emergency nursing needs of the country. They were sent pins about the size of a quarter. In the center was a red cross on a field of white, circled by a blue band with the words "American National Red Cross" and a band of leaves.

They were advised not to give up their positions. They would be given two weeks' notice in order to arrange their personal affairs. While they waited for their orders, the young women worked at the Multnomah County Hospital where they had trained.

The two shared an apartment on southwest Hall Street. It was a dingy little place, with a Murphy bed folding into the living room wall during the day. A few pieces of old heavy furniture filled the room. The unit included a bathroom, closet, and a tiny kitchenette.

They used a wringer washing machine in the basement for their laundry and strung their wet garments about their tiny apartment. Still, for a few months, they enjoyed the luxury of private quarters.

They were lucky to get it. All available housing was filled by workers pouring into the Portland and Vancouver areas to work in the shipyards.

In April, they were called to enroll in the army at Camp Roberts, California. Thrilled, the two young women boarded a train for Oakland, where they were to stop off for a visit with Aunt Freda Bauer and her friend, Monica Lewis.

After the greetings and introductions, Aunt Freda asked about their trip. "Were you sidetracked for troop trains or hospital trains?"

"Only a couple of times for troop trains."

"You're lucky. A friend of mine also met several hospital trains bringing the wounded back right after the attack."

The two older women took their guests on a round of sight-seeing in San Francisco, across the bay. They saw buildings sitting on steep hills, cable cars that crawled up and down those frighteningly steep hills, and dined at the famous Cliff House when they finished their tour.

As they watched a pink sunset on the water and seals outside on the rocks, Freda invited them to order a drink before dinner. Alice and Dana looked at each other blankly, wondering if they should admit they had never had a drink before dinner, and had not the least idea what to order.

Freda, who was treating the young women to the meal, suggested they order pink ladies. Alice and Dana were delighted with the drinks.

"Tell me about the family." Freda presented a slightly older version of Emma, with pleasant blue eyes and light blond hair. "I like to hear about Juniper. Tell me what's going on."

"Dad says trucks are hauling off loads of young men from Juniper for the service."

"So soon?"

"We have a lot of catching up to do in this war."

"Of course. What about the family?"

"Well, I'm afraid Fred is eager to join up. Mother is trying to get him to wait until he is drafted, or at least until he graduates in a few weeks. Of course, Emma's marriage is the big news. She's finishing the school year teaching in Springdale. You know that Aunt Edith has been teaching in the valley now for some time. Dad's back at work in the mill since lumber is badly needed for the war effort."

"Isn't he a little old for that kind of work?"

Alice shrugged. "He's gained a lot of experience with the WPA. He thinks he might get on as foreman. He tried to enlist with the army, but they turned him down because he's too old."

"I wish I could have attended the wedding, but I just couldn't get off. Several of the young nurses I've been training have already left for service in the army or navy. They just keep coming. I may enlist myself. What does Tess hear about Ernst? He never writes to me."

"Tess says he likes the army and got into the service at a good time, as far as promotions go. She didn't want him to go, of course. Uncle Louis has joined up with the navy." Alice relished her crab salad, the first she'd ever had.

"Goodness, soon there won't be anybody left on the home front. Does Emma still work summers at the hotel?"

"She was, but now that she's married, she might decide not to."

"Does Grant Hunter still own the hotel?" Freda could not get enough news from her hometown.

"Yes, and there is talk of an air base outside of town. They say Mr. Hunter is thinking of expanding the hotel to include a smart restaurant, maybe remodeling and extending into the building he owns next door. He's a fine man, came to the wedding. Emma liked working for him."

"I believe he owns a lot of property in Juniper. A good eating establishment would help the town, maybe bring people from neighboring communities and get more money circulating. Grant used to date Kate, you know. John said they were quite serious at one time. Did he ever remarry after his wife divorced him?"

"Not that I know of. I've heard of him dating someone now and then. It usually creates a lot of interest in our little metropolis. But it never lasts."

"And what about Kate? Does she date these days? She never mentions seeing anyone in her letters."

"She never mentions it to me either, and we see her quite often. She surely has opportunities. Of course, she spends many of her holidays and vacations visiting us."

"Not much like her sister Freda, is she?" Monica asked. "Freda dates every chance she gets."

"And why not?" Freda grinned. "Here in California, thousands of men have been sent to army and naval bases. They're everywhere. Why not take advantage of it?"

"Why not?" Alice laughed. "Maybe Kate should be in California. She helped pay my tuition, you know."

"I'm not surprised. She loaned me money to start my training too. And she's helped Edith qualify for teaching."

* * *

The train carried Alice and Dana to San Miguel. All along the way, they noticed troop trains filled with young men. At Camp Roberts, the guard had to call headquarters to get clearance to admit them. They were sworn in and began their lives as army nurses.

That evening several nurses sat in the barracks getting acquainted. A nurse named Marjorie told them that Camp Roberts was named for Corporal Harold W. Roberts, a hero in World War I who gave his life that his tank gunner might live.

"It's one of the few US Army posts named in honor of an enlisted man. Construction took only a few months—from November 1940 to January 1941. Regular training began in March, and in June of that year the camp was completed."

"The whole camp completed in eight months?" Alice brushed off her new army jacket.

"Yes. Situated about halfway between San Francisco and Los Angeles, the entire camp is more than fifty-eight square miles."

When Marjorie finished her informal geography presentation to the new recruits, another nurse, named Ellen, rolled her eyes. "Marjorie is our walking encyclopedia. Pay no attention to her. Just enjoy the camp as much as you can because we probably won't stay here very long. Training camps like this are being built all over the country."

"I'm glad we'll be wearing lighter outfits on the wards." Dana was trying on the dress uniform. "These wool uniforms are hot. Not very classy either."

Alice hung hers in the closet the way they had been shown, all hooks facing the same direction, shoes shined, laced, and placed toe inward. "How often do they inspect the barracks?"

"Weekly," Ellen said, "and your beds better have tight square corners and all 'feminine junk,' as they call it, tucked out of sight. Dresser drawers have to be in good order.

"And even though you start as second lieutenant, you can only get as far as major. You'll get about half the pay of men with those ranks, and you'll get few military privileges. For instance, don't expect anyone to salute you."

"I can do without the salutes, but more pay would be helpful." Alice was already figuring out how much money she could save to help Fred and Jennie with training beyond high school.

"And if some guy asks for a full-body rub," Ellen said, "tell him to eat grass."

Their chief nurse was a regular army captain, who, while kindly, seemed overwhelmed by all the recruits.

"I hope she gets used to all the new nurses." Marjorie grinned. "We're going to get a lot more of them. I see appeals for nurses in recruitment posters and in all the magazines. And Mrs. Roosevelt is calling for more nurses."

Alice peered out the window at the bare hills, just beginning to turn green. Was this where they would serve during the war?

Across from the camp's main gate, army troops kept coming and going at the Southern Pacific Railroad Depot. Marjorie told them that the men came for a seventeen-week training cycle. In the camp were service clubs for enlisted men, theaters, a laundry, a post office, a sports arena, and chapels staffed with chaplains.

The hospital complex contained hundreds of beds. The patients were all young males in generally good health. Even under normal circumstances, young men tended to think they were in love with their nurses. To complicate matters, at camp they were away from home, lonely, and vulnerable.

Some of the nurses dated the newly released patients as well as officers on the base, but Alice refused to get involved. She reasoned that none of the men would be in the same place for very long, so eventually they would have to separate. Besides, her last experience in Juniper with Chet had made her very cautious.

Sometimes a group of nurses would dance at and visit the officers' club. They all liked to jitterbug. If Marjorie came along, she always insisted that they leave in a group, no trotting off for private dating. "We're better off together," she said.

Alice danced with zest. As she talked to the young men, she was often surprised to find how nonchalant they seemed to be about going to war. Were they denying the possibility of injury or death? Did they believe they would be the lucky ones? Or was it all just show?

At the hospital, some of the enlisted men from small towns and rural farms seemed excited to be somewhere else. In just a few months their humdrum lives had changed into exciting adventures.

Alice often worked in the central supply room where supplies were sterilized and surgical packs were made up. It was a quiet place to work, but the surgery ward, where she also worked, buzzed with activity, especially on Saturday nights. The main causes were automobile accidents and knife fights.

Ellen, working the same shift, commented, "Even without a war, we'll always find work, as long as men keep fighting each other."

* * *

The government, in order to encourage patriotism and recruitment, bombarded the population with posters showing the Germans, Italians, and especially the Japanese, who had made the sneak attack on Pearl Harbor, as evil people. John Bauer cautioned his family in Juniper that the propaganda didn't apply to all the people in the Axis countries.

"The ordinary people in those countries are probably much like us, frightened of war but unable to do anything about it." He remembered Helmut's letters, his concerns about his Jewish colleagues. "The government used the same propaganda in the last war. They called the Germans 'vicious Huns.' Some people around here even stopped talking to my family while I was off fighting in the war with the US Army. And a German-owned grocery store in Portland was damaged by vandals."

John had no such empathy for the leaders of the hostile countries—Hitler, Mussolini, Hirohito—who were reviled by millions of people.

* * *

David Walker slipped into the small house on the ranch where Emma cooked their evening meal. Planting feed grain required long hours, and it was almost dark. Still in his overalls, he washed up and found Emma in the kitchen, pretty in her soft pink-flowered cotton dress, her long blond hair pulled back and tied with a ribbon.

He was tempted to come behind her where she stood at the stove and wrap his arms around her for a kiss, but that would delay their meal. As they ate, she told him about her trip to Juniper that day, the letter she had received from Alice at Camp Roberts, and news from her family.

"Mother's been 'invited' to help out with all kinds of war committees—rolling bandages, helping at the USO, sewing. Fred's signing up for service as soon as he graduates. He hopes to get into the US Air Force and start flight training. Mother worries about him and about Alice too."

"Sooner or later Fred would have been called up anyway. Men are being drafted or joining up by the thousands," David said.

"I know, but that doesn't make it any easier."

In spite of their initial worries, David was not drafted yet. They had no idea when he would be. He had repaired the roof, and he and Emma had wallpapered the old ranch house where they lived. Emma had even painted the kitchen cabinets.

"I could join up." He put his arm about her waist as she gathered dishes from the table. "But I hate to leave you, and I don't know what Dad would do for help. It's humiliating to see the looks that strangers give us ranchers and farmers for not wearing a uniform."

"They just don't realize what you do." Emma deposited the dishes on the counter beside the sink.

"Some of the ranchers think that we won't have to go because the country needs us to raise beef."

"Please don't join. What would I do without you? I should start teaching next fall because of the shortage. Male teachers have joined the services. I might not be able to finish the year though."

"You wouldn't?"

She looked down. "We're going to have a baby sometime next winter."

"What? Are you sure?" They both wanted children. But to have their wishes granted so soon seemed too much to ask.

"Oh yes." Emma gave him a triumphant little smile. "I saw Dr. Weber today, and he confirmed it. I'll have to stop knitting blankets in the Bundles for Britain program and start knitting booties for baby."

"It's wonderful." David swept her up and whirled her around the kitchen. "Oh, I love you, Mrs. Walker," he said as he set her down. "How shall we celebrate?"

She smiled at him over her shoulder as she headed for the bedroom. "I have an idea," she said. He quickly followed.

Many pregnant teachers were not allowed to teach at that time, but Mr. Walker scoffed at that and made sure his community had a schoolteacher. Emma was ready to teach the whole year. The baby obliged by making his appearance at the start of the Christmas holidays.

Of course, everyone knew that Emma was Walker's daughter-in-law, but with teachers in such short supply, the community felt lucky to have her. Only Meredith Pearson, Chet's older sister, complained about the school board's action.

Mrs. Walker did her part by looking after young Davy during the day.

* * *

At Camp Roberts, Alice and the other nurses eyed the war news almost continuously.

"Look here"—Ellen's legs swung off the end of the bed as she read the newspaper in mid-May—"the three carriers that escaped the Pearl Harbor raid are in operation. They've stopped Japan in New Guinea after a two-day battle in the Coral Sea."

"Oh, thank God." Dana got up to look at the map that hung on the wall.

In June, the nurses cheered the naval victory against the Japanese at Midway Island, which would have been a stepping-stone to Hawaii and the United States mainland.

"What a great battle," Marjorie said. "And they did it with those three aircraft carriers."

Alice read from her paper. "It says here that they destroyed four Japanese aircraft carriers and two hundred seventy-five planes. Maybe the Japanese won't get to Camp Roberts after all."

Marjorie stitched up a seam in her underskirt. "Ladies, this may be a turning point in the Pacific war."

When the US Marines landed at Guadalcanal in August, the West Coast no longer appeared so vulnerable.

And Stalingrad, supposedly an easy victory for the Nazis when the Russian army left the city, turned into a bitter battle, a siege, when the German conquerors, cut off from their supplies and forced to eat their horses, were surrounded in November by the returning Russian army.

On January 31, 1943, Field Marshal von Paulus and fifteen of his generals defied Hitler's orders and surrendered what remained of their twenty-two divisions.

"My father thought the Germans would never take over Russia," Alice said. "It seems he was right."

Chapter 13

During the spring of 1942, Jennie Bauer talked to her parents about working in Portland when school let out. The Kaiser Shipyards were recruiting workers. With her husband gone off to the army, Naomi Davis planned on getting a shipyard job, and she had invited Jennie to stay with her.

Gloria shook her head. "You're much too young to be off by yourself like that."

"I won't be off by myself. Naomi will be with me. I'll be sixteen in June. Alice and Emma were working when they were sixteen."

"But they worked here in Juniper. They lived at home. It's out of the question."

"It's for the war effort." Jennie stormed from the room.

But when she calmed down, she persisted. She had arguments on her side: workers were needed badly, it was to help the country win the war, and the money was better than any pay in Juniper. In time she found her parents wearing down.

When she brought up the topic one day, John said, "Tess wrote that, since Ernst is gone, she's working in the shipyard herself now. All of the housing up there is full. They're building new housing for the workers, but even the new places are crowded. Tess will be renting out one of her rooms. If you take her room, where she can look after you and Naomi, you can go."

"Oh, yes, yes." Jennie danced around the room. She didn't mind staying with Tess as long as Ernst was not there. "That would be perfect, thanks. I can't wait to tell Naomi. She's waiting until my June birthday so that I can go with her."

How ironic that the war nobody wanted provided jobs, raised salaries, and pulled the country out of the Depression. Couldn't the government do that some other way?

"Tess says to bring plenty of work clothes." Gloria pointed to a small traveling bag that she had pulled out. "The workers are snapping them up as fast as they appear on the store shelves. Bring anything else you need too, because, with thousands of workers in Portland, supplies will be low. I'm hemming you some scarves out of flour sack material. She says you'll need them to hold your hair out of the way."

When they were alone, Gloria gave way to her worries. "Do you think she'll be all right, John?"

"With all three of them together, they'll be fine, and they'll be company for Tess," John assured her. "How can we not support the war? With the draft taking all the young men, the shipyards desperately need workers. I hear they're advertising all over the country. I'd go myself, but I'm doing fine as foreman at the mill, and it's a necessary industry too."

Before dawn on the first day of June, Jennie and Naomi boarded the bus to Portland, their lunch sacks and small bags in hand. John had insisted that they wear heavy work shoes. They also wore slacks, ready to work the moment they were hired. Crowded together with other potential workers headed for the cities of Portland and Vancouver, Washington, they stood most of the way.

Fragrant roses and rhododendrons bloomed in the city of roses that warm spring day. The lush beauty contrasted sharply with the tragic scenes of fighting all over the world portrayed in the newspapers. Jennie viewed the beauty with a touch of bleak sadness.

The Portland bus terminal was packed with people, and the streets, even so early in the morning, were jammed. Everything was busier and more vibrant than Jennie remembered from her rare visits to the city.

Grocery, clothing, and dime stores did a brisk business as the workers rushed to buy supplies. One woman emerged from a dime store carrying a sack of colorful items. "Ten headscarves," she told them.

"I'm a sweeper, and I need them to protect my hair. There's junk in that air. I'm lucky today. Usually they're all sold out."

When they stood in front of the busy shipyards, they were astonished by the activity. Far off at the wharf they glimpsed the outlines of enormous structures being built, with workers crawling around them, and in and out of them, and working on tall ladders. Huge cranes rose high in the air.

Hundreds of workers moved purposefully among several buildings: administration, mechanical, cafeteria, and a building with an amateurish sign on it that read Employment.

The girls were handed forms to fill out. When they finished, the woman who took them asked their ages. Jennie answered proudly that she was sixteen.

"Well, you're too young to work in the shipyards, but you can work in the cafeteria, if that suits you."

Jennie, slightly disappointed, told her, "That suits me, but we'd like to get the same shifts."

"That might be possible for tomorrow's swing shift. You can go over and talk to the cafeteria manager, and I'll take Naomi to the lead cleaning woman. They'll probably put you both right to work. We're short everywhere today. You should plan to meet this afternoon at the café. Right now, we need to get your fingerprints and pictures taken. Keep your bags with you."

Jennie was overwhelmed by the scents of attractive, colorful food in the cafeteria—so different from the somewhat bland diet they often ate at home. Workers could choose from great platters piled high with succulent browned chicken slices, beef roast, and pink hams; white fish with lemon wedges and parsley garnishes; cheese-covered casseroles with green peas inside; ivory creamed potatoes or mashed potatoes with brown gravy; beans with rich slices of pork; shredded cabbage and carrot salads; bowls of fresh lettuce with slices of purple cabbage, radishes, and green onions; tomato-flavored vegetable soup; almond-colored custards; butterscotch puddings; Jell-O of every flavor—strawberry, lemon, grape—enhanced with sliced carrots or pineapple; cakes with creamy frostings; apple pies; and walnut cookies.

Her dad had said that food might have to be rationed during the war as it was in Britain, but it obviously had not happened yet. She'd never seen such quantities and varieties of food, not even at the church potlucks.

Her mouth was still open in fascination when she was led to the back of the cafeteria and shown piles of dirty dishes and pots and pans. "We'll see how you do with these," the woman said. "Ever seen so many dirty dishes?"

"No, but I come from a large family, and I've washed plenty of them." Though she was disappointed not to be working in the shipyards, she was excited about her first job, her first time away from home. The pay was good, and everything was new and interesting. She scrubbed the pots and dishes diligently all day until her hands were white and wrinkled from the hot water, and her face was flushed from the steam rising from the huge sinks.

As they left the cafeteria at the end of the shift, Naomi told her about her job. "There's nothing to it. We just clean where the electricians and welders have worked and dropped stuff."

"What stuff?"

"Oh, bits of metal, electrical snippets, asbestos, and other junk they throw away. I swept up hundreds of empty gum wrappers, candy wrappers, and cigarette packages."

"You clean up after all of them?"

"No. Not just me. Dozens of cleaners sweep up after the thousands of workers building the ships. At least that's what the lead lady told me."

The two managed to get swing shifts, starting the next afternoon. Wearily, they went off to catch a city bus that ran near Tess's house.

Aunt Tess had expected them sometime during the day, but she worked the swing shift so she left a note: *Welcome to Portland. Please make yourselves at home. I've left some food out for you. Use the bedroom with the green furnishings.*

On the table sat cheese sandwiches, a thermos of coffee, fruit, and cookies. They happily devoured the food and then fell into bed in the room assigned to them. It had been a long day.

As the three women lingered over a late breakfast the next day, Tess gave them advice. "Cover your heads at all times when you're sweeping because the air is filled with dust, and rust dust that even keeps you from seeing. If the dust gets too bad, cover your noses and mouths with extra scarfs. I was a sweeper, but I'm helping an electrician, and I hope to learn enough to become one myself."

"Really? You could become an electrician?" Jennie asked, surprised.

"Yes, most men have the skilled jobs, but women can get them if they learn how because of the shortage. Even now some men are leaving the shipyard to join the services."

When Jennie reported to work that afternoon for the swing shift, she was greeted by the head cook who told her, "I hear you're a fine worker. I'm going to have you make salads for the dinner rush. Tom will show you what to do."

Tom Hansen smiled in greeting. "I'm only going to be here a short time or I'd be working in the shipyard. I've been going to college. I'm twenty and I'm joining the air corps." A friendly fellow with twinkling blue eyes, he carefully showed Jennie how to arrange the salads on individual plates—dozens of them. Then she cut fruit pies, chocolate and vanilla cakes, and cobblers and set the desserts on individual plates. At least the work was more appealing than washing dishes, and much easier on the hands.

When the dinner crowd thinned out, she was allowed her own meal break, and Tom joined her at her table. He said he was from Hood River and had been working at the shipyard only a short time himself. "We grow apples, pears, and cherries over there, even some peaches.

Hood River Valley is one of the prettiest places in Oregon, especially during cherry blossom time."

He and his friend had rented a small apartment that was available before the flood of workers began to crowd the cities. "Where are you living?" he wanted to know.

"We're renting a room from my Aunt Tess, or my folks would never have let me come up here to work. Her husband's away in the army."

"That's lucky for you. They're building housing units at Vanport now." He referred to a huge complex of units to house workers. "They might be ready by the end of the year. Have you heard about the medical insurance?"

"I've heard about life insurance."

"Mr. Kaiser is going to make cheap medical insurance available for those who want to buy it. I won't need it, of course, because I'm leaving for the air corps." Tom told her about his plans with enthusiasm while Jennie finished her coffee.

Does every boy in the country want to fly planes?

* * *

Friday evening after work, Tom invited the two young women to a party at his apartment for other swing shift workers. Jennie found Tess and told her they wouldn't stay long. Tess said, "Well, if you really want to go."

"Tom is pleasant. I'd like to go."

"Well, at least promise to stay together, and don't drink any beer if they offer it. Don't leave with any men, and don't smoke cigarettes."

About twenty young people crowded into the small basement apartment, chattering and comparing work notes, munching cheese and crackers. Tom's roommate passed out snacks. "The landlord lives upstairs, but he works the graveyard shift so the noise won't bother him." He laughed, obviously intending to make his share of noise.

Some of the older men and women drank beer, including Naomi, but Jennie took Aunt Tess's advice and drank Coke. She hadn't liked the small sip of beer she'd had. Soon the air was filled with cigarette smoke.

A fellow named Jess sat beside Jennie and talked about his entry into the army soon. "You should have a drink," he said. "I'm having one."

"Well, that's your choice. I don't care for the taste."

"I'll be risking my life for the country when I get into the service. In fact, I'll be risking it for you."

"You're very brave."

"Don't you think I should get something to help remember my country and what I'm fighting for?" He put his hand on Jennie's knee and waited for her answer as he moved his hand up to caress her thigh.

Jennie moved his hand away and stared at him. Did he seriously believe it was her duty to give him what he wanted—because he was going into the service? Did he think her a child, susceptible to exploitation? Never again. "I don't think it's my fault that there's a war on."

"But it will be dangerous as hell. I need fun now."

She shrugged. "That's war, I'm afraid."

"But I might die."

Jennie refrained from commenting that, at the moment, she could not care less. She got up and joined another group.

* * *

Tom left a few days later for the service. After that Naomi often went out to parties or dancing after work, but Jennie usually went home. Tess would write and tell her folks if she went out too much. And, since most of the other workers were older than she was, she felt uncomfortable at their parties. They all seemed so worldly-wise and confident.

Besides, she felt the sobering war news hardly encouraged partying. Instead she wrote to Tom, Fred, cousins James and Mark, and a few other young men she knew in the service. She also knit blankets and caps for the servicemen.

Tess disapproved of Naomi's activities, but Jennie knew that Naomi missed Roy terribly. They had been best friends for years.

Tom wrote that some of his Japanese-American friends in Hood River County had been sent off to an internment camp called Tule Lake just south of the California-Oregon border. It was dry, barren land, surrounded by barbed-wire fence and filled with tar-paper shacks for them to live in. Fruit growers in the Columbia River Valley, they were thought to be security risks. Tom complained:

> How could they be security risks? Most of them have been here for years. My dad has stored some of their most precious possessions on his property, but they've had to give away or sell most of their things for much less than they're worth. God knows what will happen to their orchards while they're away.

* * *

Back in Juniper that autumn for the school year, Jennie found her family, as usual, taking a keen interest in the war news. John hoped it would all be over before his son went into battle. He followed the actions of the navy and the marines in Southeast Asia. He cheered when General Eisenhower's forces and Lieutenant General Bernard Montgomery's British pinned the Germans against the Mediterranean Sea in May 1943 and captured a quarter of a million prisoners stranded on the coast of North Africa.

To celebrate, he took Gloria to see the war movie *Casablanca,* set in Morocco. The film revived the song "As Time Goes By" and thrilled audiences. Soon everyone was humming the tune.

"It's a wonderful film," Jennie said. "Why wouldn't it be with Humphrey Bogart and Ingrid Bergman starring in it? I wouldn't be surprised if it won the Academy Award."

Later Gloria said she had read that Hollywood utilized the skills of several cast and crew members who were exiles from Germany.

As a result of the Reichstag fire in 1933, dozens of artists and dissidents in Germany were arrested. Many of them were Jews. But earlier, some had fled to Paris and other countries, unable to take much of anything with them. As the Germans marched to Paris, those who could do so left for the United States or London.

* * *

When Jennie worked at the Portland shipyard cafeteria her second summer, butter, margarine, sugar, and meat were all rationed, but the food still tempted her. While her mother excelled as a seamstress, it occurred to Jennie that she was a good, but somewhat indifferent, cook.

Whenever Uncle Ernst came home on leave, Jennie spent the night with friends she knew from the cafeteria. She had no wish to see him at all.

The crowds in Portland were hard to ignore. The population of the metropolitan area swelled with shipyard workers by the thousands from all over the country. The workers raced to produce enough ships to win the war, and there was competition among the three shipyards in Portland and Vancouver to see which could make ships the fastest. They surpassed all previous records.

Stories circulated about the laughs Kaiser generated when he stated that a shipyard ought to be able to build a ship a day, a seemingly ridiculous goal in prewar days when it had taken several weeks. In the end, the workers came close to meeting that challenge, producing a Liberty ship every few days.

To help relieve the food shortage, Tess and most of the nation tore out lawns and put in victory gardens, weeding and watering in their spare time. They shared fresh vegetables with their apartment-bound friends. At the peak of the harvest, the women canned beans, tomatoes, and squash.

By the end of the summer, Jennie took excess produce home with her—as much as she could carry. The women produced some crops that John and Gloria could not grow well in the drier climate of Juniper.

To conserve water, they all used rinse water from the laundry, the dish washing, and floor cleaning, for it seldom rained in the summer. The Juniper Bauers, though, had one advantage. They happily secured dried manure for their vegetable plot from Emma and David Walker, who trucked loads into town from the ranch.

*　*　*

Once, Ernst returned to Portland on furlough. To avoid him, Jennie slept overnight with a friend. Naomi scrubbed the breakfast dishes while Tess shopped at a corner market. Suddenly Naomi felt a hand on her buttocks. She swung around, hitting Ernst in the face with her wet dishcloth.

"What do you think you're doing, you pig? Keep your hands off me or you'll feel something a lot worse on your head."

Ernst scurried off, muttering, "Just being friendly."

"Stay away from me!" she shouted after him. "You're a louse!"

Naomi watched him with disgust. *So that's why Jennie is not here. Should she tell Tess? No, what purpose would that serve? He'd been warned, and he'd soon be gone. No sense worrying Tess or making her angry. She needed a place to stay. Tess would probably get wise to him eventually on her own.*

Until Ernst left, Naomi spent most of her time in the victory garden. The carrots and corn had never been so well weeded. Later, coming in one day with a basket of cucumbers and ripe tomatoes, she said to Jennie, "Is he the reason you spent those days with your friend?"

Jennie flushed. "Yes, I didn't have a chance to tell you. And I didn't think he would bother you. You're so self-assured. I thought maybe it was just me. I was young and vulnerable when he kissed me on the lips. I know now it was a horrible French kiss. Rather turned me off French kissing for life, I think."

"What a snake. To prey on a young girl like that—and his own niece too. Well, I don't know what he was thinking. Just because I like to see other people now and then doesn't mean I'm cheating on Roy, or would be interested in another woman's husband. Roy and I've been in love since our first high school date, and there will never be anyone else for me."

"Do you worry about him?"

"Yes, but it doesn't do much good, does it?"

"I worry about Tom and Fred. The papers say airmen go down all the time. I don't want them to be killed." Overwhelmed by her thoughts, she stared out the window, imagining fiery planes falling from the sky.

Chapter 14

While she was based at Camp Roberts, Alice volunteered for special flight nurse training in case the army needed to evacuate the wounded by plane. She wanted to be ready to work where she might be most needed.

By the spring of 1943, the war news was encouraging. US forces were finally on the offensive in the Pacific and the Mediterranean. All the nurses waited expectantly to receive orders overseas. It was believed there would be a final push in Europe.

Brad wrote that he was now flying bombers:

> It was tough training, but we have to win this war, and I want to do my part. I wish I could see you, Alice. I dream of those few happy days we had together in Oregon, and I miss your smile and your pretty face. Someday we'll be together.

Alice held the letter to her breast. She had long considered him one of her best friends—maybe even a boyfriend. She remembered that last kiss, when he had held her for long moments. Now she feared for his safety.

* * *

In September, Alice sat reading a letter from Emma, relating the progress of young Davy Walker. He was crawling, almost walking, starting to talk—a child prodigy, according to Emma. Alice smiled at what was probably some motherly bias.

"Aren't you going to get packed? We have to leave first thing in the morning." Ellen began to sing. "We're going o-ver, we're going o-ver." She danced a little jig.

"Yes, yes, I have to write a letter to my mother first." In the letter, Alice told her family as much as she could and then wrote: *I'm fine, feeling great. Don't forget to collect my insurance if I don't get back.*

Marjorie cautioned Ellen and the other nurses. "It's not going to be some great picnic, you know."

"Oh, we know, Miss Serious. I'm ready, willing, and unable to do my duty." Ellen grinned. "But is there any law that says we can't enjoy the travel and the fun?"

"I certainly intend to enjoy it." Dana eagerly packed her belongings. "After all, we've just struggled through a Great Depression and years of nursing preparation. Now we're ready for excitement."

It was a miracle that Dana was even allowed to go overseas. At a slight five feet two inches tall, she was judged too thin. But Dana talked to all those with authority and finally convinced them that she was extremely healthy and 103 pounds was normal for her small frame.

The petite woman reminded Alice of a lively child at times. When they walked, she actively tapped her hands together, using up excess energy as she vigorously preceded the other walkers or waited for them to catch up.

Alice, Dana, Ellen, and Marjorie took the train route made out by the camp transportation officer. The crowded train traveled slowly through the South. Soldiers and sailors joined the train all along the way, en route to new stations.

Finally, they stopped in New Orleans, where the four nurses were to change trains after a long layover. They struggled through the packed, stuffy depot. Servicemen slept on benches, and tired young mothers held sniffling babies.

Four young soldiers approached them in the waiting room and suggested they all go to lunch in the French Quarter. The girls walked off and talked it over.

"It would be like a pickup," Dana said. "Should we let ourselves be picked up? My parents would die if they heard about it."

"I don't think we should go with them," Alice said.

"Oh, where's the harm, Miss Goody-Two-Shoes?" Ellen patted her hair and eyed the soldiers. "I like the tall one with the brown eyes and the cowlick."

"We could offer to pay for our own lunch." Marjorie tapped her toe. "Anyway, what can happen in broad daylight? They all seem very nice."

So they told the soldiers they would pay their own way, and all eight of them set off. It saddened Alice to see the miserable, run-down sections of town where most of the colored people lived. Segregation of the races was ingrained in the South.

As they rode the city buses, they noticed the colored people all filed to the back. They saw separate drinking fountains and separate bathrooms and signs reading No Colored Allowed. What a terrible way to live—for both groups.

Colored people lived in Portland, she knew, and they tended to live in separate areas. But nobody told them where to sit on the buses. And Jennie wrote that they handled the same jobs as the others in the shipyard. No community-sanctioned discrimination existed.

Eventually the young people found a place to eat in the French Quarter that they thought they could afford.

"Now we can say we've been in the French Quarter," Ellen said. "I can't wait to write home and brag about it." The day turned out to be a fine lark, the young men pleasant and polite.

Their train for the rest of the journey, though, was worse than the previous one. The cattle car with benches nailed down to the floor was extremely uncomfortable and dirty as well; it dismayed the young women. The fresh animal smell assaulted their senses.

Ellen stood up for periods to escape the benches. "I'd give them a piece of my mind about these trains, but I don't have any of it to spare." At least Ellen could often make a joke to lighten things up.

"Aren't we a wretched lot?" Marjorie asked as they arrived, tired and miserable, at Fort Bragg, North Carolina.

Ellen, much irritated by then, snapped, "Oh, for God's sake, Marjorie, this is no time to be prissy. Who cares what we look like? I just want a bed to fall into."

Marjorie raised her eyebrows. "My, my, aren't we touchy when we're tired."

As they joined nurses from all over the country, their papers were recorded, and their new equipment was issued: clothing, bedrolls, duffel bags, blankets, fatigues, a helmet, and a gas mask. They were instructed to send all their belongings home: civilian underclothing, uniforms, shoes, and dresses.

Ellen complained bitterly about giving up her attractive shoes, dresses, and especially her white lacy undergarments in exchange for dingy-looking, government-issued undergarments. "My mother made my undies from the softest white flour sacks. Who the hell's going to be looking at our underwear anyway? This is the most asinine requirement yet."

"Please don't be afraid to give us your complete and honest opinion, Ellen," Marjorie said, with a bland smile.

"Don't be sarcastic. I'm having trouble dealing with this place."

"And we aren't?"

"Nobody will see your underwear if you don't let them," Dana said. "So what difference does it make?"

Since Alice's underwear was somewhat worn, she didn't mind the exchange. In the end, all four of them slipped a couple of civilian outfits into their luggage.

"I'll bring my last pair of silk stockings," Ellen said. "If you treat me right, you can all borrow them sometimes for special occasions."

"Oh, yes," Alice said. "I'm sure we're going to find plenty of those in the middle of a war."

Besides giving up most of their garments, they had to spend the next sweltering day practicing camping, marching, and sleeping in a tent. Perspiration rolled down their faces and dripped between their breasts. Tired as they were, they didn't welcome this practice. Alice wondered how often she would use all that mess gear.

Following brief training at Fort Bragg, the nurses were shipped to Camp Kilmer in New Jersey to wait for transportation overseas. Something had happened to the ship they were expected to board. Rumors flew that it was getting a major overhaul. "I hope it's not the hull," Marjorie said with a laugh.

To keep the young passengers busy while the ship was readied, they were given twelve-hour passes so they could visit New York, thirty miles away. Alice called her aunt Pearl, who rushed to gather her up, along with her three companions, and show them the sights of the city.

In Grand Central Station they sent telegrams to their parents. From the top of the Empire State Building, they looked out at the Flat Iron Building, the New Yorker Hotel, the Statue of Liberty, and Ellis Island.

They strolled along Broadway and looked at all the theaters, lit up after several years of blackout because of the fear of bombing raids. Aunt Pearl and her husband escorted them to dinner at the Plantation Room of the Dixie Hotel, where the orchestra played "Wait for Me, Mary."

Alice felt a small wave of homesickness when they played "Miss You." As she looked at her friends, she saw not a dry eye among them. Each had a special boyfriend somewhere, at home or in the service.

They were given additional passes when the ship was still not ready. A nurse named Sally joined their group, and she asked Alice to carry a sack for her.

This time the nurses rode the bus through the Lincoln Tunnel under the Hudson River. Pearl's son, Norman Jackson, who was home on leave, met them and joined them for the day. Charmed to be escorting five young women, he took them for a ride on the subway, for a visit to the Hayden Planetarium, and to an automat for lunch, which reminded the nurses of post office boxes. They toured Rockefeller Center, built during the Depression years.

By the end of the day, it was evident that Ellen had intrigued Norman. He took pains to be by her side, directed his comments to her, and got her promise to write to him.

On all their excursions, Sally Stuart asked one of the others to carry her packages.

One day Marjorie said, "Sally, why do you ask the rest of us to carry your bags? Why don't you carry them yourself?"

"Oh, I couldn't," Sally said. "Ladies don't carry bags." Her words were greeted with complete silence.

Ellen looked at the other three and rolled her eyes. When Sally left them, Ellen burst out in indignation. "So she's a lady and we're not? Well, that's the last time I carry anything for her. She can go to Halifax. She is one peculiar woman. Who does she think she is? Did she have a maid or something?"

The others agreed that they were through toting bags for Sally.

* * *

Finally, they boarded the *Queen Mary* and settled into their crowded cabins for the trip across the Atlantic Ocean. "At last." Ellen stretched out on an upper bunk. "I'm so tired of trains, buses, trollies, and subways. And we can wear slacks until dinnertime."

"I don't mind the uniform," Alice said. "I like to dress for dinner." Their uniforms were now olive-colored and redesigned. All the nurses thought they were slimmer and trimmer than the old navy-blue uniforms.

Dana unpacked a few items. She glanced at Ellen. "Aren't you going to miss all the attention from Norman?"

"He's charming." Ellen was oblivious to Dana's teasing. "But it doesn't pay to get too involved with anyone. I may write to your cousin though, Alice, if you don't mind."

"Why should I mind? He obviously has very good taste. I hope to keep in touch with him myself."

"I heartily agree with you. Norman has very good taste." Ellen said, smiling. "He's a most discerning fellow. And modesty is vastly overrated."

When she got a chance, Alice wrote to her aunt Kate.

> How strange it is that, because of this horrid war, I'm able to see Aunt Pearl again and the sights of New York. Her daughters work for the USO so we didn't see them. Her son, Norman, home on leave from the navy, escorted us around. He's quite interesting, bright, and friendly—took a liking to my friend Ellen.
>
> The journey across the country has been difficult at times but exciting as well. We passed miles and miles of fertile fields. What a bountiful country we live in.
>
> Mother fears that our cousins, James and Mark Turner, may be fighting in the African campaign. Fred, of course, is still in flight training.
>
> Here on the ship, we have to use salt water to bathe and we have drill every day. We have abandon ship drills, fire drills, and air raid alerts.
>
> At first most of us were seasick, not something I want to write about. We nurses help out in the dispensary giving shots, and we rotate shifts working in the surgery and sick bay caring for surgical and medical patients.
>
> It's chilly on deck, although it's invigorating to get out there. The food is good. We often have filet mignon, poached

halibut, or stuffed turkey with fresh garden peas or asparagus, hearts of lettuce, exotic desserts, fresh fruit, and ice cream. Even Ellen, our own critic companion, is impressed.

We talk with enlisted men and shavetails (second lieutenants to you civilians), and romance appears to be blossoming between some of the passengers. (Not me—I'm not interested.) We also play cards, especially pinochle, and watch old films.

We're excited but also eager to find out what awaits us.

The nurses soon learned that on July 10, allied troops had invaded Sicily, aided by the new landing ship-tank (the LST). By the end of the thirty-nine-day campaign, they had swept the German and Italian defenders from the island and prepared to strike at the Italian mainland. Alice waited to hear about James and Mark.

Meanwhile, Allied planes bombed Rome. The Italians, unhappy with Mussolini, imprisoned him and formed a new government, disbanding the Fascist Party.

Chapter 15

Late Friday afternoon Kate caught a bus to Juniper. With rationing in effect, gasoline was too valuable to waste on unnecessary travel for one person. Signs proclaimed, "When you ride alone, you ride with Hitler." Edith was seeing a young marine on furlough and had decided not to travel with Kate.

Getting around the country was becoming more difficult all the time. The trains and buses bulged with passengers. In some rural areas, people brought out their old buggies and hitched them to horses again.

As she got closer to Juniper, Kate wondered what Grant would say when she talked to him. After he returned from service in the Great War, they were so happy together. They waltzed at the dances, hiked over the countryside in the late afternoons, and took in the exciting new movies. He said he loved her. They strolled on warm summer nights, when a cool breeze could stimulate the senses and a soft touch could set them on fire.

Then his mother became ill. Kate heard nothing from him for weeks.

At length she heard that he had married her classmate. Her grief almost paralyzed her. Love and trust were gone. It felt as though someone had died.

When Kate discovered she was to have a child, Gloria, her friend and sister-in-law, suggested she come to Wyoming with her and John. At least her parents, busy caring for four younger children, would not have to hear of her predicament.

Kate thankfully accepted their offer, and the three struggled together to prove up the homestead. She and John found work to see them through.

Would Grant now be surprised? Or did he know or suspect? This time, instead of going straight to the Bauer home, Kate entered the Juniper Hotel. It was already dark when she took a deep breath and walked through the front door. She asked the desk clerk for Grant Hunter and was shown into his office.

He watched her enter, her green suit molded to her trim figure, revealing a crisp white blouse at the collar. Smiling broadly, he rose and walked to her, his heart racing. How often he had imagined her being willing to see him again. Now here she was. Why was she here? He took her hands in his and studied her face. Her blue eyes were troubled.

"Kate, how good to see you. Did you just get to town?" He led her to a chair, concerned, and quite willing to let his voice show it.

"Well, yes," she said, her body stiff, her face set. "How are you anyway?"

"I'm fine, thank you."

He saw she had difficulty stating her reason for coming. "And how is your family? Your lovely nieces and your nephew? Of course, I see Emma now and then when she and David come to town. They're a fine couple. It was such a pleasure having her work here."

"That's what I want to talk to you about." Kate wondered how to start now that she had arrived.

"Yes?" He waited.

He raced over the possible scenarios, but he was utterly dumbfounded when she burst out, "Alice is our daughter. She's been sent overseas. She may be in danger. I thought you should know."

Stunned, he knelt down and put his head in her lap with a moan of anguish or a sob. She could not tell which.

After a time she said, "I thought you suspected. It didn't seem right that she might die, and you never knowing that she was yours."

He raised his head. "I did suspect the truth, Kate, after John and Gloria returned from Wyoming with a redheaded daughter. I didn't see her for years, of course, but when I did, I noticed that she didn't quite look like the blond one or the parents. I wish I could tell you how terrible I felt. My sick mother was determined that I marry her friend's daughter, but if I had known you were expecting a child, I wouldn't have done it. We would have been married. I loved you. I shouldn't have married her. It wasn't fair to you or to her."

She waved away his remarks, although they soothed her heart. "It's all in the past." He had been so desolate when he first returned from the navy. She would have done anything to help him recover. But when she heard that he was to marry, she thought he did not want her.

Luckily, she had Gloria and John to sustain her during those years of hardship in Wyoming. Even when they held school for three neighboring children in their two-room cabin the first year, she nursed the baby in the bedroom while Gloria worked with the students.

Since Gloria looked after Alice the next two years, while she taught a larger class in an abandoned mine shack, it seemed natural for her and John to let the Juniper community assume Alice was their daughter when they went back. Unable to get work nearby, Kate finally secured a position in the valley. She sent money, and visited them and the child often.

Then something clicked in Kate's mind. "Are you the anonymous donor who left food and money on Gloria's porch?"

Grant winced. "It was so little. But I had to do something when I suspected that Alice was my daughter."

"Oh, Grant." She smoothed his hair. "That was wonderful of you. The extra money and food has made a big difference to all of them. I'll keep you informed about Alice. The nurses are not on the front lines, but anything could happen."

She told him more about Alice while he sat beside her and listened carefully, daring to touch her wavy chestnut hair, her hands, and her shoulders. He wanted to protect her, to brush away her pain and worry. "Why did you decide to tell me now?"

"It didn't seem necessary before. Oh, I suppose I thought that sooner or later you would find out for sure. But now, with the danger she faces, it's important that you know the truth."

"I'm glad to know. And I'm grateful you decided to tell me. She's a beautiful, intelligent, young woman. Looks a lot like her mother." As he had hoped, this brought a smile to her face.

At last she rose to go, and he followed her, observing her straight back and fine form. He walked beside her to the Bauer house, the early darkness lending an air of enchantment to the high desert night. Despite the sobering news about Alice, his step was light and his heart exuberant.

"Is there any reason that I can't see you again, Kate?"

"I don't know, Grant. With gasoline rationed and the buses so crowded—"

"I don't care. I'll come wherever you are. I'll manage somehow."

"Why don't I write to you and let you know when I'll get to Juniper again?" He got her address so he could also write to her. And he had to be content with that.

But as he turned away, a breeze touched his face, and a small smile lit it. Here was a start. He had already heard from Emma that Alice was overseas, and he had adjusted to the unsettling news. Now he could plan to see Kate again.

* * *

John and Gloria greeted her when Kate knocked on their door.

"Is that Grant Hunter?" John asked, as Grant strode away.

"Yes, John, it is. I've told him that Alice is ours and that she is overseas. I thought he had a right to know that she could be in danger."

"And about time too. Had he suspected?"

"Yes. And he had heard about Alice being overseas from Emma and David. He also said that his mother insisted he marry before she died."

"I'm not a bit surprised. Mrs. Hunter was a domineering woman and a pompous snob. We kids all avoided her. She probably thought that rich girl was the only suitable wife for her son in the whole town," John said with disgust.

"I never realized that."

"Well, Grant is a simple family man. We've sure noticed how he dotes on Emma. As an only child, he probably felt obligated to his family, his mother."

Gloria broke in. "Have you eaten?"

"Not much. Maybe some fruit?"

"Yes, I've apples and a cake I've made. The coffee is still hot. I want to show you the new washing machine that John bought me. You've seen these wringer washing machines that you crank? Well, this one is electric."

Gloria pointed to the machine, sitting in the far corner of the kitchen. She poured the coffee and walked over to demonstrate how it worked.

"You put the clothes into this big drum, they're swished around by an agitator powered by electricity, and then you feed them through the wringer to get the wash water out. And after you rinse them in rinse water, you run them through the wringer again to get the rinse water out. It saves me so much work."

"Wherever did John get it when all industry is making armaments?"

"He bought it from a family that's moving away. Of course, it's quite old but still works."

"Oh, I'm so happy for you." Kate munched on an apple.

After a silence, Gloria went on. "You know, Grant never married again. I saw him looking at you at Emma's wedding. I'm sure he still loves you."

"He wants us to write to each other. I can't imagine us getting together after all this time."

"He's a good man, Kate, respected by everyone. Why not let bygones be bygones?"

Why not indeed?

* * *

Some weeks later, in the valley, Kate escaped from Mr. Conner, the sixth grade teacher, who had cornered her in the school hallway. The lonely widower constantly looked for excuses to talk to her about school activities. He usually managed to include a suggestion that they have coffee, go to a movie, or have dinner together. She always politely declined. She was not interested in Mr. Conner. He had an annoying habit of talking incessantly and rarely waiting for a reply or comment from his audience.

Kate returned to the valley apartment she shared with Edith. She found the younger woman sprawled on the couch, shaking with tears.

"What is it?" She dropped her files and purse as she rushed to her.

Edith raised her head. "It's Oliver. His mother wrote to me. He's been killed in the Pacific. In the Gilbert Islands, Tarawa. Just an atoll, really. But it was heavily armed with Japanese. They attempted to keep the Allies from advancing onto other islands and to the mainland of Asia."

"Oh, how awful. He's…was…such a nice young man."

"We were just getting close. Almost engaged. I promised to wait for him."

"I'm so sorry, Edith."

"His friend Paul is coming over. We're both in shock." Edith sat up and dabbed at her eyes with her handkerchief.

"Do you want me to leave for a little while?"

"No, no, we're just going to talk. He has some of the details of Oliver's…death from marines who wrote to him."

"I'll put on some coffee." *How much more bad news will we have to take before this cruel war is over?*

* * *

Out in Springdale, Emma Bauer watched the children playing on the school ground one Friday afternoon at school. She might have joined in skip rope. But she was heavy with child and did not want to take any chances of hurting the baby she carried.

Clouds covered the sky, but the air was calm. At the bell, the children, rosy-cheeked from the chill, filed into the two classrooms. Miss Shafer had left early for a dental appointment in Bend, so Emma monitored her classroom as well as her own.

She sent one of her older students to read a story to the fifteen younger children until they settled down. Next they had penmanship assignments and spelling exercises.

She moved back and forth between the two rooms as she put the eighteen students in her classroom to work after presenting their lessons.

In the afternoon, snow began to dust the school yard. Within minutes it was swirling around the building and had completely blanketed the ground. It looked as though winter had arrived early. Emma put more coal in the potbellied stove.

When it had been snowing for an hour, she began to worry about the children getting home. Most of them walked anywhere from a mile to four miles to school. Was it safe for them to undertake the walk?

Mr. Walker had warned her that in such an event the parents came after the children. The snow kept falling, and it blew in such a way that visibility was limited. The road—everything—was completely covered.

At dismissal time, none of the parents arrived to pick up their children. Emma tried to call Mr. Walker on the telephone, but the phone line was down. She could not reach any of the parents. Perhaps the storm was already too dangerous for them to travel to the school.

The children fidgeted. They watched the windows in fascination as the silent snow steadily fell. Emma knew she risked worrying the parents and perhaps angering them if the children did not arrive home on time.

Still she could not send them out into such hazardous weather. She had heard about the terrible blizzard of 1888 in the Midwest that hit at school dismissal time. Dozens of children became lost on their way home and froze to death in the snow.

She made a decision, gathering the younger children into her classroom so that she could tell them all together. "Children, it's not safe for you to walk home today. You'll have to stay here until your parents come after you. You may play cards or checkers, or draw pictures. To save coal, we'll all stay in this room. Bring chairs from the primary room so you can all sit down."

She hoped the coal would last. A load was due the following week, but they might have to heat the school for several hours. As a precaution, she allowed the fire in the primary room to go out and let the other one die down some.

"I could get home in the snow," Tommy said. "Let me go home, Mrs. Walker."

Emma passed out crayons and games. "No, Tommy, you might be able to make it home, but others might not be able to reach their homes. We need your help here."

"Oh." Tommy hadn't thought of that.

"I'm cold." Penny, a precocious first grader, shivered and crossed her arms over her chest.

"Let's put on our coats and hats and pretend we're living in the olden days before they had nice warm stoves. Anybody remember who built the first modern stove?"

Tommy raised his hand. "Benjamin Franklin."

"You're right. They named the stove after him. The Franklin stove."

"Can't we go out and play in the snow?" an older student asked.

"It's too dark and cold. Tomorrow you can go outside."

The unexpected pleasure of games in the schoolhouse was enough for most of the students. They divided into groups, and soon the room was noisy with their chatter and laughter.

But the hours dragged on, and the snow kept swirling around the building. It had to stop eventually. And when it did the parents would come after the children.

Penny pranced up to Emma. "Mrs. Walker, I'm hungry."

Emma had thought of that. "I have some dried apples and dried plums. We'll pretend we're soldiers in the war and these are our K rations. They have to carry the rations with them, you know."

"They do?"

"Yes. Would you like to pass them out?"

"Oh yes."

"Let each person take two apple pieces and two plum pieces." Thank God she had thought to bring that fruit last week. She told the children to get a drink of water to go with the dried fruit.

* * *

At the Walker ranch, David paced the kitchen floor. The wood cooking range kept the room cozy while a pot of coffee simmered on the top. He challenged his father. "Couldn't we at least try to get through?"

"You know better than that. In a blizzard like this, we wouldn't have a chance. We couldn't even see the road. And if we took the horses, they couldn't do much better."

"But what about all those children?"

"Let's pray that Emma didn't send them home. The snow was high even at dismissal time, so she probably didn't."

"Emma shouldn't be responsible for the children. Would the parents have taken them home by now?"

"No, David." Mrs. Walker was rocking little Davy to sleep. "They probably couldn't get through either. It came on so fast."

David groaned. "My poor Emma. What can we do?"

"Nothing. You should get some sleep. It might be a difficult day tomorrow."

Mr. Walker said, "Don't you remember this happening once when you were a boy? That time, the teachers kept the children at school who lived a long way off. The others made it home. Some of you spent the night in the schoolhouse with the teachers."

"I remember." Sarah, dressed in her overalls for chores, entered the kitchen and removed her boots at the door. "It was great fun."

David scowled. "For you maybe. But not for the teacher, I'll bet."

Chapter 16

At the schoolhouse, the children grew sleepy. "Let's pretend we're cave people and sleep on the floor. We'll need to put all our wraps on," Emma said.

This thought intrigued the children less than the other ideas. She led them in songs, however, and they joined in, sitting around the stove. Then she told them stories: *Ali Baba and the Forty Thieves* and *Cinderella*. As their bodies grew weary, they spread out and drifted off to sleep. Emma also dozed off on the chilly floor outside the circle of children.

She dreamed of a great mist encircling her, and though she struggled to run out of it, she could not see well enough to do so. She awoke several times during the night and crept to the windows to see snow still falling. The children slept.

When morning finally came, she was gratified to see it had stopped snowing. The sun shone brightly. As the children woke up, she allowed them to play outside to distract them from their hunger. They made snowmen and chose up sides for snowball fights. The coal held out, so she was able to maintain a fire to warm them when they came in to dry off.

By midmorning the snow started to melt. Frantic parents came to pick up their children.

"We couldn't get through yesterday," one father said. "I've never seen the snow fall so fast. We couldn't even see the road to drive. When I tried, I went in the ditch."

"Thank God you didn't let them walk home," another told her. "You kept them from getting lost in the snow."

But Mrs. Pearson, visibly upset, scowled at Emma. "We've been worried sick about our little boy. We only live a mile away. You could have sent him home."

Emma recoiled. "I'm sorry, Mrs. Pearson. I thought the children would be safer here."

"Well, I don't agree with your judgment." Meredith, eyeing Penny, left with her son in a huff.

Emma knew she was Chet Southwick's older sister and just as disagreeable.

Finally, only Penny was left. As Emma stood in the entry peering out the small window, a gray-haired man strode in. "I'm here to take Penny home." Emma recognized him as Mr. Southwick, Chet's dad.

"Are you her father?" Emma was guarded. Penny's mother had brought her to school the first day. The woman had told her that Penny's father was away. She glanced over her shoulder into the classroom where Penny was drawing on the blackboard.

The man glared as Emma hesitated. "Mr. Southwick, I'm very sorry. But I believe I should wait until Penny's mother can come after her."

"I'm her grandfather."

"What?"

"I don't think her mother can come after her," he said, wavering.

Emma thought quickly. Whatever the story was, she couldn't let the child go with this man.

"Mr. Southwick, it is good of you to come after her, but my husband will be coming after me soon, I'm sure. We can take Penny home. You needn't concern yourself."

"Look, Mrs. Walker, I do concern myself. It's not generally known, but Penny is Chet's daughter. Her mother's a maid and her maternal grandmother's a cook. They both work at the ranch house for the Glass family."

Emma stared in disbelief. "It's true, Mrs. Walker. They were teenagers at the time. She claimed rape; Chet denied it. I don't know what to believe, but Penny resembles my deceased wife. She can't be denied.

I worry about the child as any grandparent would. Chet went to town last night. He's probably trapped there by the storm."

"I…understand."

As they stood in silence, Penny ran up to the man and was lifted into his arms. "Hello, Mr. Southwick. I didn't know you were here."

He chuckled and kissed the girl on the cheek while she giggled. Turning to Emma, he explained, "She knows me. I often visit her."

Suddenly a horn honked outside. At the window Emma saw David and his father. They got out of the truck and began tramping toward the school.

"Mr. Southwick, my husband's here. We drive right by the ranch where Penny lives. Let us drop her off. You can count on my discretion about this matter. It will go no further."

Reluctantly, he put the child down. "I appreciate that. If it's no inconvenience then, you can take Penny home." He put on his hat, bid them good-bye, and walked out the door, nodding to the Walker men.

Relieved to see that Emma was all right, David said, "What was he doing here?"

"He was concerned about Penny not having a ride home. I told him we could drop her off. Her mother and grandmother work for the Glass family at their ranch house."

"Fine." David looked around. "Did the other children spend the night here?"

"Yes, but their parents came after them."

"Then let's go, Mrs. Walker and Miss Penny. Dad's here to drive the Model-T home. I suppose you're hungry. Be polite to me, and I'll give you apples and cookies that I brought for you."

"Aren't I always polite to you?"

"By golly, you are. Here." He handed the food into their eager hands, and they ate as he drove off.

* * *

Penny's mother, Nina, met Emma and David at the ranch house door. "Thank you so much for bringing her home, Mrs. Walker, Mr. Walker. Mother and I've been worried sick but figured you'd keep the children at school."

"You're right on our way, so it was no trouble. Mr. Southwick came by to pick her up. Shall I let her go with him if something like this comes up again?"

Nina kissed Penny, holding the child in her arms. "Go to the kitchen and see Grandma," she said. Let down to the floor, the child scampered off. Nina turned slowly toward Emma. "He's a friend of ours. He wouldn't hurt her. But I'm not sure about his son. Don't let her go with Chester Southwick."

"Very well," Emma said.

As she and David turned to leave, Odette Glass walked into the room. She surveyed the serious group. "Is something wrong?"

"No, no," Emma said. "David and I just dropped Penny off. It was right on our way."

"On Saturday? There's no school on Saturday."

"Because of the blizzard. The students spent the night in the schoolhouse," Emma said.

"Really? I did hear something about her not coming home from school."

"Good-bye." Emma and David walked off to the truck.

"Can you imagine? She's not even concerned about her maid's child being off in the blizzard."

"Typical," David said, caressing his wife's cheek as he settled her in the front seat of the truck. "I'm so relieved you're all right."

Within a few days, Emma heard more from Meredith Pearson.

* * *

The complaint arrived in the form of a letter. A group of Springdale parents and board members planned a meeting at the school to discuss her action during the blizzard. She was told to attend and inform the group why she kept the children at school overnight.

Dismayed, Emma showed the letter to David, who promptly showed it to his father.

Mr. Walker, indignant, fumed. "I'm the board chairman. They're completely in the wrong. I should have been consulted." He telephoned other community members and suggested they attend the meeting if they wanted to say anything.

On the day of the meeting, all three Walkers arrived at the packed schoolhouse.

Since she had instigated the action, Meredith Pearson took it upon herself to begin the meeting. Indicating her friends, she said, "We parents find fault with Emma Walker for not sending the children home early. At the very least, she should have sent the children who live nearby home. My son and several other children could have made it home if the teacher had had sense enough to send them when it started to snow. As it was, we suffered a miserable night worrying about our youngsters. We believe the teacher to be incompetent. She should be fired."

A murmur went around the room.

Another mother stood up. "Nobody could have predicted how much snow would fall. I believe Mrs. Walker saved lives by keeping the children at school."

A man stood up. "It's impossible to find your way in such a blizzard. How could children do it?"

Another asked, "If you knew how the storm would turn out, Mrs. Pearson, why didn't you come after your child when it started to snow?"

Several more parents spoke in favor of Emma's decision. Finally, Mr. Walker stood up. "I'm the chairman of the school board. I can tell you how difficult it would be to get another teacher during a war. Teachers can make more money by working in the Portland shipyards or in war plants.

"Furthermore, I believe Emma did the right thing. She saved your children's lives. Yes, you spent a night of worry. But that was nothing compared to years of grief. I suggest you go home and think about that."

People got up, smiled and nodded at Emma, and shuffled out. At last, only Meredith Pearson and her friends glowered at the Walkers as they rose and stalked out after the others.

"You wouldn't have your job if you weren't his daughter-in-law," Meredith fired at Emma as she left.

Distressed as she was, Emma breathed a sigh of relief. "Thank you," she said to Mr. Walker.

"Thank you for staying. Those Southwick kids are never happy unless they're stirring up trouble. Their mother died young, and they were left with one parent. Maybe that explains it. Mr. Southwick is a fine man. I'm sure he did his best with them, but they're always causing trouble."

* * *

Alice and her friends disembarked at Scotland, where the *Queen Mary* had pulled into the Firth of Clyde. From there they traveled all night to Holton Park, Wheatley, Oxford, England. Here they lived in small brick huts, six women to a hut. Little iron stoves without grates or dampers challenged their ingenuity, but they finally got them to give out some heat.

"Nasty little beasts," Ellen said, kicking their stove one chilly morning.

They slept on six-legged cots where they spread out their bedrolls. They used footlockers placed at the foot of their cots as chairs, and they put their gear away in their allotted space of one large and one small drawer apiece in the chest.

They were given no choice of roommates. Alice shared a cottage with five others, including Sally Stuart and Dana. An older roommate planned to go to medical school and become a doctor. One well-liked Irish girl soon left them for a requested transfer. Another woman came from Canada.

    Air raid sirens screamed their warnings. When they did, personnel of the unit reported back to duty. Sometimes several sirens screamed during the course of an evening. Blackouts were common. During heavy air raids on London, they observed the eerie sky as bombs fell on the city. They could only imagine the devastation.

Chapter 17

Aunt Freda Bauer, now an army nurse, wrote to Alice from Australia. Her letter was dated August 1943, but it took some time to catch up with Alice.

We still live in a tent and do our washings in our helmets. The paint is wearing off on the inside of mine, so I have to be careful of ruining it.

We do calisthenics and drill and drill. Today the sergeant wanted us to drill in front of the shavetails in order to show us off. We agreed, so we did column lefts and rights, right and left flanks, rear marches, etc., and I guess the shavetails were surprised all right.

The schoolchildren are on vacation for two weeks now. This is winter, and it seems funny to see school in session during June, July, and August.

We have been entertained in some excellent Australian homes and have become acquainted with some nice nurses (sisters here).

We take turns at latrine duty, office duty, and ground police. We pick up butts and more butts.

A cousin on my mother's side, Bill Becht, who lives in Idaho, came to see me. Because he's an enlisted man, we were not allowed to eat together, go to the officers' club together, or even go to a movie together.

We can hear taps every night and reveille every morning.
Love,
Aunt Freda

In April, Alice and her friends trained at a camp in Cirencester, England. Afterward they were sent to their final destination: a tent hospital near the southern coast.

Built by the army unit, enlisted men poured concrete for cement walks and foundations for the ward tents. The nurses lived four to a tent, with small potbellied stoves in each one. Alice was reunited with her three friends from Camp Roberts.

"Oh no, not you three again," Ellen said, greeting them with open arms nevertheless. "What have I done to deserve this?"

"You probably got us because of your sweet nature," Marjorie retorted, smiling. "We'll try to live up to your high standards of deportment and vocabulary."

"You're too kind." Ellen beamed. "I was angry to be off in another tent. How dare they take me away from my friends like that? Who do they think they are, the US government?"

Their patients never stayed long in their station hospital. Those who needed surgery or extensive care were sent on to specialized army hospitals. Minor wounds and illnesses were sent to general base hospitals. Only those who could not be safely moved remained.

After long hours at work, the nurses just wanted to relax. But sometimes, when they were off duty, they visited and danced at the officers' club on base.

As they planned their first visit, Sally said, "Remember not to wear your bras."

They all stared at her in disbelief. Ellen put her hands on her hips. "What are you talking about?"

"Lieutenant Dillon told me that women are not allowed in the officers' club if they are wearing bras."

"How naive can you be, Sally? He was just pulling your leg."

"Really? Why?"

Ellen rolled her eyes. "Because men are full of lust and like to trick people, especially women."

Red-faced, Sally wore her bra as did the others.

* * *

"It's too bad that we can't date enlisted men," Sally Stuart said, as the nurses hurriedly ate breakfast. "I've noticed one handsome fellow, and he's been looking me over. It isn't fair. Why couldn't he be an officer?"

"Don't ponder the mysteries of the universe too deeply, Sally," Ellen said.

"I'm sure he wants to date me."

Date you or something. Ellen chuckled. "I heard a couple of enlisted men assert that nurses were made officers just so that the male officers could keep the women to themselves. It rings true. We don't do much besides fetch and carry."

"We do more than that," Alice said.

Ellen gave her an indulgent smile. "Of course, Miss Florence Nightingale."

Alice laughed at the moniker. It was impossible to be upset with Ellen.

"Florence Nightingale is remembered for her care and compassion to soldiers," Alice said. "She was also a renowned statistician who used epidemiological data to document the effectiveness of nursing practices. And because of this work, disease and death were greatly reduced in the armies of the Crimea."

"My God! You've been hanging around Marjorie too long. You're beginning to sound like her."

Alice merely smiled. "You pay me the greatest compliments."

* * *

Nurses were being shifted all the time. Their head nurse was ordered to southern Italy where the Allies had invaded, and Marjorie took her place. Because of the tremendous buildup of American bases and army personnel in England, everyone assumed that there would be an invasion of the northern, Nazi-occupied European mainland before long, but no one knew when.

One day Marjorie called Alice outside the hospital. "There's someone to see you." She indicated a tall, young captain standing a short distance away. When he saw her, he removed his army hat.

"Brad," Alice whispered. Thinner and more serious-looking than the youth she knew from four years ago, he carried a look of weariness about him. She took his extended hand. "How good to see you, Brad."

His eyes licked over her. "Your hair is shorter. You look very professional in that seersucker uniform."

"Brown stripes aren't my favorite color design, but…you're still flying?"

"Yes. We're making bombing runs over Germany and the Continent. How long have you been here? I've been hoping you'd be sent over. Selfish of me, but I wanted to see you."

"We haven't been here long, just a few months—training, waiting for the big event. Tell me about your flights."

"Not a lot to tell. I pilot the bomber. We leave early, in the middle of the night sometimes, and get back in the afternoon. Not every day. The weather doesn't allow it. There's a lot of fog—or something else grounds us."

"It must be terribly dangerous."

"Well, that's war." He shrugged. "The worst part is losing those guys who fly alongside of us in other planes. So far we've been lucky."

"I'm so glad to see you, Brad, but I need to get back to work."

Brad squeezed her hand. "Look, let's get together. I'm at the next base over. I have some days off duty and you must too. Let me know when you're off work. You can send me a note." He gave her his location and took her number.

"Will we be going to the Ritz?" Alice asked, with a teasing smile. She remembered him calling their picnic stop the Ritz on the way to Juniper.

He laughed and walked her back to the hospital entrance. "We would if my pay would allow it. How about a park instead?"

"That would be lovely."

Before he let go of her hand, he impulsively kissed the back of it.

Sally Stuart noticed her flush as she entered the hospital ward. "Is your boyfriend an enlisted man?"

Alice laughed. "No, and he's not a boyfriend. Just an old friend who's flying missions over Germany now." But was he just an old friend? She had thought of him so often and cherished his letters. They had been so comfortable together, old friends from another life.

But she also remembered his strong arms around her, his body close to hers, and his lips kissing her. She had been overjoyed to see him, ecstatic in fact. And she felt thrilled that he had looked her up.

Sally soon met her own officer at the officers' club. They dined together there and saw movies on the base. They often traveled into London.

Following their lead, Dana, Ellen, Marjorie, and Alice took the train together to meet Brad and some of his officer friends, all on stand-down time, in the dining room of the Ford Hotel in London.

The group stuck together to visit the sights, but Brad often dawdled, and Alice lingered behind with him. When they visited the Tower of London, she shuddered to think of all the people beheaded there.

"Monsters appear in every age," Brad said. "Henry VIII could hardly have been worse than Hitler and Mussolini. Modern dictators have all the power of kings, if not more."

"Perhaps, with this war, we can change that."

"If I didn't believe that, I wouldn't be able to do what I do. I think of the guys we've lost and those German airmen in their downed planes, and I want to believe that all their deaths are for a greater good.

"Our gunner has been killed, and all of our crew has been hit by flak except me and the navigator. Our radio operator was shot down with another crew. I've seen my friends go down in flaming planes and crash.

"Enemy fighters hit our planes, and the havoc they create is hard to believe. I've seen flak so heavy and thick you think you could actually land on the smoke puffs. Planes come home so badly beaten up they couldn't fly again for a month."

He stared into space, as though he saw the doomed men in front of his eyes. He seemed to forget she was there. Then he suddenly snapped out of it and talked of visiting Trafalgar Square and Piccadilly.

When the officers put the nurses on the train for the ride back to their base, Alice could not help wondering if they would ever see the young men again. The fatality rate for airmen was extremely high.

* * *

Mail from home greeted them the next day. Sent to North Africa by mistake, it was several months old. But packages of cookies and other treats were still edible, and any nurse who received some shared with the other women.

Alice eagerly opened her letters. Emma was expecting a second child. Fred finished his flight training and was anxious to get overseas. Jennie answered her recent letter. She wrote:

> Mother is in a civilian watch for enemy planes in Juniper. People expect the Japanese to attack the coastal states, but I believe they're too busy in the Pacific fighting our forces. Of course, folks still talk about those two bombs that dropped near Brookings a couple of years ago. They didn't do much except make craters.

Iris Reynolds, your high school classmate, married a navy officer. I hear she's following him from base to base. I remember that she made fun of you for going into nursing, thinking it messy work.

I hope she finds quarters for military wives neat and clean, but I've heard differently. That's one reason why Aunt Tess decided not to join Uncle Ernst. Some service families are even living in converted chicken houses because housing is almost nonexistent around the bases.

Thanks so much for your kind offer to help me financially at college. It's so thoughtful of you. The truth is that I haven't decided whether or not I want to go to college at this time. We're needed in the shipyards, and I think I should help my country by working there until this stupid war ends. After all, "we're building a better world."

Also, I probably won't need your help. I've managed to save quite a bit of money working during the summers. We've made good wages, and I've bought war bonds and put the rest in the bank. Since I started school early, I will be a young high school graduate. I could spare a year to work, to help win the war, and save more money.

Alice smiled ruefully. Now that nurses were finally paid the same as men in the army, and she had a little more to spare, her help was not needed. Still, Fred would need help when he returned from the war, and so would little Linda and Marie eventually.

Now, though, it was likely their parents could help them with further education. Her father earned good wages and was even in the process of buying their Juniper house.

Not all the news was good. The death of her cousin Mark in the Italian campaign shocked Alice. Her mind flashed back to the young boy who ran with Fred, golden hair flying in the clear winds of central Oregon. Suddenly the war intruded on her as it never had before.

Other nurses received bad news too—about friends and classmates they knew. With serious faces, the nurses went back to their duties. Most of the news was sad. And the strain of waiting and preparing for a big offensive took its toll on the whole base. But the worst was yet to come.

Chapter 18

Sally spent more and more time with her officer. She seemed to have trouble concentrating on her work. One morning Alice found her with morning sickness in the latrine.

"Are you pregnant?" she asked in surprise.

Sally nodded, her face contorted in misery. She cleaned her face and then covered it with her hands.

"Couldn't you have prevented this?" Alice asked. "After all, you're a nurse."

"I just never thought it would happen to me."

How careless. "Will you get married?" Alice tried to sound sympathetic.

Sally grimaced. "He's already married. He has a wife at home."

Alice's face became bleak. "You realize they will send you home now. Is there anything I can do?"

"No thanks, Alice. I think I'll be glad to go home. My father will be angry, but he'll help me. I don't want to have a baby."

When the other nurses heard that Sally was leaving, Ellen said in a sarcastic voice, "Oh, we're really going to miss her, aren't we?"

"Ellen, have a little compassion," Dana said.

"You're right. I'm being boorish," Ellen said contritely. "Well, why send her home? We have some of the best doctors in the country right here on army bases. And we need every nurse we can get. Despite her reluctance to carry packages on our little trips, she's a good nurse. Why not abort right here and let her get back to work?"

Marjorie agreed. "Yes, and the army has spent a bundle training each nurse. It doesn't make much sense. But abortion is illegal, and many people think it's immoral too."

"She doesn't seem too unhappy about going home," Dana said. "Perhaps it's for the best."

* * *

At Brad's urging, Alice rented a bicycle to meet him in a nearby town. The trees sprouted new buds, and the green meadows looked lush and inviting. What a macabre contrast the land presented compared to battlefields in Italy, Russia, the Continent, and the Pacific where guns and explosions were blasting off and bombs burst in raids.

They sat under a tree and listened to insects buzzing around them. For the first time she noticed how large his arms and hands were, how fascinating the small dark hairs on his tanned forearms were, and how his hair, parted neatly on one side, framed his angular face.

Brad stretched out his long legs. "We had an early mission this morning."

"Why don't you take a nap?"

He grinned at her, his eyes running over her trim figure in her black-and-white cotton dress. "Could I use your lap for a pillow?"

Alice felt her face redden. Excitement coursed through her veins. "Of course, if you'd like."

"If I'd like?" He sank down against her. "You're soft and you smell like lavender."

He told her about his plans to finish his college classes in Oregon when he got out of the service.

"My family sent me to Portland in the first place, you know. Even my big brother insisted that he wanted me to get a college education since he couldn't go to college. 'Bradley,' he said, 'one of us in this family has to go to college. Since I barely made it through high school, I guess it's up to you.' Actually, he made good grades in school. Steve joined the CCC, and some of his wages were sent home to the family. He's in the marines in the Pacific now."

"What will you major in?" Alice ran her fingers through his black hair, silken, thick, luxurious.

"Business, I think. My dad was in business, do you remember? He owned a hardware store, but it failed early in the Depression. Two hardware stores couldn't make it in Juniper." He laughed ruefully. "Then he worked at the mill off and on."

"Yes, I remember the store."

"Dad usually had no work. Grant Hunter sometimes gave him work on small jobs in exchange for the rent. Mother sold magazines to take up the slack. When he started working, Steve handed over his pay to support the family. Dad finally got a WPA job. If Grant had not waited for the rent time and time again, we'd have been out on the street."

"He's a good man," Alice said.. "When Emma worked for him, he often helped her in little ways—gave her extra food, bed linen that was no longer usable in the hotel. He gave her a torn bedspread once that Mother made into coats for the little girls."

"Some people say—that's my mother and her friends—he's trying to make up for his failed marriage. According to Mother, though, his wife was a flighty thing who didn't want to settle down to a mundane life in Juniper."

"Interesting." Alice pushed her auburn hair back. "My dad thought Mr. Hunter never made any money on those apartments he owned because he was always helping the tenants."

Brad sat up and touched her red hair. "Your hair is beautiful."

Slightly embarrassed, she went on. "My dad worked for the WPA too. He thought it was charity though. He was raised as a farmer. Grandpa settled on a farm outside of Juniper, but he had to sell it."

"Lots of farmers couldn't make it during those years," Brad said.

"Things were bad for us in town too. One time Dad gave me a nickel for a loaf of bread. He said, 'Don't lose it. It's all the money we have.' I hurried through the sagebrush, so proud to be trusted with the money on my first trip to the grocery store alone. As I jumped over a small ditch, the nickel flew out of my hand.

"I searched for hours, it seemed, but the nickel had disappeared. I hated to go home to face Dad's anger. But when I told him, half crying, that I had lost the last of our money, he gathered me close and wiped my tears and said, 'Don't cry, Alice. It's only money.'"

What had they eaten that day? Probably potatoes.

"One thing you can say about the Depression, Alice. Almost everybody had it bad."

She nodded. "Dad worked at several things: farm work, the mill, sales work. Aunt Kate worked as a housemaid while she trained as a teacher."

"Folks said they were hard times, but they were nothing compared to this war, Alice."

She dimpled. "When she was a child, Kate says the family was too poor to buy coconut, so they had to use string instead."

Brad chuckled. He reached out to stroke her smooth cheek.

"You know, Brad, I'm surprised that you aren't writing to a real girlfriend."

"Aren't you real?"

"Am I your girlfriend?"

"I hope so. I did meet a couple of women I dated while I was training in the United States."

"Well, tell me about it. I'm not surprised. You're very handsome and personable."

Brad laughed, obviously pleased. "One was the widow of a navy officer killed at Pearl Harbor." He refrained from telling her that he had stayed overnight at the widow's place. "She was older than me."

"Oh?" Alice said with interest.

"She married an army major even before I left."

"Bad luck for you, eh?"

"Probably for the best. She was ambitious and eager to remarry."

"And the other one?"

He had stayed over with her too. "She wrote me a Dear John letter a month after I left the States," he said in a wry tone, referring to a type of letter sent to servicemen telling them their girls couldn't wait for them.

"Oh, I'm sorry."

"That was probably best too. How about you, Alice? Who have you been dating?"

"Me?" Alice snickered. "My long hours have not permitted much dating, unless you count a chance encounter and dinner with seven other people in New Orleans on our way east. At Camp Roberts we nurses often visited the officers' club as a group, but I never dated. I haven't really dated since high school."

"So tell me, Alice, what are your goals? What do you want?" They lolled on the grass, savoring the quiet.

"I wanted to help myself and my family out of the Depression. I wanted to make a decent living as a nurse. And I wanted to leave Juniper.

"Fortunately, my family is getting along fine now. Dad's had steady work since WPA days, Jennie works in the Portland shipyard, and even Mother makes money sewing and substituting in school. Emma and David are prosperous enough to start a family. But what will happen when the war is over?"

"I think the government will never turn its back on a depression again. Surely the experts have learned some things from the Great Depression. Maybe the Federal Reserve will help moderate economic cycles."

He took her hand. "Your determination has certainly helped you stick with nursing. I wouldn't mind settling in Juniper. One of my goals is that you and I be together."

Alice shook her head. "We're both in very dangerous jobs. You know I've trained as a hospital flight nurse. I may be called for that duty soon."

Brad hugged her tightly. "God forbid."

* * *

Over tea in a small teahouse, she told him about Mark's death. He mentioned mutual acquaintances killed in the fighting. "Mother wrote that Roy Davis died in North Africa," he said.

"Oh, poor Naomi. They waited so long to marry too."

"So why wait, Alice? I'm twenty-six, you're twenty-four. Let's get married here."

"Oh, Brad, you don't even know what you want. It's impossible."

"I know what I want. I want to marry you. And I want to get out of this crazy damn war, get my college degree, and then settle down in Oregon."

"When we were in Portland, you wanted to see the whole world."

"Yeah, well, I've seen enough of it to last me the rest of my life. Alice, we've known each other a long time." He stroked her arm and spoke softly. "I've always wanted you. Ever since we worked together at the old Jiffy Café and you had every guy in town after you."

She laughed. "Well, that's an exaggeration." But she stirred with excitement at his touch. Then she sobered. "We wouldn't even have time together. If the invasion of Europe starts soon, my days at the hospital will be longer, and yours will be too. There's no way for it to work now."

When they parted, he kissed her and held her close, reluctant to let her go.

* * *

A few weeks later Brad took Alice to the officers' dance on his base. Waltzing figures covered the dance floor. As Brad whirled her through the cheerful couples, she could almost forget about the war, the worries.

During intermission, the young people attempted frivolity and most succeeded, especially those away from home for the first time. The war seemed a great lark.

But eventually the conversation turned to the fighting in Italy and in the Pacific, friends they had lost, where they all might be going, and when the invasion on the Continent would begin.

"When we finally get over there, we'll whip the socks off the Krauts," one young, green officer boasted.

"I wouldn't be so sure," another said. "Haven't you heard about the Atlantic Wall? The Germans have installed fortifications all along eight hundred miles of coast, from Norway to Spain."

"Oh hell," another new man said. "I've heard rumors about specially designed tanks to get over those jerry-built mines and stakes. Our engineers will figure it out."

"The British-Canadian raid on Dieppe, France, in the summer of forty-two turned out to be a disaster," Brad said. "Fifty US rangers were involved too."

"Aw, that was just a test. They've learned some things since then. Good God, we've got over one hundred fifty bases all over England. The country is inundated with our servicemen. Why, the island might sink any day from the weight."

"I read a column by Ernie Pyle," a flight veteran said. "Those poor chaps in Italy damn near froze in the mountains last winter. Got frostbite. They sometimes don't get baths or hot food for weeks. I'd sure hate to be in the ground forces."

"Wonder what's taking so long for us to get over there," one man mused.

"We'll probably invade France in May, when the weather clears," another chipped in.

"We'll beat Fritz by Christmas, and we'll all be going home," a new officer said.

"Oh, sure. Once the invasion starts, you'll probably turn tail and run," his buddy said in a teasing voice.

"Aw, go to hell. You, of course, will be Mr. Hero," the officer snapped in a sarcastic comeback.

One thing the nurses noticed: servicemen on the trains and the buses usually sang "Lili Marlene" on the way home.

"What is it about that song anyway? Why do they sing it all the time?" Marjorie wondered.

"I've been told it came from a German love poem about this girl standing under a street lantern," Dana said.

Ellen was skeptical as usual. "Probably a prostitute."

"No, no, I told you. It's a love poem written by a German schoolteacher. It was played on German radio and the Allies picked it up."

"Well, it's pretty anyway," Alice said.

Chapter 19

Brad and Alice had another daylong visit in the rural English town, but to his dismay, she would not be swayed about marriage. "Why marry when we can't even stay together?"

Despite her protests, his kisses and caresses titillated her. She longed to explore those emotions further. When they met, she could feel his glance running approvingly over her.

But she knew about the high casualty rate among airmen flying over the Continent. She wondered if she wasn't being unfair. He hated the killing, and his face often had a haunted look.

She realized that other nurses, servicewomen, or English women would have gladly dated him, slept with him, and perhaps married him. He'd grown strikingly handsome with his black hair, serious brown eyes, and long dark lashes. Still, Chet was handsome too. That meant nothing.

Many servicemen wanted to marry in a hurry. Perhaps those who did thought they wouldn't be back. Or perhaps they wanted to experience married love immediately, thinking they might be gone for years. Maybe they hoped marriage would assure them a woman when they returned.

As they faced mortal danger, did they mistakenly believe marriage would relieve their loneliness, their homesickness, and their misery?

She'd already seen or heard about wartime marriages that weren't working. She would not marry Brad in the middle of a war, but perhaps she could give him a few hours to forget it all. "Brad, maybe we could get a room somewhere?" She kept her eyes averted.

He studied her face. "When?"

She looked into his longing eyes, dark and mysterious. "I won't marry you, but we could be together if you want."

"If I want? What a stupid question. You know I want you. I love you. Are you sure?"

"Oh yes, Brad. I want to be with you. We could be separated any day, transferred or…"

They made plans to spend time in a hotel the next time they met. Back at work Alice wavered between feelings of longing and excitement, and others of shame and trepidation. But, after all, if she did not lose him in the air over Europe, she would probably marry him someday. She wanted that. Now that she and her family had escaped poverty, a life with Brad was her greatest wish.

This was wartime, she told herself. Brad might die any day in the sky, and she would never see him again. Then she would wish she had erased the horror from his eyes, at least for a little while, and had known his love. Why wait for that, when they had so little opportunity.

She put on one of the two dresses she had brought to England, the teal blue she had worn as Emma's bridesmaid. Brad welcomed her in the hotel lobby in the late afternoon, looking as cheerful as she had ever seen him in Britain. He was determined to help her relax.

"I'm so glad to see you, Alice." He took a hand, touched her cheek, and then smoothed her hair. "You look wonderful. I was afraid you wouldn't come."

"Thanks, Brad. I thought about you all week."

He'd brought wine with him to drink in their room. The taste of it reminded Alice of the pride her parents had felt when they served their homemade wine at Emma's wedding. The memory of her home sent a wave of homesickness washing over her, so strong she felt like crying right there.

But Brad smiled and talked. She soon forgot about home. His presence thrilled her.

He sat beside her on the bed, caressing her arms and shoulders as he admired her auburn hair. "Where did you get your beautiful hair?"

Alice chuckled. "I don't know, thank you. All the members of my family have blond or light brown hair, but I'm the only redhead. We all have blue eyes though."

"If we had a child, it might have red hair."

Alice frowned. "Oh Lord. I hope you brought something to prevent that."

He kissed her forehead. "Of course I did. I wouldn't put you in that kind of predicament. And I wouldn't want any kid of mine brought up in an orphanage. I'm just hoping you'll change your mind about marriage someday."

"Someday, when the war is over," she mumbled. Would it ever be over? It dragged on and on.

"You know, I love you for more than your fabulous beauty. I love you for your bravery and your devotion to your family."

He gently brushed her mouth with his. Her excitement mounted. "I love you, Alice. I hope you know that."

"Yes, and I love you too." Sensations filled her body. He was close, handsome, and stimulating. And he loved *her*. Hungered for *her*.

"I know, and I'm so grateful."

He buried his face in her hair, inhaling the scent of perfume. He knew she was inexperienced, but her kisses and reactions told him that she felt passion. He anticipated an awakening for her and a night of extreme pleasure for both of them. And he was not disappointed.

His caressing hands felt sweet and sensuous as he helped her undress. His strong shoulders, silken skin, and lustrous black hair made her throb with anticipation. She felt encircled in a bed of glorious intimacy. Completely consumed, she cried out with joy and surprise.

Afterward, he held her close and told her how pleased and happy he was. They spent the evening in their hotel nest, loving again.

* * *

At her train, he kissed her hungrily, hating to see her leave. He held her close until the last minute. "Let's meet again next week."

"Oh, I hope we can. I'll certainly try, Brad, but we're very busy right now. New supplies and surgical dressings and even more beds keep coming in all the time. We're still moving in, crowding the beds close, preparing for the mass casualties. God knows how many there will be. Most of our patients have been moved out recently—the diseases, accident victims—making way."

"There are plenty of bombing flights going on now too, since the weather is better. But if we get unexpected stand-down time, I'll get in touch with you."

"Aren't your thirty missions about over?"

"Soon. Then I'll be working somewhere on the ground."

* * *

The next morning Ellen observed her happy demeanor. "You must be having a lot of fun with Brad. Nurses are allowed to be married now, you know. Do I hear wedding bells in your future?"

"Oh no." Alice colored. "He wants to marry, but I don't think it's a very good time, with everything so uncertain. It would be impossible."

"I see…" Ellen said, with a knowing look.

Alice strode cheerfully off to her ward. Let her speculate. Though in truth, it was hard to keep anything from the worldly-wise Ellen with her sharp green eyes.

Most of the nurses dated officers, at least occasionally. Even Ellen was dating an army second lieutenant who was so enthralled with her that he barely noticed her cynicism and admired her sense of humor instead. And one of the single doctors seemed to be spending a lot of time with Marjorie.

"Discussing treatments, I suppose," Ellen said, straight-faced, to the others.

Dana regularly saw Alan Cooper, who navigated planes out of a base nearby. Alice sympathized with her constant worry about him. All of them might not come back. Will any of them come back?

Alice and Brad had another day together before all leave was canceled on June 4. Marjorie suggested they write letters and take care of personal business before the onslaught of patients started coming in. The nurses stocked shelves, sorted medical forms, and scrubbed everything. Nothing happened.

Then in the predawn hours of June 6 and all day long, formations of warplanes droned overhead. The sky was black with them. They learned that the invasion of France had begun: D-Day—the launch of Allied forces across the English Channel to the beaches of Normandy to drive the Germans out of France, out of the Low Countries.

The nurses continued their work with grim faces, thinking of relatives and hometown friends, the young airmen they had met since they had been in England, as well as members of the ground forces. Alice worried about Brad. She knew he flew one of those bombers in the pre-attack flights.

Chapter 20

In their briefings and in scattered talk in low voices, Brad and other officers gleaned bits of information about preparations for D-Day.

"It sounds as though around nine thousand planes will be going over before dawn," one major speculated.

"All bombers?"

"No, no. I think they'll be dropping thousands of paratroopers first behind enemy lines from hundreds of planes and gliders. They'll secure bridges and crucial sites and try to slow the German effort to reinforce the coast."

"Oh damn," groaned a tail gunner. "My brother's a paratrooper."

Brad whistled. "Good God. That's going to be dangerous."

"It will be. Probably only a small number will return. Next, we bombers are to hit German fortifications—concrete and steel bunkers making up the German Atlantic Wall, as well as rail, road, and communication targets. We'll need to knock out German radar stations too, or at least snow the screens with strips of tinfoil."

"Sounds easy compared to the job of the paratroopers."

"Well, the Germans will have fighters out. You can count on that, and they'll be firing from the ground too. Meanwhile, thousands of vessels carrying ground troops will set out from England. Let's hope the fog will obscure them from the enemy. There'll be warships too and a naval bombardment on the coast."

"The men will have to be loaded into landing craft, won't they?"

"Oh yes, and they'll probably be under fire as they board the LSTs. Then they'll have to get around beach obstacles and mine-tipped stakes that the Germans have set in the sand."

Brad grimaced. "We've heard about some tanks with long, front-extending frames holding chains with rotating iron balls. Those balls are supposed to clear the mines harmlessly."

"Don't count on those tanks clearing all the mines," the major scoffed. "We also have special tanks, called carpet layers, to roll out walkways for the men over the wet sand. And they're preparing an artificial harbor. From England, underwater pipes will supply petrol to the invasion forces."

"Won't those soldiers face enemy fire from the coastal bunkers?"

"Of course they will. It'll be dangerous as hell. We bombers can't disable all of them, for Christ's sake. Aren't you glad you're in the air force?"

"Those dirty Krauts. They'll be sorry they started this goddamned war."

Everything did not go as planned for the Allies. On Omaha Beach, one of the five beaches chosen for landing, the American troops were forced to scale cliffs under heavy fire because the bombers had not been able to knock out the fortifications.

Despite ten thousand Allied casualties, by midnight on June 6 there were one hundred thirty thousand troops ashore and the stage was set for the arrival of five thousand vehicles—tanks, jeeps—and tons of ammunition and supplies.

And in the days following, thousands of troops came each day in their dogged advance. In six days the Allies had secured an area several miles from the beaches.

When details of the invasion were available to the population on the home front, Jennie, working in the Portland shipyard, thought about all the precision planning going into such mass slaughter. What could humanity accomplish if it put the same effort into solving hunger, poverty, and disease?

* * *

At the hospital in England, Alice had little time to think about Brad. By late afternoon on D-Day, the rush of wounded soldiers started arriving in ambulances lined up in front of the tent hospital. By the end of the day, their station hospital had cared for more than a thousand wounded. The seventy-five nurses, forty doctors and 250 enlisted men worked late into the night, caught a few hours of sleep in shifts, and then got up to relieve others and work another round of twelve- and sixteen-hour days.

The injuries ranged from superficial wounds to mangled and broken bodies that hardly seemed capable of recovering. Alice was touched by their patience as the soldiers waited for the nurses to care for them. Most were polite and grateful. Some were in shock, and others had been given morphine by the first medical providers in the field.

More than one soldier died in her arms. An eighteen-year-old asked Alice, "Am I going to be all right, nurse?"

"Of course you are," she said, taking his pulse.

"Good." He turned his face and quietly died. She brushed away the tears that rushed to her eyes and moved on to the next patient.

Doctors worked hours over some patients in surgery only to have them die shortly afterward. After one such struggle, the surgeon sobbed in the operating area.

Chapter 21

Meanwhile, back in Juniper, the Bauers anxiously read and discussed the war news all spring. With Alice in England, and Fred now in England too, copiloting planes over the Continent, they feared bad news every day. They also worried about Freda Bauer in Australia and Ernst Bauer in Italy and James Turner in France.

John and Gloria grieved her nephew Mark Turner. They heard of the children of friends who were also killed or injured—Arnold White, Roy Davis—and more now with all the fighting. They tried to do their part: collecting metal for the war effort, saving grease and tinfoil gum wrappers, growing victory gardens. And they waited, struggling with their fears, reading the newspapers for the names of those killed or wounded in action.

* * *

Jennie hopped on the predawn bus to Portland on her birthday, the first day of June. This year she wanted to work in the actual shipyard instead of the cafeteria. Now that she was eighteen, she would be allowed longer hours, and she could save more money. Some of her work clothing waited for her at Tess's house.

She noticed that young men had disappeared from the shipyards. Now older men, those rejected for military service for some reason, and women did the work. When she arrived at the shipyard, they handed her a broom and she became a sweeper.

The lead woman greeted her with a smile. "Welcome to the best sweeping outfit in the good old USA. I'm Bertha Schneider. We get to clean up after all these messy pipe fitters, electricians, and welders. We'll start you out easy." All day Jennie, along with the other women, swept up trash left by the workers as they moved along.

On her second day, she was sent down to clean a soggy mess of water and oil beneath the engine room because she was little enough to get through the small hole to the job. With rags and a bucket, she mopped up and handed buckets of slop to a woman who waited at the cavity entrance, who carried it up a ladder to another woman, who carried it up on another part of its journey to the outside, where it was left for removal. Bertha joined her for short periods and took over while she had a meal break.

"I thought you were starting me out easy," Jennie said, with a pleasant smirk.

Bertha chuckled. "Don't believe everything you're told, especially around here."

They cleaned all day, and when they left at the end of the shift, they met the painters who were scheduled to paint under the engines. She and Bertha were pleased to be ready for them.

She learned about the scaling jobs on tanks deep down in the ship that held water, oil, and gasoline. The tanks needed to be painted with protective paints, and before they were painted, all rust had to be removed from their steel. With scraping blades, wire brushes, a whisk broom, a dustpan, and a bucket, the scalers tediously cleaned the tanks for the drinking water or the oil they would hold. In the summer, the heat was almost unbearable, and in winter it was bitterly cold. Rust dust floated in the tanks, and fresh air was not always piped in.

Tess now worked as an electrician and Naomi as a welder. The three women, to save money, often brought their own sandwiches and coffee. During one dinner break, already tired, they lingered a few minutes over the meal.

Jennie said, "People wonder why the government froze wages but not profits."

"Well, Jennie," Naomi said, with a sarcastic edge in her voice, "surely you wouldn't expect the rich to sacrifice anything in this war. They'll just get richer."

"I'm exhausted, but we shouldn't complain," Tess said. "Think of those guys in Italy wallowing in the mud and eating cold rations, trying to drive the Germans back. They seem determined to hold it, even though the Italian government has surrendered. Ernie Pyle tells it like it is."

"Have you heard from Ernst?" Naomi asked.

"Yes, but he can't really tell me much because of the censors. We have our own code. When he's going into battle or moving forward, he writes that he's hungry for apple pie. But I learn more from the columns Ernie Pyle writes from Italy."

"Wonder what people are doing back in Juniper."

"I'll tell you what they're doing." Jennie packed her thermos away in her lunch bucket. "They're saving scrap metal, knitting blankets for the troops, and watching for Japanese attacks. It's hell for everyone."

"But is it really?" Naomi asked. "What about the rich? The Reynoldses, the Glasses, the other rich ranchers?"

"I've heard that Odette Glass is working at the USO they've set up for the men at the Juniper Air Base."

"Oh, sure," Naomi said, snickering. "It must be tough to dance with all those servicemen every night."

"And awful to have to wear pretty clothes instead of grubby work duds," Aunt Tess said.

"I suppose," Jennie said, conceding to their remarks, "sitting down to eat a leisurely meal must be a real sacrifice."

"Say, who is this Odette?" another woman chipped in. "Does the poor thing have to get her hair done every week too?"

"And how about her nails?" another asked. "Does the little darling have to sit still to get her nails all fixed up?"

"I'll bet she is forced to wear those miserable silk stockings, instead of the cotton and rayon the rest of us get to wear," a third said as they tramped off to their heavy work.

Jennie no longer scorned the war—a great hungry monster that devoured men, women, and children indiscriminately. Her isolationism was gone. The war was deadly serious business. The sooner the ships were built, the sooner the navy could help win the war.

The workers cheered on June 4 when American soldiers liberated Rome from the Germans.

Two days later, when the invasion of Normandy started, night shift workers were among the first to hear about it. Hundreds of workers knelt down on the decks of partly finished Liberty ships to pray. Almost all of them had husbands, sons, brothers, or sweethearts now fighting in Italy, France, or the Pacific.

Some, like Jennie, had sisters in the women's services, many of them nursing the wounded.

Chapter 22

In England, Alice wrote letters and handled other small jobs for the most severely wounded patients. Sometimes the patients wanted to talk about their experiences—the horrors, the nightmares. Then all she could do for them was listen.

When Brad contacted her about meeting him, she almost wept with relief to discover he had survived.

Soon after, she got a letter from her cousin Norman Jackson, serving in the navy. She, Ellen, and Brad met him for dinner in a nearby town. He was delighted. "I was hoping to see you again," he said, with his eyes on Ellen. "I've often thought about your visit to New York."

As they chatted, he reminisced about his family trip to see Alice's family in the Pacific Northwest. "I remember you well from our stay in Oregon when I was a child. You taught us how to play kick the can."

"You never played kick the can in New York?"

"Never. In New York we kicked other things. I thought kicking the can was great fun."

Brad burst into laughter, then sobered. "The navy played a big role in the invasion. Do you want to tell us about it?"

"I hope someday I can forget about it. When the engineers cleared a narrow strip through the mined beach obstacles, we ran rope and cable lines from our landing craft in a path for the soldiers to hold on to, to help them ashore. Some were shot before they got to the beach." His voice broke, but he managed to continue. "A few of our craft were destroyed. I went back to the transport and picked up another load of men to get to the beaches. I made twelve trips from the transport to the beach that day."

The others shook their heads, tears formed in their eyes, and it was some time before the conversation became light again.

* * *

During the summer, Alice and Brad made another jaunt to London. Everywhere they saw military uniforms. Trains filled with supplies for the war rumbled to southern ports.

They visited the art museum, shared a picnic in a park, and spent hours in a hotel room. She treasured their time together but would not agree to marry him.

"Yes, there are lots of wartime marriages, but I think we should wait," Alice said. "It's no way to start a life together."

"Surely you don't think we're too young," he said teasingly.

Alice laughed. "I guess we're old enough, older than most people who marry. But I've volunteered for hospital flights. Next week I may be evacuating patients from France. I could be gone a lot."

"Do you have to?"

"I want to. I joined the Army Nurse Corps to serve. I'll come back."

Dana and her navigator sometimes spent time with Alice and Brad. Alan announced cheerfully one evening that he and Dana were planning to marry as soon as they could arrange it. The two were obviously in love and happy to have made their decision.

Alice was pleased for them since Dana clearly wanted to marry. Brad envied them. *Why couldn't Alice see things that way? She loved him, didn't she?*

When the couples separated, Alice and Brad spent time together in a small hotel. "I've been waiting to have you all day," Brad said, drawing her close.

She smiled. "And I love you too."

* * *

One day later Marjorie pulled Dana off the ward into her small office. Alice wondered what was going on. The nurses were so busy that only exceptional circumstances kept them from their tasks.

Soon Marjorie hurried to Alice. "Please go to Dana in the office. Alan's plane has been shot down by an enemy fighter. It caught fire as it went down. He's been killed. You're her best friend. See what you can do for her."

"Oh no!" Alice cried, aghast. She felt she was almost in shock herself. Woodenly, she walked to the office and took Dana in her arms. The small woman shook with sobs. When she at last grew quiet, Alice urged her to go to their quarters and rest.

Dana refused. "That wouldn't serve any purpose. I'll do what I can here." For the rest of the day, she controlled her emotions and smiled at the patients as before.

Her friends watched her in sympathy. Marjorie said, "I hope this is the last death among our acquaintances."

As the days went by, Dana gradually accepted Alan's death and remembered his love. Though she was quiet on their off hours, on the ward she performed as before. Weeks later she confided to Alice in a worried tone that she was pregnant.

Alice, shocked and dismayed, said, "Oh, Dana, how awful. What can you do?"

"Alan and I were to be married, of course. But now I'll need to get an abortion. I have no intention of having an illegitimate child. It wouldn't be fair to the child. And it would cause my parents so much shame."

"None of our doctors will do it," Alice said with regret.

"I'll have to talk to some of the locals."

"How did it happen? Surely you took precautions."

"Of course we did. But no birth control works all the time. The condom broke, that's all. We knew it at the time and hoped for the best."

"I'm so sorry. How can I help?"

"Well, the first thing I have to do is find a doctor willing to do it."

"I could talk to the lady who rents us a room. In her business she's probably learned about such things."

"Thank you, Alice. I'm going to see an English doctor and see if he'll recommend someone."

"That's probably the best way. When you have it done, I'll go with you. You shouldn't go alone."

"Oh, Alice, that would be so helpful."

But before the women had a chance to start asking around, Dana suffered a miscarriage. Enduring much pain, she stayed in their sleeping quarters for two days. Despite the misery, she and Alice were greatly relieved. To be sure of her recovery, Alice accompanied her for a checkup with an English doctor.

It seemed fitting that, after everything Dana had gone through, she was now free to continue her chosen career, serve her country, and begin her life anew.

* * *

Soon after, Marjorie rushed to Alice on the ward and said, "Brad has some news for you. He's right outside." Without stopping to question her, Alice hurried to see Brad.

His face was grave. "What is it, Brad?"

"It's your brother. He's safe but badly injured. I've got permission from Marjorie to take you to him at my base. I didn't even know he was there until I heard some of the guys talking about how badly his plane was hit."

"Fred's hurt? I've got to get in touch with Mother."

He took her arm. "The service would have telegraphed his parents. Let's go see him. Then you can write to your folks."

"Yes, of course. They'll want to know how he is. How is he?"

"The doctor says he'll recover, but it will take a long time. He's broken some bones, taken some flak."

But when they saw Fred, his most pressing concern seemed to be getting back into the air. "Blast it," he said through heavy bandages on his face. "I just got over here. They're talking about sending me back. I've only finished a few of my missions."

"Oh, Fred." Alice kissed his forehead. "You have to get well. There's always time for flying later."

"The war will be over by the time those damn doctors think I'm ready. I've waited all my life to fly. It's all I've lived for."

"See here, Fred," Brad said. "You've given a lot already. You've done your duty. The war is probably over for you."

Fred sobered. He had heard that before. Once you're badly wounded, you're done.

Outside Brad told Alice, "Most of that is bluster, you know. In a way, he's lucky he's wounded. He'll be out of danger for several months."

Alice knew Brad was right, but it hurt to see her brother so maimed. That evening Alice wrote to her parents.

> It's just a matter of time. He's lucid, eager to get back in shape so that he can get into the air. He's broken a leg and an arm and has suffered other injuries too. But he is in good hands.

For the next few weeks, Alice spent as much free time as possible at Fred's hospital.

* * *

One day Alice received a letter from Rose Perkins, the tall nurse she had trained with in Portland. Rose nursed in the combat zone in France.

Dear Alice,

I was glad to hear about you and Dana and your work with the invasion casualties there in England. You must be thrilled with the new penicillin.

The French people are very friendly. They always smile and help us when they can. They're glad to be liberated.

We're way behind the front now because we ran out of gas. And our food is not very tasty when we're too far behind.

Also, I suppose they need the space on the ships for supplies. If only they could send over some Kotex now and then. Has the army no concept of female physiology? We're always out of them and have to use cloths, which we launder over and over.

Lima beans and stewed tomatoes don't make the best meal. We're glad to get fresh fish when the men throw grenades into the water. And some of them shoot ducks and other wildlife. I feel as though we're camping.

Sometimes enlisted men scrounge tomatoes, potatoes, and onions. They cook up a big pot of stew with any bits of meat they can buy or barter. We're invited to the feasts, and the stew sure beats the K rations and the beans.

We play softball with the enlisted men, and we nurses go swimming in a river that flows by our tent hospital. It's refreshing. Enlisted men join us for water fights, although we try to avoid them because when they are around, we have to wear more clothes. We do our laundry in the river too.

The patients are heartbreaking. We just do what we can for them while they are with us. I hope you can do a lot more for them when they get over to England. Combat soldiers often donate their blood for the patients when we run out of plasma.

Friends always ask about my pay. I suppose it's the same as yours. Our base pay is $166.67, additional pay for foreign service

$16.66, mess allowance $21, for a total of $204.33. Government insurance costs $6.60 per month.

Considering all our training and our long hours, it's not much. But there's nowhere to spend our money here anyway. Don't spend all of yours in one place. Ha!

Now we are beginning to dread the winter ahead, as our tents are not much protection from the cold. I hope we don't see a lot of frostbitten patients. On top of everything else, that would be horrible for the soldiers.

When Alice read the letter to her friends, Ellen said, "Spend your money? That's a laugh. Why, Alice won't spend a dime on keepsakes whenever we have an outing."

Alice felt defensive. "I don't need those trinkets that all of you buy. I'm saving my money."

"Leave her alone, Ellen. She wants to help her little brothers and sisters," Marjorie said.

"One brother," Dana said.

Ellen, sorry she had spoken, said, "Well, you're smarter than the rest of us, Alice. What will we do with all that junk we pick up anyway? I notice you always have money for things you *really* need."

* * *

Marjorie looked doubtfully at Alice. "Are you sure you want to volunteer for this?"

"I said I did. That's why I took the hospital flight training."

"Along with the UC-64s and the C-47s, they're evacuating patients in any aircraft that is available, even those with no special markings. It's very dangerous since they are legitimate targets for enemy artillery. If you're shot down, you could be killed, wounded, or captured in France or the Low Countries."

"We know the patients need to get to England faster for treatment, Marjorie. They need nurses to come back with them from the battlefield."

"But why you?" Marjorie wore a bleak expression. "You're my friend."

"It has to be done. You know that. I'm sure I'll be back."

Alice's first few assignments as a flight nurse on a hospital plane went well. Their patients were evacuated safely from hospitals in France and carried to station hospitals in England. Sending them quickly to better medical facilities in England was important. And space had to be made for the new casualties on the Continent.

It was a chilly autumn day when Alice climbed into the plane for her fifth flight to pick up wounded near the fighting. With her flew a surgical technician, Buck Jones, and four crew members. After takeoff, she unbuckled her seat belt and settled down for a nap.

Much later she awoke when the plane began to jerk and pitch. She heard metal tearing around her. They began to lose altitude. Alice looked out the window and realized that the left engine was on fire. Cold air swirled in through a large hole near the fuselage. A piece of flak hit Buck in the arm. The plane dipped and swerved.

Explosions burst around them as Germans on the ground fired ack-ack rounds at their airplane. Two members of the crew were hit and slightly wounded. The plane wobbled and shuddered and then went into a dive and crashed nose first onto the ground.

Chapter 23

Alice was tossed across the plane and nicked her arm, spilling blood onto her slacks. Suddenly flames burst around them. Someone shouted, "Get out!" In panic she and Buck followed the crew out through the top hatch.

Immediately a small group of German soldiers appeared with rifles pointed at them. They seemed surprised to see a woman. One of the soldiers found supplies in his pack and administered first aid to Alice and injured crew members.

Then they pointed in the direction of a nearby road and followed the Americans as they walked in that direction. Alice was badly frightened, but the brisk exercise provided an outlet for her excess adrenaline and anxiety.

Soon they came to a town nearly empty of civilians. Later they learned that the army had ordered the civilians to leave. German soldiers and vehicles moved around, and a sign indicated that the town was Aachen in Germany. They were put onto the back of a truck and taken farther down the road to a larger town.

In an imposing building, an officer speaking perfect English interrogated them one by one. The others watched as each of the Americans gave name, rank, and serial number.

Afterward they were led to a nearby house where they were fed black bread and butter, soup, and juicy ripe pears. Since they were handed the same serving bowls as the officers at the next table who had helped themselves, they decided it was safe to eat the food. They had had no nourishment all day. The food tasted delicious.

More officers came in, looked at their identification papers picked up at the site of the crash, and discussed the situation. They were saying *swester*, which means "nurse."

Once again, in the back of an old, open truck, they were driven to another German town farther on. "Thank God they aren't Secret Service," a crew member said. "They probably would have shot us right away."

"They seem quite decent," Alice added. But she felt very vulnerable. Wartime propaganda had painted the Germans as savage beasts with no morality.

Several horse-drawn wagons passed their truck going in the opposite direction. "Amazing," Buck said, "a country with the latest wartime technology, and the farmers still use horses."

They saw people harvesting nuts, late vegetables, and fruit—apples, pears, and plums. The green countryside seemed bountiful. Still, they had heard that farmers were allowed to keep barely enough produce for their own needs. The rest was taken for the country's wartime requirements.

They were driven to another house where they were led upstairs to sleep. Two men were given a room, three another, and Alice was given a third. She propped a chair against the door handle as a precaution. Though she ached with fatigue and anxiety, she slept fitfully. She kept remembering what they said about prisoners of war: "For them the war is over." The war maybe, but not their struggles.

The next morning, after sponge baths and a breakfast of bread and sausage, they were once again taken farther into Germany in a truck. At midday they stopped at a large house that had been turned into military quarters. As they and their guards were fed sausage, sauerkraut, and potatoes in the kitchen, planes roared overhead and bombs exploded nearby. Everyone took cover. An officer speaking English remarked, "Strange for all of you if you are killed by your own fighters."

Little did he know how gut wrenching it was for Alice as she wondered who flew the bombers overhead. Was one of them Brad

Mayfield? Had he heard about the crash of her hospital plane? Was he still alive? Since she had seen him, he could have flown another mission and been killed.

* * *

"We've got to let him know," Ellen said. "He has a right."

"But we have no news about what happened to the plane," Marjorie said. "They may have escaped. They could be on their way here right now. Why upset him needlessly?"

"You're dreaming," Ellen scoffed. "They've been captured or killed. I'm sorry too. But we may as well face it and let him know."

The problem was taken out of Marjorie's hands when Brad came by that afternoon. He had wondered why Alice had not visited her brother.

"Oh God, I was afraid of this." Stunned, Brad sat down near Marjorie's desk. "What are her chances?"

Marjorie's eyes filled with tears again. "If she's been captured, she may be all right and return when the war is over."

He fought for control. "I'd hoped we could be married before I go on furlough. I've completed almost all my missions." He stood up, staring vacantly around the office.

"Don't go back to your base right now. Stay and have something to drink."

He sat back down, almost too shaken to stand. "I probably wouldn't have known if you hadn't told me. They would have telegraphed only her parents."

He sipped coffee while Alice's friends came in one by one to commiserate with him. When he returned to his base, he told Fred what he had learned and tried to put a hopeful note on it, as much for himself as for Alice's brother.

He gathered up his few possessions for the day he would be leaving for home. There would be no reason to hang around England when he got furlough time. If Alice got back somehow, she would not be sent to work at her old base.

* * *

His last mission. Brad got up in the middle of the night and joined the others for mess. These days he sometimes had trouble getting food down.

How many would be going out that day? The briefing seemed to take longer than usual. His mind kept wandering to Alice—in Germany or dead. Still, if she came back, he did not want her to find him gone forever. He concentrated on the order of taxiing, the place in formation—necessary information for bomber crews. At last his group was driven to the center of the airfield to their ship. The engineer sniffed the fog. "I bet we don't go today." Brad and the copilot did their preflight checks.

The notice arrived: "Ninety-minute delay." Perhaps the engineer was right. If the mission was canceled, he would struggle through another night of anxiety about Alice; then, during the final mission, he'd suffer fears, tremors, and thoughts about the horrors the bombs were causing on the ground. And everything was worse now. Alice could be in their target area.

The word came. The run for that day was canceled. It would be another long, miserable wait.

Chapter 24

John Bauer burst into Grant's Juniper hotel office and said, "You've got to come. My brother Ernst has been killed in France. Gloria and I have to go up to Portland to be with his wife. Jennie called at the neighbors' house and said Tess is completely devastated. We're taking the little girls. Tell Kate all the bad news when she arrives this evening."

Grant stood. "I'm so sorry."

John took a deep breath and continued. "Alice is missing in action in France or somewhere. Her hospital flight ship went down on its way to pick up patients. They haven't been heard from."

"Good God! Did the crew survive?"

"They just don't know. There's no word of Alice or any of the others. We have to break that news to Jennie and Tess too."

"What should I do?"

"Tell Kate when she gets off the bus. Make sure she gets to our house. She'll be as upset by all this as Tess and Gloria are. Stay with her as long as you can. You can stay in our room. She won't be in any condition to be left alone."

"OK. Anything else?"

"Kate will have to go out and tell Emma and David tomorrow or call them from somewhere. Then she'll have to tell Edith when she gets home, and get in touch with Freda and Louis if she can."

"Of course, of course," Grant assured him. "Anything else I can do?"

"Not just now. I've got to go. Gloria and the girls are waiting in the car." And he fled the room, leaving the shocked Grant staring after him.

Grant pictured Kate sitting at that moment on the bus, her wavy brown hair shining in the dim light. For a time he mused on her background: her sturdy German-born peasant parents settling in the dry Oregon country, their life in Germany in the late 1800s, and their efforts to emigrate.

He saw a procession of German ancestors through the centuries farming the central European plains. Tragically, their descendants now fought other descendants who lived in America.

Grant was waiting as Kate left the bus at the hotel. When he approached her, she could tell by his expression that something terrible had happened.

"What's wrong?"

"Your family rushed to Portland to be with Tess and Jennie. Your brother Ernst has been killed in France."

"What?"

"I'm terribly sorry. Come into my office for a minute."

Kate sat and covered her face with her hands.

Grant sat down beside her and waited. At last she looked up, tears in her eyes. "I was so afraid he would be. All those months in Italy and now this. We weren't really close. All the others are much younger than John and I. Do they have any details of how he died?"

"They didn't tell me any. They were in a hurry to get going."

"Poor Tess. Now she and Naomi are both widows. Is Jennie all right?"

"Apparently she is. John talked to her on the telephone next door. Ernst's wife is devastated of course. They felt they had to go to Portland to be with her. That's why John asked me to meet you and let you know."

"Thank you, Grant. I'll be fine. You don't have to stay with me."

"I'm not about to leave you alone with this news. My car is right outside. Let's fix some dinner at their house. John asked me to spend the night in their room."

"Some dinner?" Kate spoke as if she'd never heard of it. "I'm not very hungry."

"You have to eat."

Grant coaxed her into the car, and when they arrived at the Bauer house, he led her to the kitchen. "Looks like Gloria left some food to eat. If you don't want it, we'll go to my new restaurant, though I'd hoped to entertain you there under better circumstances."

A pan of stew and a pot of coffee left on the stove were still warm. Fresh rolls waited in the oven. "Sit down," Grant said. "I'll fix you a bowl." He ladled out two servings of stew, set rolls on the table, and poured coffee.

He watched Kate closely as they ate, trying to see if she could take more grim news. To improve her mood and to get her to relax, he told her about Emma and David's visits to his restaurant and their chats.

He asked her about her work. She told him how she and her fellow teachers helped feed students who came to school hungry—not so many now as during the Depression.

Construction of new buildings had almost ceased due to wartime shortages of materials. Thus her district was on double shifts. Textbooks remained in the classrooms so that more than one class could use them.

He related some of his humorous trials expanding his food business—the difficulty getting materials and scouring the town to buy up used tables, chairs, and other supplies that people were willing to sell. He even demolished an old shed on one of his properties to salvage the lumber. He brought her up to date on the latest gossip around Juniper.

She saw again the man who had fascinated and seduced her years ago, the boy she had known all through school. Though his auburn hair was graying, his green eyes and lithe body had changed very little, and she remembered falling in love with him. He exuded energy and purpose.

"I'm so glad you answered my letters," he said. "I look forward to them."

Kate smiled, embarrassed. "I'm always glad to hear from my friends and family in Juniper."

"David finally got an essential occupation deferment. He's needed on the ranch raising beef."

"That's good news. He'd hate to leave my niece and the children. I feel bad for the thousands of men who have had to do just that."

Grant buttered a warm roll. "He says he still feels guilty when he comes to town in his civilian clothes and meets up with airmen from the base."

"He would. Such a responsible young man."

"The air base is busy. Mrs. Mayfield organized the whole USO up there. They hold dances and social events for the airmen and invite women to attend. Makes things more normal for the young fellows."

Over coffee in the living room, they discussed the war news.

"With the Germans kicked out of Italy and driven out of Russia and France, and with the Japs retreating in the Pacific, it's hard to see how this war could go on much longer."

"Maybe it'll be over by Christmas. Then Alice could come home. They've already decided to send Fred back to the United States for treatment. He won't recover soon enough to do much good over there."

Grant got up and began to pace back and forth. "There's other news."

"Is Fred back already?" Kate stood.

"No, it's not Fred."

He hesitated but finally said, "Alice is missing. She was in a hospital plane attempting to evacuate wounded from France. The plane crashed."

Kate startled Grant as she leaned toward him. He quickly realized that she was fainting, and he caught her before she fell to the floor.

He carried her into the nearby bedroom and laid her on the bed. Her white face frightened him, and he rushed to the kitchen for some water. When he returned, he saw that her eyes were open, wide and dazed.

"Drink this," he said and she complied. "You fainted. Shall I send for the doctor?"

"No, no, I'm all right. I'm just…" She burst into tears and began to shake with grief.

Grant reached out and put his arms around her. "She might be alive. We have no reason to believe she's dead."

"She's been my whole life, mostly," Kate said between sobs. "Oh, I've loved the others too, but she's my own daughter."

"Our daughter."

At last she quieted. "You should sleep," he said.

"Don't leave me. Lie down with me."

So he did, holding her while her tears covered her face. Finally she fell asleep. He removed her shoes and placed her under the fresh bedding that Gloria had thoughtfully provided. Leaving the light on in the next room, he removed his own shoes and jacket, joined her, and eventually dozed.

He awoke when she moved close to him. He felt her silken arms around his waist, smelled her lavender-scented perfume. Stimulated, he turned, pulled her close, and stroked her hair and her face.

"Are you awake?" he whispered. He kissed her nape and murmured love words in her ear as his questing hands moved lower to slowly caress her thighs. His touch made her skin tingle with desire and excitement.

"Yes," she said.

"Tell me that you want this." His voice was hoarse.

"Yes," she whispered and sighed with pleasure.

He stood to remove his clothes. "I've wanted you for so many years, Kate. Tell me again that this is what you want."

Her excitement built at his words. The soft light outlined his muscular shoulders, the well-toned body, the red-gray hair matting his chest. "Yes," she breathed.

Pulling a condom from his wallet, he placed himself over her and began to kiss her full lips, her light honey-colored skin on her soft neck and shoulders.

The old magic surrounded them, and they gloried in its power.

Afterward they slept naked, close, his front to her back, his hand over her breast. During the night, Kate awoke to his sensual caresses, soft kisses, and urgent lovemaking.

* * *

In the morning she could hear him in the kitchen making breakfast. By the time she had dressed and entered the kitchen, she found fried eggs, toast, and hot coffee on the table. He greeted her with a long kiss. He was sorely tempted to linger with her, but they had things to do.

He urged her to eat, for they needed to drive out to see Emma and David with the bad news. "You're spoiling me," she said. "I usually make breakfast for Edith and me."

"You can use spoiling. You've been looking out for the young people in your family for a long while. Emma told me once that you bought shoes for all of them."

"Oh well, for Christmas…"

For Kate the day had an unreal quality. She felt depressed about Alice and Ernst but cherished by Grant, the one person who could share her concern about Alice in the same way. His kindness and thoughtfulness impressed her.

* * *

Emma and David Walker, playing on the lawn with little Davy and Nancy, watched them drive up.

"That's Grant Hunter's Chevy," Emma said, surprised. "Who's that with him?"

"Looks like your aunt Kate."

"What?"

"Has he been out before?"

"Never."

Grant and Kate joined them on the lawn. Kate hugged them all. She studied the children. "The little rascals have grown like weeds."

"Come inside," Emma said. "I don't believe you've ever seen our little castle, Grant."

"Looks very cozy," Grant said as they followed her into the house.

Kate told Emma and David about Ernst's death. It was hard for Emma to be too saddened. She hadn't liked him for a long time, ever since Jennie had told her about their uncle French kissing her when she was a child. She and Alice and Jennie had avoided him, and managed to keep the little girls away from him too. But she thought of Aunt Tess and of how the loss would affect her.

When it came time to tell them about Alice, Kate's voice broke, and Grant had to finish for her. "They have no news of her or the crew. She's essentially missing in action."

"I was so afraid of this," Emma said. Her eyes were moist, her voice shaking. "We thought, with Fred coming home, that our family had missed the worst of the war."

Grant said, "Kate needs to get back and inform Edith. She'll want to write to Freda. We will have to depend on you to get in touch with your aunt Dorothy and Russ Turner."

"Of course," David said. "We'll drive in to see them later this afternoon."

"Poor Brad," Emma said.

"Brad?" Kate looked up.

"Well, yes, he's piloting bombers from England. Alice has been seeing him."

"Oh yes, I believe she did mention him in one of her letters."

Mrs. Walker arrived and said to the group, "Now come on over to the big house for a meal, all of you. I have a roast cooking. We'll feed the baby and put her down for a nap. Follow me."

Grant told the older Walkers and Sarah about Ernst and Alice. Subdued, they all gathered around the table. Still, despite the sad news, Emma felt something between the two visitors—an understanding, shared feelings? What was it?

At the dinner table, they talked of other things: the fighting, the shortages, and the economy.

"I've been reading about a bitter fight our troops had at a German town called Aachen," Mr. Walker said. "Seems it's an old historical city, and the Germans tried hard to hold it but were driven back. We're finally into their country."

"The war can't last much longer," Grant said. "The enemy is being beaten back everywhere."

"Have you been able to get any silk stockings in your town?" Sarah asked Kate. "I wear anklets or long johns since I'm doing the work of three men." She looked pointedly at her father. "But I'd like to have a pair for church and special things—such as a date with the one in a hundred men who's still available on the home front."

Kate clucked in sympathy. "No, I wear rayon or cotton stockings. We can't get anything else."

"Guess it's time to give my girl her due," Mr. Walker said. "She works hard. I don't know what I'd do without her. She and David keep this place going. We're having a devil of a time securing equipment and parts though. Hope our machinery holds out as long as my young ones do."

"I fear the country might fall back into a depression as soon as the war is over," Mrs. Walker added. "And what about all this war debt?"

"Well, much of it is in war bonds," Kate said. "We owe it to ourselves."

"Munitions makers and factories must be making a bundle of money with all those government contracts," Mr. Walker said. "Old Southwick tells me a few people in Juniper invested in munitions. He's wishing he had. Still, he's doing all right with beef prices high and his boy helping out some on the ranch."

"From what some of the servicemen write home, many of the contractors are cheating," Grant said. "Providing shoddy goods, cheap supplies, uneatable food. They suspect widespread graft."

"According to what I read, the Truman Committee in Congress has prevented much of that." Mr.Walker referred to a Senate committee, chaired by Senator Harry Truman, which was looking into the matter.

All the Walkers saw Grant and Kate off and waved as Grant drove away. Emma said in a puzzled voice, "I didn't know they were…well, whatever they are." To which David raised his eyebrows.

"Grant is always polite, but I just never noticed him so attentive to anyone. Did you see how he held her chair and opened the car door and couldn't keep his eyes off her? And *her*! She smiled at him constantly."

"Maybe they just ran into each other and decided to ride out together."

"No, there's something more than that. I just can't figure out what it is."

"Sweetheart, if you can't figure it out, no one can." David lifted Davy, threw him up in the air, and caught him again, while the boy laughed with glee.

Chapter 25

Across the ocean, Alice and the five men were driven in open trucks deeper into Germany every day. They were always housed in private homes with the German soldiers taking over the buildings and guarding the prisoners. They were relieved to be treated so decently. Alice remembered posters at home showing German soldiers grinning over masses of charred human bones, a child crying in their midst, or of a German soldier threatening a partially clad woman with a knife.

When they arrived at a military complex, the Americans were treated individually at the hospital for their wounds. The doctor told Alice, "They don't know what to do with a captured woman." At this stop, the nun-nurses fed them a sauerkraut dish.

In the evenings, after sponge bathing in a basin of water, Alice rinsed out her undergarments and hung them over a chair to dry. Although they still felt damp in the morning, she wore them anyway.

One morning an English-speaking officer told her that her five companions were being sent to a POW camp. She would be taken to a prisoner-of-war hospital where she could help tend the injured. As she and Butch exchanged home addresses, she felt more alone than ever. They promised to write to each other when the war was over.

On the day she was to arrive at the hospital, she had a sickening headache, along with a sore throat and a fever. It was just as well she was going to a hospital, where she would find help.

When they got to the huge facility, she stood in front of an officer seated at his desk in a private office. A distinguished-looking man in his midthirties, he examined the papers that had been sent with her.

Suddenly his head jerked up. "Bauer? Bauer from Oregon?" he asked in perfect English.

Alice hesitated. "Yes…"

The officer walked around the desk and stood in front of her. She cringed.

"I'm Helmut Bauer. Have you heard of me?"

She stared at him, unconvinced. "How is that possible?"

"My cousin is John Bauer in Oregon," he said in astonishment. "He wrote to me and gave me the names of all his children. Alice is his daughter. You are my cousin."

"Well…" Alice said, recovering quickly. "How very good to meet you."

"My dear, I'm sorry you're a prisoner here. But you are perfectly safe."

He looked at her closely. "You are flushed." He reached over to feel her forehead. She flinched.

"I only want to see if you have a fever. You do. You should be in bed right now. Come, I'll introduce you to our head nurse. I'm the administrator of this hospital. It might be best not to mention our relationship."

In the hospital Alice met Ursula Wist, a blond-haired, blue-eyed woman who fit Hitler's vision of the perfect Nordic. Helmut spoke to her for several minutes in German. It seemed to Alice that he was giving her special instructions. He touched Alice's shoulder gently as he left.

With a brisk nod, Ursula led her to a bed in a far corner of a ward. She pulled a curtain hung from a ceiling wire to enclose Alice's bed and small table. It was obvious why she did it. The other patients were all men.

Alice changed into the gown she had been given and fell into the bed. She slept feverishly off and on for several days. Now and then a meek, stubby young woman came to walk with her to the latrine and wash her feverish face and hands.

She found soup left at her bedside table, but she ignored it at first, drinking only water. She had no appetite. From the ward, she heard moans and conversation in German and several other languages.

Eventually she began to feel better. She looked forward to food, and she ate everything they left her. Within a few days she had a healthy appetite. She asked the young woman for more food, but the attendant made a helpless gesture and rushed off.

Suddenly a fist knocked on the wall beside the curtain.

Chapter 26

"Can I come in?" asked a low male voice that was obviously American.

"Please do." Alice sat up.

From the other side of the curtain emerged a pale American youth in his twenties on crutches, grinning broadly in welcome. "I heard you ask for food," he said. "I thought I'd better let you in on a few things. I'm one of the few American officers here. I'm Billy Swift."

"So glad to meet you."

"The others are officers too—French, Dutch, English, etc. No Russians. They don't want us to fraternize with them."

"How did you get here?"

"I was taken prisoner in France. The fighting was awful."

"I heard. Won't you sit down?"

Billy took a place on the edge of the bed, setting the crutches aside. He spoke in a low voice. "One thing I am pleased about. The rest of my buddies and I managed to help a Jewish fellow from New York escape. We were afraid he would be shot if the lousy Germans suspected he was Jewish. The ruckus he created put the rest of the guards on alert, so no one else could follow. We beat the bastards on that though."

"That's an inspiring story."

"It perhaps makes up for the treatment he got from bigots in his own army unit. Fellows hollered at him and made derogatory remarks."

"That's sad. Have you been treated well?"

"Fairly well. I was the only one wounded. Our group surrendered to the regular soldiers. We might have suffered worse if we'd been taken by the SS."

"Have you been here long?"

"No, just a few days. When I recover I'll have to go to work for the Germans. The thing is, Ursula rules supreme here. Food and other supplies are running low. She has the power to dole them out as she pleases. Stay on her good side."

"How could I? I haven't seen her but once since I've been here. I'm Alice Bauer." She offered her hand.

"Bauer. That's funny," Billy said as he shook it. "The head man of this place is named Bauer."

"A common name." Alice tried to be nonchalant about it, heeding Helmut's advice not to mention their relationship.

"Well, Ursula seems to hate Americans especially, maybe because of the rumors coming in from delivery workers. Some of them are in contact with people in the underground who listen to the BBC," he whispered. "She has relatives near the French border. How is the invasion going?"

"I can't really tell you much. I nursed at a base in southern England. Then I signed up for a hospital flight that was evacuating patients by air from the Continent to England. Our plane was shot down."

"Did others survive?"

"Yes, the five men aboard were taken somewhere else." Her voice shook. *Butch and the others? Were they killed?* She had no way of finding out.

"I'm so sorry. Did the invasion succeed, do you think?"

"Thousands were killed and wounded. But they did establish a beachhead where they bring in more troops and supplies. I think we are advancing through France, but it's slow going. The Germans fight savagely, I hear.

"Paris was liberated in August and put into the hands of the Free French, headed by Charles de Gaulle."

"Yes, we heard about the liberation." Billy rubbed his hands together in appreciation.

Alice smiled in agreement. "Several officers at our base speculated that the Allies must have had secret cooperation from the German commander in order to save the historic city from ruin; it's believed that Hitler orders total destruction when his army can't hold an area. Then an Allied invasion in the south of France in August was hugely successful too."

"The way things are going, Alice, the Russians may get here from the east before the Amis, as some call the Americans. They're driving the Germans out of their country. I hear they are now in Poland."

"I hope the Americans make it first." The Russians were an unknown quantity. "Where are you from, Billy?"

"I'm an Iowa farm boy. Joined up in 1939. I just hope my girlfriend waits for me."

"What's her name?"

"Patricia, and pretty as a peach. How about you?"

"I dated an air force pilot. I guess I hope the same thing."

"I'd better leave. I hear our oh-so-helpful nurse coming to give us warm and friendly care. Best not to anger her. Beware of collaborators." He hobbled off on his crutches, and she heard him give Ursula a cheery greeting.

The nurse moved slowly from bed to bed, apparently checking on each patient, exchanging a few comments here and there. At last she pushed aside the curtain around Alice's bed. Alice smiled and said, "Good morning," in a pleasant voice.

Ursula stared at her, unsmiling. Alice raised her hand to her mouth to show that she wanted food. Ursula looked at her for some time, closed the curtain, and walked away.

No food arrived the whole day. In the afternoon, as she napped, someone left a pitcher of water and a glass, but no food. Her meek young helper pretended not to understand when she indicated hunger. By evening her stomach growled. Did Ursula mean to starve her to death?

Chapter 27

The next morning Helmut Bauer came to see her. His sharp eyes examined her soiled night garment and the empty table beside her. "Are you well?" he said.

"Yes, yes, I am. I'm getting better. But I'm hungry. I think they forgot to feed me yesterday. Could I get some food?"

"Of course you can. We don't starve people here."

To her amazement, he called Ursula and, in an angry tone, berated her in German, pointing to Alice's soiled gown and empty night table. Ursula hurried off, and within a short time, a basin of water and a towel arrived followed by a bowl of cereal.

"I'm sorry about this, Alice," Helmut said. "It won't happen again."

"Thank you. I'm really hungry."

"I was as surprised as you were to meet up with you. My father often talked about his older brother in America. When your father wrote to me, I was excited. I'm sorry I never got to meet him."

"Dad looked forward to your letters." Alice eagerly ate the cereal.

He stared out at the drab buildings. "My wife has some relatives, but I don't have any others. My sister died young. Our parents are both gone."

"That's too bad."

He turned to look at her. "I've been thinking about your situation. After the war ends, you'll surely go home. And I'm working on something else."

"Couldn't I go home now? I'm a noncombatant."

"I'm sorry. I have no authority for that. For now, since you're better, you'll help care for the patients in this ward. No Germans, just prisoners of war. Officers. That's why you were sent here. I've arranged for you to have a small room to sleep in."

"That would be wonderful. Of course I'll help the wounded."

"You could work a few hours a day until you gain your full strength."

He touched her arm, smiled, and left her.

And she'd get to work under Miss Ursula Compassionate. A big comedown from Marjorie's enlightened supervision.

* * *

Back in the United States, Mrs. Mayfield prepared her most delicious steak dinner for her pilot son when he returned to Juniper. Though the meat required several ration stamps and put a large dent in their food budget, she'd been saving for the event. Along with other American mothers, she had spent months listening to the news every evening to hear how many American bombers had not returned to base that day. At last Brad's ordeal was over.

His first question was about his brother. "Have you heard from Steve?"

"As far as we know he's all right. Where do you go next?" Mr. Mayfield took his son's army jacket and hung it up.

"I'll be going to Bowman Field for reassignment."

"I'm so glad to hear it." Mrs. Mayfield breathed a sigh of relief. Out of the carnage for good. Her prayers were answered.

Brad breathed the clear desert air. "I've longed for that desert air again. I swear I smell sagebrush, right here in the middle of town."

His parents laughed.

"Have you heard anything about Alice Bauer?" he asked.

"Alice?" Mr. Mayfield frowned. "Wasn't she killed? I heard her hospital plane went down."

"But that doesn't necessarily mean she's dead. Maybe she's in hiding somewhere or a prisoner."

"Did you see much of her in England?" He'd written his mother that he'd dated her.

"Yes, yes, I did. I just can't believe that she's dead. I'm going to see her parents and find out if they have any news."

"Of course. You can go see them after we eat."

* * *

"We don't know anything more about Alice than you do," Gloria told him when he stood in her living room. "All we can do is hope for the best and be ready if she comes home injured."

Brad stumbled back down the path toward town, through the low sagebrush and the few Juniper trees. He needed to get control of himself.

Now that he was home, it seemed doubly bitter that Alice was not here with him. They had talked often about their plans in their hometown after the war—places they'd visit, friends they'd see. He decided to get a cup of coffee at the hotel.

"Hello, Captain," Grant said, offering his hand. "Welcome home. The whole town's proud of you."

"Thanks." Brad shook hands and gave him a weak smile. "I'll have coffee."

Grant poured a cup and examined his haggard face. "You must be very weary."

"Truth is, I'm concerned about a friend of mine—Alice Bauer." Brad took a seat. "She went down on a hospital plane over enemy territory. They have no word about the fate of the crew or of Alice."

"I know about that. I wish there was something we could do."

* * *

On the street outside, Odette Glass glanced into the window of the hotel café and noticed Brad Mayfield sitting at the counter. She admired his wavy black hair and his handsome face. He had possibilities, being a captain now.

She decided to have a snack herself. Luckily, most of the seats were taken, except for the one beside Brad. She sat down, exclaiming as she did so, "Brad Mayfield. How fantastic to see you. I hear you're a captain."

"Well, yes. Good to see you, Odette."

"Welcome home, Captain. How long can we enjoy your company?"

"I'm on furlough a month."

"How delightful for us. Why don't you come to a little party I'm having at the ranch tomorrow night around seven. Lots of your old friends will be there."

Brad seemed hesitant. "Thanks. Maybe I will."

"None of that maybe stuff. I want your promise to be there. The women will outnumber the men," she said, with a teasing smile.

Brad laughed. "Well, in that case, I'll be there."

"You'll be the life of the party." Odette ordered coffee and continued to gush over Brad.

When he left, Odette told Grant, "He's so handsome."

"That he is. He's been dating Alice Bauer in England."

"Really? I heard Alice was killed in a plane crash."

"They don't know for sure. She's just missing."

"Is that so?"

* * *

When Brad mentioned Odette's invitation to his parents, his mother said, "You should go, Brad. You're not helping yourself by moping around here. It will do you good."

Without deciding, Brad pitched in to assist his mother with fruit canning. The aroma of sweet boiling jam filled the air as he tackled small repairs around the house. Since the owner was short of help,

Mr. Mayfield worked long hours at the hardware store and let things slip at home.

The next day Brad's thoughts returned to Alice again and again. He saw her auburn hair swirling around her bare shoulders, her blue eyes, smiling and enticing. He remembered her generous nature and her innocent, kind heart. She had become his best companion, his hope, his life.

He couldn't accept that their days together were over. Finally, in desperation, to get his mind off the thought of her death or capture, he drove out to Odette's party in his father's car.

A makeshift bar stood in one end of the long living room. The rugs were rolled back, and people were dancing to recordings of the Glenn Miller band and Frank Sinatra.

Just as Odette had told him, there were not many men present—just a few young officers from the nearby air base and some ranchers, exempt from service because of their essential occupation. Most of them were on the dance floor. Chester Southwick, Alice's senior classmate and would-be rapist, was immaculately dressed in pressed cords and a silk shirt. He gave Brad a hateful look and thereafter avoided him.

Women sat around conversing in small groups. Feminine laughter drifted through the large room. Iris Reynolds greeted him with a big smile. "Captain Mayfield, how good to see you."

"You too, Iris. I heard you married a sailor."

"I met him in college."

"And you lived on base?"

"Yes, I lived with him at several bases until he went overseas. It was horrible. Housing was terrible at all of them. Dank little apartments, squalid little rooms, and then we had a baby, which made it even more difficult. I didn't know anyone."

"So are you living here with your folks?"

"Yes, and I'm so happy to live in a normal house."

Brad refrained from mentioning that the spacious Reynolds home hardly qualified as a normal house.

Sarah Walker approached him. "Hello, Brad. Remember me?"

"Of course, Sarah, even though you were still in grade school when I left. Your brother David married Emma Bauer."

"Yes. It's good to see you home safe."

"Believe me, it's wonderful to be here."

"I'm surprised to see Chet. He usually prefers socializing out of town. Has quite a reputation for tomcatting about. Some people even say that Chet is violent. He likes to carry a pistol, fancies himself a movie cowboy. I suppose Odette didn't want to omit invitations to any of her neighbors."

"Yes, well, there are some stories about him."

"So I've heard. I'm sorry about Alice missing. Emma tells me you were a good friend of hers."

"I'm terribly concerned. I'm hoping she's a prisoner and will be released when the war is over."

Sarah wanted to help. He seemed quite desolate.

"Why don't you come for dinner with us on Sunday? David and Emma join us then. I'm sure Emma would like to hear as much as you can tell her about her sister."

"That's kind of you. I'd like to talk to Emma."

"Maybe you can grab a ride or share gasoline ration stamps with someone else. Several people come out to Springdale on Sunday."

"That's a good idea. Do you know anyone who could give me a ride?"

Sarah gave him several names. "I'll be as glad as any serviceman when this damn war is over," she said. "I'm so tired of ranch work. Dad can't hire help, and next to David, I'm his right-hand guy. This is the first party I've been to in ages. Of course, there haven't been very many. People haven't felt much like it, and they've been working hard—raising beef or rolling bandages."

"Then perhaps you'd like to dance." He wasn't excited about dancing, but she was a pleasant girl. And with so few men at the party, he just had to dance.

Her face brightened. "I'd love to."

He danced with several women, including Odette, who flirted with him outrageously. "I have to drive to The Dalles on Monday to pick up some supplies and to shop. But I hate to drive that far alone. Could you drive me in my car if I furnish the gas stamps?"

He shrugged. A trip to The Dalles would take his mind off unpleasant things. "Sure. Why not?"

As the evening wore on, the party atmosphere contrasted so harshly with his war experience that it had an eerie quality. He left early and spent the night struggling with his dreams about plane crashes. In them, he saw a beautiful woman with auburn hair emerge from the wreckage and stumble to the ground. He struggled toward her but always awoke before he reached her.

In the daytime he imagined her fighting with German guards, facing deprivation, or starving in a hideout somewhere behind enemy lines.

On Sunday Brad joined the Walkers for dinner at the big house. "Tell us all you can about Alice's days in England," Emma said, after greeting him and seating him at the table.

"We toured the sights of London." He ticked off the places they had visited. "After the invasion, hospital personnel worked even longer days because of the thousands of casualties."

"How did she happen to be on a hospital plane anyway?" Mrs. Walker wanted to know.

"She volunteered for the training in the States and then volunteered for the assignment over there. It was dangerous. I couldn't dissuade her." His voice shook. "I expected to be the one who didn't come back."

"Are the Allies doing as well as the papers report?" Mr. Walker asked.

"It's hard for me to judge. The German Luftwaffe certainly isn't functioning as it was. When the invasion started, some said we'd be in Berlin by Christmas, but I think everyone has given that up."

"What a shame," Sarah said. "If Alice is a prisoner, she won't be able to celebrate Christmas, I suppose."

* * *

On Monday morning Odette drove up to collect Brad for their trip to The Dalles. "Don't you look handsome?" Her eyes shone with admiration.

"Well, I don't dare wear civilian clothes or someone will think I'm a slacker." He slipped into the driver's seat.

"I'm so happy you're driving me today. Do you have any shopping to do yourself?"

"I was thinking of getting a couple of pieces of jewelry—something for my mother and something for Alice."

"But is Alice coming back? I got the impression that she's probably been killed."

Brad swore under his breath and answered shortly. "That's not certain. No remains have been found. She could be in hiding or captured."

"Well…I'm sorry. Perhaps you're right." She bit her lip and changed the subject.

"I want to find some silk stockings or even those new nylons," she said after a moment. "They just aren't available in Juniper. And I need several other supplies. Everything is scarce."

Before they began their shopping in The Dalles, Brad drove as close as he could get to the banks of the mighty Columbia, flowing between Oregon and Washington State on its way to the Pacific.

The river would soon no longer be so mighty due to the dams being built upstream, providing the area with electric power. But even so, the sight of the huge body of water always amazed those from the dry central part of the state.

"I've heard the dams might affect the salmon runs," Brad remarked. "The Indians have complained."

"Well, they use electricity too." Odette held her black hair down in the breeze.

Brad imagined Alice sitting with him on a nearby slope, her red hair blowing in the wind, their picnic spread out before them. Had she ever been here? Would it ever happen?

In the jewelry store he found a costume pearl necklace for his mother and a bracelet of shiny polished stones for Alice. Then he followed Odette from store to store as she tried on clothes, picked over underwear, and insulted clerks. Bored, he longed for the day to end. By the time he and Odette reached his house in Juniper, he had determined never to repeat such a day again.

Where was Alice? Why hadn't they heard anything?

Chapter 28

After Helmut's visit to the hospital ward, Alice's meek helper, named Gerta, led her to a room that served as a storage room in the past. Located in a small hallway just beyond the end of her ward, it lay at the back of the entire hospital building near the latrine.

Shelves had been knocked out. She was barely able to close the thin doors. The small cot and tiny end table filled the space completely. It didn't matter. Alice had no possessions here. She supposed this was the best Helmut could manage. It would have been difficult for her to share quarters with German nurses.

The one blanket would not keep out the cold of the approaching winter. She would have to sleep in some of her garments, along with the hospital gown, in order to keep warm. Her only source of heat came from the nearby ward, where a coal-burning stove stood in the middle.

In the morning Gerta brought her some dark bread, white cotton stockings, and a white nurse's uniform. Later she led Alice through the ward to the hospital kitchen on the other end.

Trays were being set up for the patients. She indicated that Alice was to carry them into her ward for her patients. Alice noticed that the other wards were located down the hall from the kitchen, opposite her own ward.

The trays held bowls of warm cereal, black bread, and water. When she approached Billy's bed, he handed her a small package of chocolate candy. "It's from the Red Cross, provided by the United States. They send them from Switzerland."

Alice slipped it into her pocket. She was to appreciate these Red Cross parcels as time went on, and as food at the hospital became extremely scarce.

After the meals Alice removed the trays and was put to work bathing the patients and changing their beds. In a few hours she was exhausted, still feeble from her illness.

There were no windows in her small storage room, but from the few in the ward, she glimpsed a forest of tall trees beyond the barbed-wire fence. She longed for a quiet walk among them, but she didn't dare go outside the hospital. And she did not want to ask Ursula or Helmut for permission, to impose on their authority.

Later Billy told her that the prison commandant's house was tucked among the trees. He and his family reportedly lived in luxury with prisoners serving as household help.

In the opposite direction stood the rest of the camp, a good distance from the hospital. A huge place, the barracks stretched off to the horizon. Guards patrolled constantly and watched from the guard towers.

Eventually Gerta led her to the kitchen where the two women ate a short meal of black bread with a few bites of pork. The moment they finished, Ursula appeared, giving orders to get the patients fed, fold the linen, and clean the workstation. Ursula was apparently planning to work her all day despite her weakened condition.

Alice carried the trays out to the patients for the next meal. When she approached Billy's bed, he said, "You're pale. You must be tired."

"I am, but I don't dare say anything. Bauer said I'd work a few hours at first, but Ursula's going to work me all day, I guess."

"She thinks you're his mistress. I heard her talking to someone in German. I understand it a little. We've all noticed that she seems to have a soft spot for Bauer."

"But that's ridiculous. We're..." Alice started to say, "We're cousins," but remembered Helmut's warning. She was silent for a moment. "That's not true. He's married," she finally said.

"Well, that wouldn't stop a lot of men. Anyway, Ursula will believe what she wants to believe. We've seen her do nasty things to patients she didn't like. Watch your back with her."

"Thanks, I will." She moved on.

She fell into bed at the end of the day. The next morning she rose early, determined not to complain to Ursula. She'd sleep better if she were worn out. She'd struggle without complaint through the long days of work.

There was little to do in her small room anyway. As the days passed, she continued to work early and late. When the patients were cared for, there was always endless cleaning to tackle.

As she became better acquainted with the patients who spoke English, they seemed to look forward to seeing her. The highlight of all their lives was the arrival of the Red Cross food parcels, which contained canned meats and fish, powered milk and coffee, cheese, margarine, dried fruits, and sweets. They also held cigarettes and soap.

Billy bartered with one of the delivery workers from outside the camp to take his, Alice's, and other nonsmokers' cigarettes for extra vegetables from nearby farms.

"We need to 'liberate' these vegetables," Billy said with a laugh.

Alice then washed them in the ward and added small amounts of the turnips, carrots, and cabbages to the trays as she readied them for the patients. It didn't amount to much for each patient, but she knew the nutrients were important for health.

Nevertheless, many patients died from wounds that wouldn't heal. She attributed deaths primarily to poor diet over time and lack of proper medical care. Medications were scarce. The doctor rarely was allowed to visit the patients. A Hungarian prisoner, he conversed poorly with the patients, although he did try.

The best care and facilities were kept for the sick and injured Germans at the front of the hospital.

Then the Red Cross parcels stopped coming.

Chapter 29

Without the Red Cross parcels, the diet at the POW hospital consisted of dark bread, potato or rutabaga soup, and what root vegetables Billy could scrounge up from outside.

Cleanliness was a problem. It was difficult to sterilize supplies. Alice tried to see that each prisoner got a bath at least weekly, but water too was scarce. She constantly changed soiled bedding for patients too weak to move or to ask for bedpans. Despite the efforts of Alice and the other nurses to keep it clean, the ward often reeked of human waste.

Their supply of coal diminished.

Alice had little contact with the German nurses, except to pass them in the ward. They watched her with suspicion in their eyes, and their exchanges were limited. Since they had duties in other hospital wards, her help allowed them to concentrate their energies elsewhere. When Ursula came through, she watched Alice with vindictive hatred.

More patients arrived all the time, but few gained enough strength to leave. Even with the food parcels, they had often been hungry. Those who did recover were taken over to the camp barracks for work details.

Alice sometimes saw the wretched prisoners being marched away from the camp early in the morning to work. It was usually dark when she heard them return, weary, dragging, and famished. Billy had learned that they were not fed all day.

She and Billy were surprised to hear about a couple of local German women who dropped palm-sized bundles of oats where the prisoners would be passing. The hungry men quickly scooped them up. The women had to be careful, of course, not to attract the attention of the guards.

Helmut brought her a book in English: *A Tree Grows in Brooklyn* by Betty Smith. When she had read it aloud to a couple of American patients too sick to read, she shared it with the other English-speaking patients. Some of them also passed around books sent by the YMCA and the Red Cross.

Billy spoke in a low voice to Alice and other trusted patients about information he'd received from outside. He explained why the Normandy invasion had caught the Germans by surprise. Apparently the Germans expected an invasion at Calais, not Normandy, and at high tide, not low tide. To complicate matters, Rommel was off visiting his wife at the time. And a counterattack was delayed several hours because orders had to come from Berlin.

The days became colder and shorter. During the long winter evenings, Alice heard the wind moan and cry in the trees beyond the fence. Once she thought she heard a wolf howl.

She shivered and tried to move faster to keep warm. The patients seemed warm enough, but each of them had been issued two blankets.

Alice often wondered about Brad. Her memories of their meetings in England helped to alleviate the drabness of the long winter days. If he hadn't been killed, he would be working on the ground in England.

Or he could be home on leave. A few lucky airmen were reassigned back to the States after they finished their missions.

One night Alice, tired from the day's work, trudged to her private storage space. As she reached to open the door, she heard a faint sound inside. A rat? A mouse? Not her favorite animals but probably harmless. Surely it would run from her. She definitely did not want to call for help.

The dim light from her ward down the hall gave her courage. A prisoner medic was on duty during the night in case of any emergency. She could scream if she needed him. Emma always accused her of being reckless and impetuous. Now she could live up to those words. Cautiously, she opened the door of her room and quickly flicked on the light.

Chapter 30

On her bed sat a young man in striped POW garb. He was pitifully young, nineteen at the most. He stood and watched her expectantly. The dark bruises on his cheek and neck did not hide the intense fear on his face. Blood soaked his shirt on one arm. For a moment they stared at one another. She swallowed.

Then slowly and carefully, with a slight smile to show friendliness, she raised his sleeve and looked at his arm. It was a superficial wound but needed attention.

"Speak English?" she whispered.

"Yes," he answered the same way.

"Stay here. I'll get some water and supplies to fix you up."

The French medic paid little attention as she reentered the ward for bandages and a container of water. Back in her room, she coaxed the POW to let her wash and dress his arm. "How did you get this?" she whispered.

"The guard hit me with a shovel." His voice trembled. From his speech, she knew he was American.

"And the bruises on your face?"

"His rifle butt."

"Do you have any more injuries?"

"Just minor."

"Do they know you are gone?"

"I don't know. They might in the morning. They don't count every day though. I've got to get out of here. One of the guards hates my guts. He's going to kill me sooner or later." The boy averted his eyes. "He thinks I'm Jewish—called me a dirty Jew."

Alice struggled to hide the fear gripping her stomach. Was this a test? Had Ursula sent the boy to tempt her to act and thus get herself killed? Was he a collaborator? Her mouth went dry.

As she stared at his wound, she thought of her commitment as a nurse: to heal and help sustain life. Despite the possible consequences, she must act to save him, as though he told the truth.

She pondered the situation. The prisoner would have no chance of climbing over the high fence. How could she hide him until they could think of something? An idea began to form in her mind. "What's your name?" she asked.

"I'm Joel, Joel Green."

Alice suspected he was Jewish. It hardly mattered whether he was or was not. If the SS thought he was Jewish, it meant extra danger for the young man in front of her.

"Look, Joel, I have an idea. I expect one of my patients to die soon, probably tonight. The poor man has several medical problems. We can't save him. Once he dies, I might be able to get him out of his bed and put you into it during the night or early morning."

"In a hospital bed?"

"I'll need to put your clothes on him. And when you're in his bed, you'll have to pretend to be very sick for a long time. Until he dies, you'll have to stay here in this room and be quiet."

The boy shook his head. "I think I can get over the fence. I don't want to put you in jeopardy."

"No, you can't get over the fence. Another patient here told me that the guards have shot over twenty prisoners trying to escape. Not one has made it. I'm the main nurse on this ward. Others seldom come in here. This should work."

"What about my shaved head?"

"We'll keep your head covered until your hair grows. The dying patient is against the wall, half hidden. So you can keep your shaved head out of sight there. Can you do this?"

Joel gulped. "All right."

"Good. Now I'm going to get some water for you to drink and to wash, and a hospital gown so you will be ready to slip into the patient's bed when the time comes."

"What about him?"

"You'll have to help me put your clothes on him when he dies and take him out the back door right across the hall. Right there."

She pointed to the door across from her room. It had never been locked. When the latrines were not working, it led to the outhouses.

"That's where you came in, right? The guards don't have a good view of the back of the hospital. Only the high fence. We'll take the poor man off as far as we dare. When they find him they might think he's you."

So once again Alice slipped into her ward, nodded to the medic, picked up a tray, and gathered up water in a pitcher to drink, a basin of warm wash water from a pot on the stove, disinfectant to kill the lice she'd noticed, and a patient gown, hiding it under her arm. As she passed the bed of the critically ill patient that she planned to replace, she noted that his breathing was more labored than ever.

When Joel had washed, with Alice's help, and changed into the gown, she said, "The latrine is down the hall. The patients are asleep, but if anyone happens to see you, maybe they'll think you are one of the others from the ward. I'll change into my nightgown while you're gone. You take the bed. I'll sleep here beside it. In a few hours I'll look in on my dying patient."

Joel wanted to sleep on the floor, but she reminded him that she had to get up and check on the patient in a few hours, and she would have to step over him if he were on the floor.

Joel badly needed the rest. He was extremely thin, and his face, besides being bruised, was pale. He finally agreed but insisted that she take the pillow. "I'm used to doing without," he said, with a weak smile. "I haven't had a pillow in a long time."

In the early morning, Alice found that her dying patient was hanging on to life. Joel would have to stay in her room while the man lived. She sat by the patient's bed until the night medic left and she heard the kitchen workers, most of them prisoners, come on duty.

She hid some of her breakfast bread in her pocket to give to Joel later. At the first opportunity, she slipped out and handed it to the young man, who wolfed it down. As Alice guarded the seldom-used hallway, he slipped into the latrine near her room.

All day she nervously performed her duties, glancing often at the hallway leading into her room. She felt nauseated with fear.

Ursula chose that day to visit the ward. She eyed Alice curiously as she checked the charts of the patients. Alice feared that she suspected something. Nervous about Joel, she shook, fumbled, and dropped a kettle. She steeled herself to remain calm and in control. At last Ursula left her alone with her patients.

She saved a boiled potato from her dinner for Joel. In a low voice, she asked Billy if he had any candy or food tucked away, planning to give it to Joel. He shook his head.

Late that night Alice's patient died quietly. She dozed, waiting until early morning while it was still dark. "Why don't you get to bed," she said to the sleepy medic in the ward. "I'll take over early today. I'm up anyway."

The medic nodded gratefully and shuffled off. It looked as though the other patients still slept. She heard deep breathing, snoring, some fitful turning, and groaning. But finally all the patients settled down.

Quickly she summoned Joel, and the two of them pulled the man as quietly as possible into the hallway, where they dressed him in Joel's striped prisoner outfit. They shaved his head to make him look like one of the regular prisoners.

No one was about as they carried him out the back door and left him on the chilly ground several feet away. Alice said a silent prayer for the patient, hoping the man might have forgiven her for the use of his lifeless body to save another prisoner. Hurrying Joel into the man's bed, she began her morning chores.

Later in the day, armed guards stormed into the ward and began to search under the beds and in the closets. They inspected the kitchen, the latrine, and her sleeping cupboard.

Chapter 31

Alice stood aside and held her breath while the soldiers searched. *Dear Lord, don't let them look at the men in the beds.*

She relaxed when it appeared that they had no thought of looking in the beds. They rechecked everything, and then, with last frustrated looks over the ward, they stomped past the kitchen toward the rest of the hospital.

What had happened? The guards must have already found the body. Perhaps they didn't believe it was Joel. But why start looking here? Had Ursula said something to the guards? That was the only thing that made sense.

She wondered what would happen to her if her part in the rescue were discovered. From all she'd heard, she surmised it would be death. She doubted that cousin Helmut would be able to save her.

According to the chart, the dead patient was French. She had warned Joel not to speak. Better to pretend not to understand German or English. Alice told Joel to ignore the Hungarian doctor when he came around, act too sick to respond.

Nervously watching for signs that the hoax had been discovered, she went back to her work for the day. Ursula visited again, slowly examining the patients and the charts, watching Alice furtively. But she found nothing out of order, so at last she left. Alice sank into a chair, faint with relief.

Joel, spent from his time in prison, adapted quickly to the role of patient. Gradually the bruises on his face faded.

Billy occupied the bed next to him, and the two began to converse in hushed voices when Alice was alone with the patients. Billy must have wondered what happened to the Frenchman, but he wisely refrained from asking. In time Alice let him in on the trade.

Finally, Ursula stopped coming by so often. One day the Hungarian doctor, on an infrequent visit, puzzling over Joel's tag, announced as he stood by Joel's bed that he was well.

"No," Alice said, shaking her head. "He is not well. He can't leave. He'll die."

An English patient nearby unexpectedly spoke to the doctor in Hungarian. The doctor looked curiously at Alice and then Joel. He shook his head. "Not well. No leave." He continued his rounds without further comment.

"Thank you," Alice said to the Englishman, "What did you tell him?"

"That they would kill Joel. Of course, many of the others out there are going to die too. They work them hard and feed them barely enough to survive."

Alice, Joel, and Billy could come up with no plan to get Joel out of the camp. They decided that the only safe place for him was the hospital bed.

* * *

December was one of the worst months in Europe for the Allies. Billy heard about a massive German counteroffensive, hitting the Allies in their weakest point in the Ardennes Forest.

During the Battle of the Bulge, a terrible slaughter came to light. German SS troops took hundreds of American prisoners. Over eighty Americans were shot in cold blood while being held as POWs. A few wounded soldiers played dead among their dying comrades and lived to tell the story. In reprisal for the Malmedy Massacre, few SS soldiers were given mercy when captured by Americans.

Another setback in the campaign occurred when 150 English-speaking Germans, dressed as American soldiers, infiltrated the

American lines—mixing road signs and circulating false rumors, including one about a planned assassination plot against General Eisenhower, who was safely in Paris at the time. These actions created havoc in the American lines.

When word reached nervous military police about the infiltrations, they questioned everyone, asking things only Americans could answer: the name of Mickey Mouse's girlfriend (Minnie), the home of Li'l Abner (Dogpatch), and the name of Betty Grable's latest husband (Harry James). Some Americans who couldn't answer were held for several days.

As a result of the Battle of the Bulge, thousands of GIs were marched off to Germany as prisoners of war. Twenty-five hundred civilians were killed in the bombings and crossfire.

By the end of January, when the Battle of the Bulge was declared officially over and the Allied lines were straightened out, casualties on both sides reached tens of thousands.

Months of fighting followed as the Germans fought a desperate struggle to defend their homeland against the eastward-moving Allies and the westward-moving Russians, but the Battle of the Bulge was their last great offensive.

Chapter 32

In Juniper, Kate burst into Grant's office. "She's alive! The Red Cross notified John and Gloria. She's nursing at a POW camp. They're trying to get her out."

He gathered her into his arms. "Thank God."

"We can try writing to her. Some of the letters get through. Oh Lord, I'm so relieved." She was giddy with excitement.

Grant studied her face. "See here. You're all flushed. Sit down for a rest. She must be well if she's nursing."

Kate sat. "I think she must be."

"We should notify Brad Mayfield. He's been very concerned."

"John sent him a telegram at Bowman Field this morning."

"Let's celebrate. Let me take you to dinner at my new restaurant next door. Most people tell me that it's quite chic."

"Oh, thank you. But John and Gloria are expecting me for dinner."

"I'll send an errand boy to bicycle up with a message."

A smile lit her face. "Am I dressed chic enough?" She indicated her pastel yellow dress with her fitted black jacket.

"My dear girl, you'd look chic if you were dressed in a burlap bag." He took her arm and led her to the lobby where he scrawled off a note and asked the receptionist to have it taken up to the Bauer house.

He seated her at a table and ordered drinks. Kate was so happy about Alice that she would have been pleased with anything. In truth, the dinner house glowed in soft light. She heard the sounds of silver clinking against china. Laughter drifted through the dining room.

She admired the new restaurant and asked Grant to order for her. "Maybe Alice will be home soon," she said, sipping her drink.

"That would be wonderful, but don't get your hopes too high. In any event, the fighting can't last much longer. She'll be freed for sure when the war ends."

As they lingered over coffee, friends dropped by to chat. For once Grant was impatient with them. Their curiosity at seeing the two of them together was obvious. "Stay with me tonight in one of the rooms," he murmured, as one group of visitors left. "We can go through the kitchen as I show it to you and then up the back way."

She hesitated. "But John and Gloria might worry."

"They know you're with me. Please. I want to ask you something."

Her objections were overruled. Their night together had soothed her heart, warmed her spirit, and excited her body. It was impossible to feel the least bit guilty about it. Longing to be with him, she nodded.

His pulse raced. "Then let's go. We can order up if we want anything."

He led her around the gleaming new kitchen, commenting on the fixtures and work areas as the staff bustled about with food preparation. Then, nonchalantly, he led her into a hallway leading to the rooms.

They entered a suite, the best in the hotel. In addition to the bed, it contained two lounge chairs and a coffee table. As they sat and savored the wine he had picked up on their way, he told her, "I actually live in the house my folks left me, but it's not unusual for me to stay overnight here or to order food either. I usually eat at my desk or at the food counter."

He took her hand. "But I don't want us to have to keep company like this. Let's get married. I want to make up for all the years of struggle you went through alone. You know I love you. Will you marry me, Kate?"

Overwhelmed with emotion, she looked surprised. "I thought you were a confirmed bachelor now."

"Not a bit. I've been waiting for you, my sweet. We should have married twenty-five years ago. Let's make up for lost time."

She glowed with pleasure. To be Grant's wife, to share his love—she'd dreamed of him for years. "Oh, Grant, I'd love to marry you."

But she had to let him know. "I intend to tell Alice the truth. She's an adult now. She can handle it. And I want to be able to claim her as my daughter. I'm tired of keeping it a secret. It's a burden."

"Let's tell her together. I too want us to claim her."

Her heart melted. "Then I'll marry you."

He rose, walked over to her chair, and stooped to kiss her. "You've made me the happiest man in the world. What kind of wedding do you want?"

"Small. Very small."

Chapter 33

In the German POW hospital, Billy heard of extensive fighting in the Belgian forests. But the Allies eventually moved past the Rhine River and into Germany.

Alice told Billy, "Brad may still be making bombing raids. Or he could be dead for all I know."

"Try to be optimistic. You told me that he had almost completed his missions."

"Yes, but wouldn't it be awful if he was shot down on one of the last ones."

"The dread of every soldier, sailor, and airman."

"I'm also wondering about my brother. He was injured in a bombing raid, but it's possible he has recovered enough to fly again." She sat down on his bed.

"Don't think about it. If he was badly injured, it's not likely he'd be flying again so soon."

"Oh, Billy, how did we all get here?" she asked, with a bleak look.

"I suppose millions of people are wondering that very thing."

"The whole world must be weeping," Alice said, wiping her eyes.

He waited for her crying to stop. They sat in silence for a time.

"We may have to start dividing up the food scraps ourselves before long," he said at last. "Did you know that five people out of three have trouble with fractions?"

She laughed. "Oh, Billy. You always know what to say." Chuckling, she went back to work.

But Billy worried about the end of the war. "The Russians massed along the German-Polish border have begun an offensive. It's been expected for some time. My sources tell me it began on January twelfth," he told Alice.

"Isn't that good news?" Alice wrapped a fresh bandage around Joel's arm as she talked.

"Yes, except word has filtered in that some prisoners in POW camps in their path are being marched west by the Germans to prevent them from falling into the hands of the Russians. So what happens to us? None of the patients will be able to march."

"Bauer would prevent them from moving the patients, surely. There aren't enough ambulances and trucks or petrol for that."

"But he's only in charge of the hospital. He's not making the big decisions."

"It's true we get less food coming in all the time. And I haven't seen any mail shipments for weeks."

"We'll have to hang on until it's over." Billy ran his hands through his hair. "It shouldn't be long."

"The patients and nurses seem nervous," Alice said. "The patients have nightmares, nurses forget things, and they're hysterical over nothing."

Billy nodded. "And the guards too. Some of the German officers have tried to get the prisoners in this camp to sign papers saying they have been well treated. That's just in case the Americans get here first, or if they need evidence later. It won't help with the Russians."

"Have they been well treated? Of course, Joel suffered from some maniac guard, but maybe that was the exception."

"I've heard of abuses." Billy wished to spare her some of the gory reports he'd heard from his outside sources. "We're lucky we can't march, and that we're more or less under Bauer's protection." He hoped rather than believed it.

A few days later, Billy, entering the ward on his crutches, told Alice and the patients, "Ursula, Gerta, and the other German nurses and hospital workers have rushed off to the far western part of Germany."

"They're afraid of the Russians," an English patient said.

"You bet they are. The Germans invaded their country and slaughtered millions. When the Russians come, they'll probably be ready for revenge, and they'll loot and rape."

"Who's going to look after all the patients?" Alice asked.

"I guess we'll have to nurse ourselves. Several top dogs in this camp have left too."

The loss of the nurses and staff meant even more work for Alice. Some recovering patients were put to work in the kitchen. They sat on benches and chairs and washed and sliced the few remaining potatoes.

Helmut began to assist in the other wards by carrying food trays to the patients. He valiantly tried to keep the hospital operating as before, though more patients were flooding the wards.

In March, Alice received the best news of all from Helmut. He had been tending patients, his normally neat, grayish-brown hair hanging over one eye.

"I've just received word," he told her in excitement as he entered the ward. "You are to be taken to Africa by the Red Cross. You will go to your country by ship. Be ready to go within the next couple of days."

Alice closed her eyes, breathed deeply, thankfully. "Oh, Helmut. I'm so grateful for your efforts on my behalf. What will happen to you when the Russians come?"

"We do not know, Alice. They might kill me. It does not much matter. There is no future in Germany now. My wife and child are safe in the west with her parents. You must not worry about me."

She began to weep. "Helmut, please memorize Dad's address so you can write to us and let us know how you are."

"I already have," he told her, embarrassed by her tears. "Now I need to get Billy and others to help in the kitchen. We need something to eat today."

"I'm sorry to leave you, Billy." Alice stopped to talk to him as he sat at the kitchen table scrubbing potatoes, favoring his left shoulder, his crutches leaning against the wall. "I probably should stay to look after the patients."

"Not a bit of it. Get out of here while you can, little mother. The nurses feared not only reprisals but also rape. The Germans know what to expect. The Russians already took over one town temporarily. They raped and shot hundreds before the Germans took the town back. You don't want to be here when the Russians come. They may not even give you a chance to explain that you're an ally."

"I hope the Red Cross sends some food parcels for you before I go. If only the Americans could get here first. Please write to me after the war."

Now they noticed unusual activity at the camp. Trucks piled high with goods left the gate. It looked as though the Germans, at least the top officers, were getting ready to evacuate. That meant the Allies were coming close.

"So much for the great Third Reich," Billy commented, as the trucks streamed out the gates.

Chapter 34

Alice bathed and shaved all the patients who wanted help. She freshened bandages. She scrubbed hospital floors and cleaned with a frenzy before she left with the Red Cross. In Africa she was placed aboard a Red Cross exchange ship for repatriation.

The questions, the forms, the medical checks, the long journey by ship across the Atlantic, and finally another trip across the United States tried Alice's patience. But finally she was home safe.

On April 12, in Juniper, Alice gratefully sipped hot coffee, a treat she'd been without for long periods. The newspaper headlines proclaimed that the Ninth US Army had crossed the Elbe River and was fifty-seven miles from Berlin.

Alice said to Gloria, "Do you think that Fred will be home soon now that he is back in the United States?"

Gloria hovered close. She could not do enough for her newly released girl. "He's still being treated in a hospital. It's hard to tell when we'll see him. I'm so glad he's out of the fighting."

She studied Alice. "I'm afraid I'll have to make you some new clothes if you don't put on some weight. That burgundy dress used to be a good fit, but now it sort of hangs on you."

"The way I'm eating, it will soon fit better. Everything tastes so good."

By late afternoon, shocking news came over the radio. President Roosevelt, just a few months into his fourth term in office, was dead from a stroke. A stunned nation wondered how the war could be fought without him. Gloria, tears streaming down her face, stood at the window. Alice sat glumly trying to absorb the startling information.

She decided to take Linda and Marie for ice cream at the hotel food counter after she told them about the president. Linda and Marie were too young to be much affected by the news for long.

"Yes," Gloria said, wiping her eyes, "take them for a treat. You need it too. Some ice cream would do you good."

"Are we going to the Jiffy Café where you worked?" Linda, followed by Marie, skipped beside Alice down the path toward the town center.

"No." Alice wanted to avoid Chet Southwick and any of his gullible buddies who might still patronize the place. "I like the hotel better."

At the food counter, people listened to the radio with sad, worried faces. Grant saw Alice and her sisters come in and rushed to greet them. "I heard you were back, Alice. Your ordeal has been the talk of the town." He wished he could take his daughter in his arms.

Alice laughed. "I've only been back a day. They examined me and decided I needed some rest. Suffering from slight malnutrition, they said."

"How long will you be here?" Grant settled them on stools at the counter.

"I have leave for a few weeks. Maybe the war will be over by then, and I won't have to go back at all. The news about Roosevelt is so tragic. I brought the girls for a treat."

"Well, this treat is on me. Have banana splits. They're very popular; strawberry, vanilla, and chocolate ice cream, with sliced bananas and sweet, delicious toppings."

Linda and Marie grinned in anticipation. "They won't want any supper," Alice said in protest.

"Look, it's a tough day for everyone. I want to give them a treat. After all, I'm their uncle now. Let them remember this day happily. And let's hope the new president can handle the job."

* * *

As President Truman took over the reins of government, Alice concentrated on her recovery. At family dinners she learned about significant events that she'd missed during her captivity.

John said, "You must have passed through Aachen shortly before the Allies fought a great struggle there. It was the first entry of the Allies into Germany. Today the papers are screaming that more Yanks have crossed the Elbe River."

Gloria said, "The Battle of the Bulge lasted close to two months, but the Germans didn't break through. The Allies straightened it out by the end of January."

John stood up to pace the floor. "There was some kind of conference between Roosevelt, Churchill, and Stalin at Yalta in February. Wonder what plans they made for the world at the war's end."

With a huge sigh, Gloria said, "The lovely German city of Dresden was completely devastated. It's reported that half the population was killed in horrible fires. All that beautiful porcelain and art destroyed."

"Why did they bomb it?" Linda asked.

Nobody could answer her question.

* * *

Alice wondered what life would be like for the Germans still living—Helmut, Gerta, the various soldiers who had taken her from the plane wreck to the POW hospital. Would they now starve to death? Their entire economy had been focused on war. Now it was in shambles. What about the prisoners—Billy, Joel, and the others?

She learned about her uncle Ernst's death. She found it hard to feel much sorrow. She had not even seen him in years.

A sad letter from Aunt Freda in the Pacific region caught up with her in Juniper.

Dear Alice,

I've been making some hospital flights with seriously ill patients. But I can't even talk about the worse experience I've had. Maybe writing about it to another nurse will help me deal with it.

Our army decided to use a South Pacific island abandoned by the Japanese as a base where patients could be briefly treated, evaluated, and then sent on to specialized hospitals.

Three of us nurses volunteered to accompany a Filipino doctor and several Filipino medical assistants to fly in and assess the situation. We were to be there a short time, checking the kitchen and available water, and making an inventory of supplies and other facilities.

We flew in a small plane and made a rough landing on a poor landing strip. In the hospital we were horrified to find hundreds of ill and dying Filipinos who had been forced to work for the Japanese. All were amputees. Many also had malaria, other diseases, and raging infections. They'd had no food or water or care for at least two days, and most of them were unable to respond in any way.

With the help of the assistants, who scavenged usable items, scrubbed linen, and boiled water, we made a broth that a few of them were able to take, bathed people, changed as many beds as possible with our limited facilities and water, and assisted with emergency surgery.

The doctor ordered blood typing, something RNs don't do, though we know how, of course. We did it anyway, and I was never as frightened in my whole career of nursing.

We worked seventy-two hours without relief and then needed sedation to get to sleep. I don't know how any person in the medical profession could be so callous as to abandon these people.

Alice cried when she read the letter. How did people get through such a war?

She was surprised to learn that her aunt Kate had recently married Grant Hunter in a small ceremony at John and Gloria's house. Kate refused to quit her teaching position in the valley so near the end of the school year, but she had given notice that she would not be back. She contracted to teach in Juniper the next year.

Kate had been there to welcome Alice home along with the rest of the family. She and Grant had invited Alice to dine with them in Grant's new restaurant.

Kate was to arrive on the bus from the valley, and Alice was to meet them in the hotel dining room.

"We've all eaten there by now," Gloria told her. "It's a beautiful restaurant. You go and have a good time with Grant and Kate."

Gloria was nervous. *How would Alice receive the news that they were her real parents? Would it change everything?*

Chapter 35

It felt unreal to be back in her hometown. Alice had sometimes thought in the last few months that she might never see Juniper or her family again. During the winter in Germany, she had ached to be back. Now she eyed with pleasure the distant rocky rims, the clear sky, and the hardy juniper trees. The smell of sage filled the air. The area sang with its own distinctive appeal.

She almost danced through the thigh-high sagebrush toward the hotel. The sun shone brilliantly, and she could see her beloved mountains in the distance. The air was fresh and clean. Never had it seemed so invigorating. Townspeople waved to her and welcomed her home.

It would have been as quiet as before the war, except for the bombers and fighter planes roaring and zooming overhead in training exercises from the air base.

Brad lived! He was at Bowman Field, training new recruits. He wanted out of the service as soon as the war was over.

Longing to see him, she relived the golden days they had spent in England in the spring and summer of 1944. His letter to her was filled with passion and thrilling plans for their lives when he returned. She answered in the same vein.

Kate embraced her in the hotel dining room. Grant poured wine and ordered dinner for all of them. "How are things going since you've been back?" Kate asked.

"It's wonderful to be home. I remember when I couldn't wait to get away from this town. Now everyone seems so friendly. Emma and David have been in twice, and Emma took me shopping. She said my clothes are too old, although they could hardly be more attractive with a seamstress like Mother."

"Yes." Kate nodded. "And did you ever notice that the clothes Gloria makes seem ageless? They just never go out of date—they're so beautiful. She's a designer as well as a seamstress. How long did Jennie stay?"

"Only a day. She had to get back to the shipyard. She says that as soon as the war is over she's going to return to Juniper and take time off."

"Have you heard from Brad?"

Alice blushed slightly, remembering the thrill of his letter. "Yes, a telegram and a letter. He'll be heading home when the fighting is over."

Grant offered his opinion. "He's a good fellow."

"Did you ever get my letters in Germany?" Kate asked.

"Not a one. The patients got mail, but I suspect that the chief nurse threw mine away. She took a dislike to me. There's a lot more to tell you about our cousin Helmut."

Grant interrupted, "Alice, why don't you come over to our house after dinner and visit awhile. You can tell us then."

"Why thank you. I'd enjoy that."

Several people stopped by to talk and to welcome Alice as the three finished their coffee. Peter, Fred's old friend, rejected for service because of his eyesight and other health problems, was eager to hear about Fred's recovery.

Iris and Violet, her old classmates, stopped to talk. "I certainly admire your bravery, Alice," Iris said. "You've served your country well. I'm dying to hear more about your experiences. Why don't you join some of the girls at my house two weeks from today for afternoon coffee? They'd all love to see you."

"That would be fun, thanks." When the women left, Alice confided that she had never been invited to Iris's large house before the war.

Kate laughed. "The war has changed many things. You're a war hero."

* * *

Grant and Kate lived in his boyhood home, a stately two-story brick house. Later that evening the three sat in the spacious living room. Alice sipped a glass of wine. "I'm sure cousin Helmut's cooperation was instrumental in getting me out of Germany."

"Tell us about him," Kate said.

"I was very sick when I first arrived at the POW hospital, probably with flu or pneumonia. He had me put to bed for several days. The chief nurse, Dear Ursula, would have starved me if he'd let her. When I recovered, he got me a little storage cupboard with the shelves removed. He'd had a small cot put in it, and it served as my room. Not much space, but I was happy to get the privacy. I doubt the German nurses would have welcomed me in their barracks."

"Was he good to all the patients?" Grant asked.

"A far as I could tell. The last few days I was there, the German nurses all went west to escape the Russians coming from the east. He actually helped feed and care for patients."

"He sounds like a good man," Kate said. "A cousin to be proud of. I've always thought it was resourceful of John to write to him in your grandpa's German hometown."

"I'm sure Helmut thought the Russians would kill him. But I've been watching the war news, and from what I read, the other Allies got to his camp, not the Russians. The patients dreaded the coming of the Russians almost as much as the Germans did."

"Maybe John will hear from Helmut after the war."

"I hope so. He and Billy and Joel promised to write when they can."

"Alice, we have something important to tell you," Kate said, changing the subject.

Alice sat up. "Oh?"

"You know that I was with John and Gloria when they homesteaded in Wyoming."

"Oh yes. Mother said you taught school the first year in the two-room cabin where you all lived."

"The thing is, there were few people around. We were sixty miles from town. We had neighboring midwives for the births of you and Emma."

"Yes, I heard about that."

Kate took a deep breath. "The first baby was mine."

Chapter 36

Kate's face was unsmiling, taut, and tortured. She sat straight in her chair.

"What?" *Kate is not kidding. Her face is so grim. What is she saying?* Alice's mind reeled.

A long silence fell over the room, as Alice pondered. *I was the first baby. Kate has no children. But is she saying that she is my mother? What is she talking about?*

At last Grant broke the silence. "She's your mother, Alice. I'm your father."

Kate said, "The next two years I held school in an abandoned mine shack. Gloria looked after you. When they moved back to Juniper, it seemed better for you to live with them as their daughter along with Emma. You two girls were inseparable playmates. At that time all the teaching jobs in Juniper were full, so I had to go to the valley."

Alice stood up, dazed, and walked slowly about the room, touching a curtain here, a book there. "You're telling me my parents are not my parents?"

"They've loved you like a daughter. You can't say they have treated you any differently than their own," Kate said.

"No, they certainly have not."

"You're their niece," Grant said. "Naturally they loved you."

She stared at him, taking in his graying auburn hair. "Then I'm illegitimate."

"Yes, but there's no need for anybody outside the family to know that. I thought we could spread a rumor that Kate and I were secretly married before your birth. Then we divorced. Who's to question it?"

Alice said with a snicker, "Mr. Hunter—"

Grant winced. "At least call me Grant."

She ignored that. "I can think of plenty of people in this gossipy little town who might question it. Still, what does it matter? I'm not going to be staying here long. Once I'm gone, they'll probably forget about it."

Grant, insistent, said, "It will work."

As she stared at them, while they flushed and fidgeted, she realized they were extremely nervous. She suddenly felt immense pity for the two people in front of her. *What a difficult task this is for them.*

"Well, we can try to get such a rumor going, I suppose. So that is why you were always sending us money, Kate?"

"Yes, but I wanted to help out now and then in any event. I had a steady job during the Depression. Sometimes John didn't."

"Well, Mother Kate." Alice gulped and smiled. "I'll have to get used to this idea. Do any of the others in the family know about this?"

"Only John and Gloria, but I believe we should tell Emma and Jennie and Fred. It's not right to keep such information from them anymore."

"I agree."

"We want to make this up to you," Grant said.

"That's hardly necessary," Alice said in a cold voice. "I've been well provided for. Now I would like to go home so I can think more about this."

"Take my car. You can return it in the morning."

"I can't drive."

"I'll drive you home, Alice." Kate rose wearily.

In the car she said, "I hope you can forgive me."

"Oh, Kate, there's nothing to forgive. I've always adored you. That will never change. You've been good to all of us."

Kate felt tremendous relief after all those years of guilt. For the first time since she'd decided to tell her daughter about their relationship, she relaxed and decided it might be all right after all.

* * *

The next morning John kissed Alice on the forehead before leaving for work at the mill. "I've loved you like a daughter."

"I know, and I'm grateful. You'll always be my father."

Gloria waited until the little girls had bustled off to school. "I'm not sure why they felt they had to tell you. They probably wanted redemption, although it wasn't necessary."

"It seems I have a lot to thank you for, considering the fact that we're not blood relatives."

"Alice, you mustn't feel that way. I loved looking after you while Kate worked. Of course, you always preferred her when she was at home. Blood will tell. When Emma was born, you girls were company for each other."

Alice, sullen, gripped her coffee cup. "It seems to me that Grant Hunter got off easy in all this."

"He didn't even know he had a child for sure until recently. Before Kate even knew, he'd married another woman because his sick mother wanted him to. The girl's mother was a friend of Mrs. Hunter's. Then after he was married, Kate wouldn't tell him."

"How convenient." Alice pushed her cup away.

"He's paid for it a million times over. He also helped us out with food and money during the worst times. I'm sure he feels very guilty."

"But perhaps she might have married, had children of her own."

"You are her own. She knew you were safe. That's what a mother wants. Leaving you with us was probably the most unselfish thing a mother could do. As for marrying, I don't think she ever quit loving Grant."

"It's strange to discover that my parents were secret lovers."

"When the men came back from the first war, they badly needed love and succor."

Alice stared at her. She had longed to help Brad forget the bombing, the ghastly horror. *How can I blame them, when I've been involved in the same way?*

* * *

In Europe, the Allies were pushing east into the central and northern parts of Germany as the Russians advanced from that direction. By mid-April the world was shocked to learn of the horrors of the Belsen prisoner-of-war camp. The Allies discovered some forty thousand starving men, women, and children, many of them sick with typhus or dysentery and infected with lice.

The numbers at the POW camp had swelled within the last few weeks by additional prisoners from concentration and POW camps. Their captors had marched them around Germany to escape the Russians in the east, or in an attempt to hide their atrocities from the Allies. Called death marches, they included political prisoners, homosexuals, and other so-called undesirables. Those prisoners too sick or weak to keep up were shot by the SS.

When the English reached the camp at Belsen, they found the guards had left the occupants to fend for themselves, without food or water.

Corpses lay everywhere. British medical workers labored frantically to save as many of the survivors as possible, moving them to the former German barracks, nearby hotels, and residences. The germ-infested barracks they had lived in were burned. As time went on, hundreds of miserable concentration camps were found all over Germany and conquered territories in Poland and Austria.

General Eisenhower remarked that now the world knew what they were fighting against: barbarism by the Gestapo on a gigantic scale. Allied soldiers wept in horror and pity when they liberated the camps and discovered the prisoner corpses and the appalling living conditions.

As the Allies continued to advance through Germany, Wehrmacht soldiers were surrendering in great numbers. With them were Russians, Poles, Ukrainians, and those of other nationalities who had been POWs wearing German uniforms. They had been given the choice of "volunteering" for the German army or losing their lives. In many cases, the advancing American soldiers, overwhelmed by the numbers of those surrendering, simply took their weapons and told them to keep walking west.

All were being sent in empty supply ships to the United States to work on farms, in factories, and on other projects. Ironically, the prisoners marveled at the wholesome food and the comforts they were given as American POWs. Never had they eaten so well, not even as German soldiers who got the best their country had to offer.

Those prisoners who refused to work were given reduced rations—bread and water. Within a few days, they usually decided to work for the ample American meals.

Along with the soldiers moving west came refugees fleeing the Russians. Others were returning to their homes. They filled the roads, pale, hungry, and clutching their meager possessions. US servicemen and women, heading east, were forbidden to talk to them.

The men in the SS were not so quick to surrender, fearing reprisals for their brutal reign. They discarded their uniforms and tried to pass themselves off as civilians. Not many succeeded.

The end of the war was in sight. Americans looked forward to seeing their sons and daughters again.

Chapter 37

The grown members of the Bauer family sat in Grant's living room one evening, while the little girls visited their aunt Dorothy. Emma, David, and Jennie were flabbergasted by what they had just heard from Kate and Grant Hunter. Though surprised, they had already decided they liked having Grant in the family as their new uncle.

"This doesn't really change anything," John said. "Grant and Kate thought you should know, and so does Alice. What we want to agree on is the need for discretion, secrecy if you like, for the good of all concerned."

Grant took up the explanation. "The story we'll circulate is that Kate and I were married secretly after the first war and were then divorced."

"Yes, but…" Emma faltered. "Everyone thinks she is our sister."

"She's really our cousin?" Jennie asked, still unable to grasp the details.

"We'll just let it out that John and Gloria decided to raise her here in Juniper and let everyone think she was their daughter."

"What if they discover the truth?" Jennie asked.

"I don't see how they can."

"If they aren't convinced," Alice said, "it really doesn't matter much. Kate and Grant are married now, and I'll probably move away. It might affect my…cousins more than the three of us."

"I'm sorry you are put into this position," Kate said, still tense.

"What position?" Emma sat with little Nancy on her lap. "She'll always be my sister, and I'll always love you both." David nodded in agreement.

Always ready for a challenge, Jennie grinned. "It will be fun to carry this off."

* * *

Within a few days, Mrs. Mayfield heard intriguing news as she chatted with Mrs. White at the grocery store.

"Did you hear that Grant Hunter and Kate Bauer recently got married?" asked Mrs. White.

"Really?"

"Yes, it was a small home ceremony. I heard that Alice Bauer is their daughter. Gloria said she thought that they were secretly married years ago, before Kate left for Wyoming with them."

"She thought?"

"Well, you know Gloria. She's more interested in sewing gorgeous clothes for those girls and their aunts than anything else."

"Now why would they marry secretly?"

"Because his mother was a domineering old bat. They were probably afraid she wouldn't approve. The Hunters were wealthy, you know."

"Well, someone must have gotten a divorce then, because he married another girl."

"Yes, he probably thought he had to divorce Kate in order to please his mother before she died. Anyhow, Kate moved to Wyoming. The second wife ran off to California. And he got another divorce."

"But Alice Bauer is John and Gloria's daughter," Mrs. Mayfield protested again, confused.

"Apparently not. Everyone just thought so since Alice lived with them."

Mrs. Mayfield thought about Grant's graying russet hair. Once it had been as vibrant as Alice's auburn locks.

Mrs. White said, "Kate has helped by sending them money and helping Alice through nursing school. And Gloria says Grant contributed to the household too."

"Seems strange they didn't bother to tell anyone that Alice was a niece instead of a daughter."

"Gloria told somebody she didn't think of Alice as anything but a daughter."

"Why didn't Grant say anything?"

"Well, you know how men are. Their children are not really their main interest. He did hire Emma Bauer at the hotel though. So he's been involved with the family. If they're married, Kate is one lucky woman. Grant's a wonderful man and handsome too. I'm happy for her."

The news reached Dixie as she waited tables at the Jiffy Café. What a strange story it was. Still, it could be true. It hardly mattered now. The entire Bauer family and Grant Hunter as well were liked and admired.

* * *

When Alice joined Iris and the other women for afternoon coffee, they asked her about life as a nurse and about her captivity. She told them she had read that by June 1943, forty thousand women had been recruited for the nursing services. The regulars took women ages twenty-two to thirty-five while the reserves took women up to the age of forty. They had to be unmarried, widowed, or divorced. But by the end of 1942, married women were accepted.

There were actually some frontline nurses in the initial fighting in Africa, but then the forces decided the front line was too dangerous for women. Even behind the lines there were nurse casualties from bombing. Alice had just read about Frances Slanger, a nurse who got to Normandy in June, a few days after the initial invasion, and died in October from a bombing attack. One nurse she knew of had gone to her death in a hospital plane crash.

"It's rumored that nurses in the Philippines have been held captive since the Japanese overran the area."

"Nevertheless, it must be fun to be around all those men in the hospital wards. Weren't you in England?" Cecelia White asked.

"Yes, I was on the southern coast. It was interesting at first. We traveled to London and saw the sights with air force officers. And we danced at the officers' club."

"What about after the invasion?"

"Not so much fun. The day of the invasion we treated about a thousand, and they were in shock or unconscious from all the morphine they had been given on the battlefield for pain."

Next the women wanted to hear about Kate's wedding and her own relationship to Kate. "You little minx," Iris scolded, as she refilled the coffee cups. "You never told us the Bauers were not your family."

"I always thought of them as my family." *And that's the truth.*

"Tell us about the wedding." Cecelia leaned forward, balancing her cup on her knee.

"I wasn't back yet, of course. They got married at our house with only a few guests."

"So now we learn that you're the daughter of one of the richest men in the county," Iris said.

"I never thought of it that way," Alice said, tongue in cheek. *I didn't even know it.*

"It's so romantic that Grant Hunter and Kate Bauer were married for the second time after twenty-five years apart. Are you going to be Alice Hunter now?" Lucille asked.

"Oh, I don't think so. Names aren't that important to me. I've grown used to the name Bauer."

"My cousin is so disappointed. She's been crazy about Grant for years," Cecelia said.

Eventually the conversation revolved around the anticipated end of the war. Several women waited to hear when their sweethearts, husbands, and brothers would come home.

"The papers say the blackout has ended in London," Violet said. "Doesn't that mean there's no danger from the German air force?"

"Did you hear that SS Chief Himmler has made a peace offer?" another visitor asked.

"I doubt the Allies will accept," Alice told them. "General Eisenhower has called for unconditional surrender."

"I heard a rumor that Hitler was killed. It was announced on Radio Hamburg."

"He should have been taken prisoner," Lucille said. "He should be put in a POW camp and suffer as all those other poor people suffered."

"They should treat him like the Italians treated Mussolini. The underground shot him and then hung him up for everyone to see," Violet said.

"How ghastly." Iris made a face.

"They did the same to his mistress."

"Even when Germany surrenders, we still have to defeat the Japanese," Alice said. "The Battle for Okinawa is a savage struggle. The invasion there was bigger than Normandy."

"The war has been awfully hard on the country," Iris said. "We've had to put up with gas and food rationing. And even when we have the ration stamps, the stores are sometimes out. We can't get silk stockings. We can't get enough shoes. We can't find good material for clothes. It's so tedious."

Alice said nothing but considered those deprivations hardly comparable to the trials of soldiers going into battle.

"What will your husband do when he returns, Iris?" someone asked.

"He'll probably go into business with my father. Now there are other couples in Juniper who might be getting serious." She turned to Odette, who'd driven in from her large ranch home in Springdale. "We all know you dated Brad Mayfield while he was on furlough."

Odette smiled. "Of course, we just dated. It doesn't mean anything. But I look forward to the end of the war so that he can come home."

Alice stopped sipping coffee. *Brad dated Odette? When he didn't even know whether she was alive or dead? Only a few months after her disappearance?*

She was filled with dismay. Suddenly she felt she was smothering. Pain gripped her heart. She stood up. Hastily making her excuses, she left the group and hurried off, she didn't know where.

On Main Street she saw people going in and out of the stores as if the world had not just fallen apart. She wandered through the sagebrush, passing the outlying houses. She was filled with anguish and bitterness. So she was just another wartime fling for Brad—easily forgotten, not worth waiting for, even for a few months.

Chapter 38

At Bowman Field, Brad stewed in the early summer heat. Why doesn't she write? I've written six letters since they telegraphed me about her return, and she's only answered the first one. Could something be wrong with her? After all, she was probably half sick when she returned. I'll telegraph her tonight.

Gloria watched wide-eyed as Alice tore up the telegram and threw it away. "I thought you and Brad were good friends."

"Not anymore." Alice started to sew a button on a dress Gloria had made for Marie. "While I was a prisoner, he was dating Odette when he was here on leave."

Gloria said nothing for a time. "He must have thought you were dead," she finally ventured.

"Well, he could have waited a few months to find out for sure what had happened to me. They probably found the wrecked plane with no bodies in it. That should have been a clue that we were still alive."

"Would he know that?"

"Oh, I don't know. And I don't care. I'm going out." Alice finished her sewing, clipping the needle from the garment, grabbed her purse, and headed toward the town center. She had no real destination. No shopping to do. No business in town.

She decided to have a cup of coffee with Grant. She wanted to know him better and also let him know that she harbored no grudge.

"Alice, I'm glad to see you," Grant said, rushing over. "I have some news that might interest you. Dr. Weber will need a nurse before too long. Mary is expecting a baby. She'll be taking time off. Her husband returned home on leave a few months ago."

"Golly. That was fast. Is that what we can expect when all the soldiers come home?"

"Well, millions of young men will be returning home. There might even be a baby boom. I thought you might want to talk to Dr. Weber about working for him."

"Oh…I don't know, Grant. I'm still in the service."

"The way things are going, the war will be over in Europe within weeks. Do you want to get out of the service?"

"Oh yes, and I should be able to get out of the army as soon as it's over. But I had thought of looking for work in Portland or—"

"You could take Mary's place until she decides whether or not she wants to come back to work. That would give you a chance to spend time with your family." He hoped she would stay. Now that he knew for sure that he had a daughter, he longed to know her better.

"Well, maybe…if the war ends soon. Thanks for telling me, Grant. It would certainly be a change from ward nursing for the army. I'll go talk to him. I could do it for a time, but I don't want to stay here."

"Another thing, you need to learn to drive. I want you to borrow my Chevy. Emma can teach you out in the country. When they come in next, you and Emma can take my car home and David can drive theirs."

She studied him. It was still difficult to believe that he was her real father. He was unlike John—always wanting to fix things, take care of everything and everyone. John tended to be more casual. He preferred to contemplate the world rather than alter it.

As the oldest Bauer child, she took on responsibility for others. It felt good to have someone thinking of her. "Are you afraid I'll run into something in town?"

He shrugged and smiled. "Well, there's less out there on the ranch to hit. Emma had to learn to drive right away, living so far from Juniper."

"She's wanted me to come out and visit for a few days. It would be a good time to learn. Are you sure you can do without your car that long?"

"So where do I have to go? I spend most of my time these days waiting for Kate to show up." He made a helpless gesture as he grinned broadly.

"You're happy, aren't you?"

"I've loved her for years, Alice, ever since we were children and went to school in the old elementary building. I was a grade ahead of her, but I waited for her on the playground if our class got out first. She played great softball, always hitting the balls way out in the field when we kids played workup. I can see her chestnut hair flying in the wind as she ran the bases. She and John were the best players, but I came close behind. Yes, I'm very happy."

"So you've known each other all your lives?"

"Yes, I remember the lavender dress she wore at the eighth-grade graduation. She wore her hair in long curls then. I walked her home that night."

"So…I was not just a minor indiscretion?"

"Oh Lord, no. Please don't ever think that. It was not that way for us. And I'm so proud to have you as a daughter." He looked at her with his remarkable green eyes. "And I think she's happy too."

"Seems that way."

"What do you hear from Brad?"

Alice looked away, evading his scrutiny. "Oh, we're not writing much these days."

"You're not? I'm certainly surprised to hear that. He was worried sick about you when he was here in Juniper."

"That was thoughtful of him. I guess I'd better be going. I'll stop by Dr. Weber's office." Eyes moist, she stumbled toward the entrance, leaving Grant wondering.

* * *

Dr. Weber's eyes lit up when Alice talked to him. Nurses were in short supply. His wife, a former nurse, would reluctantly manage for a time, but their school-age children kept her busy. If Alice could pitch in, he and his wife would both be pleased. Was she recovered from her ordeal as a prisoner? She assured him that she only suffered from slight malnutrition. She would keep in touch. If the war ended soon, she would try for a discharge right away.

* * *

Emma welcomed Alice for her driving lessons in Springdale. They rolled down the back roads while Mrs. Walker looked after Davy and Nancy.

"You shove the gear into second before you put it into third. Alice, your mind is not on this driving."

"Well, it was Grant's idea. I'm not sure why he thought I should learn to drive. I went along because he insisted, and I wanted to spend some time with you and the kids."

"He's trying to make it all up to you, you know."

"What is there to make up? I've had a good life with you and the rest of the family. Outside of the shock of illegitimacy, I'm still part of a loving family. And Kate has always been a second mother to me in a way."

Emma studied her hands. "You know, I always sensed you were special to Kate. I can't say I was jealous. I just noticed."

"As if you have ever been jealous of anybody," Alice scoffed. "If there's anything negative from this information, the fact that I got to grow up with sisters and a brother has more than made up for it."

"Still, Grant doesn't see it that way. Besides, he's pleased to be a father. I think he's always wanted a family. He almost adopted me when I worked for him. I was the youngest one there. The maids and waitresses all like him because he treats them fairly. Pull over here and practice stopping."

"I'm not exactly complaining." Alice put the gear in park, practicing the clutch. "In fact, it's great to have him looking out for me. He sent me to Dr. Weber. Since Mary is expecting, he'll need a nurse soon."

"That's wonderful. It will be such fun to have you near. I've missed my sister. Oh, that's right. You're actually my cousin." She ducked as Alice threw a bandana at her.

Alice turned serious. "The thing about Grant is, I'm a grown woman. Twenty-five years old. I can look after myself. It's a little embarrassing to have him doing things for me."

"Alice, you should enjoy it while you can. Indulge him. I know it gives him great pleasure. He's a father at last."

"How ironic. He's a father, but his child is grown."

"Well, he could always become a grandfather and start over."

Alice grimaced. "Not very soon."

"Grant is the same with Kate. He's bought her jewelry and a watch and a fancy purse, and some other things."

"She deserves it. She's helped all the Bauer family through the years—Freda, Edith, me, the folks. I think she lent money to Uncle Ernst and Uncle Louis now and then too."

"True, but she's as overwhelmed as you are by the gifts. Now pay attention. When you make a left turn, you stick your arm straight out the window and point in that direction. Be careful to watch for other cars coming toward you. Wait until the traffic has cleared. Then you can turn."

"Then why do I have to signal?"

"For the cars behind you and on the cross street."

Alice sighed. "It's very confusing."

"Surely a trained nurse with a background in physiology, anatomy, and chemistry can learn how to drive a car."

"You make me feel ridiculous."

"You'll get the hang of it. To turn right, stick your arm out and point right."

"Why is that car plowing along on our side of the road?"

Emma sighed. "Odette likes to take her half out of the middle. Wait until she passes. The kids should be up from their nap by now. Let's go send Grandma home."

"I'll take Davy for a walk while you feed Nancy."

* * *

Finally, when Emma declared that Alice was ready to drive on her own, they returned the Chevy to Grant.

Alice ran errands for Gloria. She carried shoes to the shop for repair, picked up elastic and trim at the dime store, paid the monthly bills. One day she saw Miss Webb, her high school teacher who had refused her scholarship, at the post office.

Miss Webb smiled broadly. "Why hello, Alice. It's good to see you back. I read about your army nursing service and capture in the local paper. Very impressive."

"Thank you. Kate Bauer gave me the money to go to nursing school. She had faith in my abilities."

"Well, yes, she's a relative. I would have recommended you for a scholarship if I'd thought the other members of the committee would approve."

"You refused to write me a reference."

"Did I? No. I'm sure I didn't."

Alice blinked. What a bald-faced lie. She'd heard that Miss Webb had been removed from the scholarship committee. At least no more students would suffer from her discrimination.

* * *

Kate came to Juniper almost every weekend, and the two women had private time together. Grant often joined them.

As her strength and energy returned, Alice visited a few friends and stopped by to see Grant. One day Alice sipped coffee at the hotel counter when Iris walked in. "May I join you?" she asked Alice as she stood by the stool.

"Please do, Iris." Alice smiled. "I've wanted to thank you for inviting me for coffee. I enjoyed seeing all the girls again."

"It was fun, wasn't it?"

"I noticed that June wasn't there. Do you know where she is?"

"She married a fellow back east who was in an essential occupation. She writes to me, has two small boys."

"I've wondered. At one time she was interested in Chester Southwick." Alice remembered how foolish she had been to date Chet just to spite June.

"Oh, she got over that in a hurry. She dated him once and found out he's crude, rude, and nasty."

"Is he?" Alice wore a bland face.

Iris nodded. "He's just like his sister, Meredith Pearson. It was nice to have company at the coffee."

"You must miss your husband."

"I do. Living near the training camps was lonely for me, and now I'm lonely for Harry. My parents are great, and the kids are a pleasure, but they don't take his place."

"I'm sure they don't. Have you made plans for his return?"

"Not really. He writes about his navy work, and I write about the kids. I'm afraid he won't be comfortable with the little ones. He's seen them only as babies. And I don't think he'll like living with my parents. I'm so fearful of how things will be when he comes home."

"I'm sure you'll work them out. After all, you lived on base."

"Yes, and I learned some things from the other navy wives—how to do laundry, change diapers, cook a little." She laughed and gave Alice a wry look. "I remember when I couldn't bear the thought of doing those things."

"Well, then, you can face anything. I never thought I would be nursing in a POW camp either. I survived."

"But we'll probably have to move somewhere."

"Think of it as an adventure."

* * *

Within a few weeks, Harry came home on a short leave. Alice approached Iris in the market as she was reading the label on a package of rice. "It must be wonderful to have your husband at home."

"Oh, Alice. I'm so glad he's back on leave. But he's talking of going to law school at the University of Oregon when the war is over."

"Really? Won't that be good? He'll be able to make a good life for you and the children when he finishes."

"He wants me and the kids to move to Eugene with him. Harry and I would have to live in an apartment, probably a cheap one, since he has to make it on the GI Bill. I don't know if I can stand all that crowded living again for three years."

"Of course you can. It won't be forever. You did it before. And you can always come home for holidays. Eugene isn't as far away as some of those bases you lived in."

"That's true." Iris smiled. "You certainly have a way of encouraging people."

"Well, three years just isn't that long." She patted Iris on the shoulder. "And you proved you could handle it."

* * *

A man from Bly, a small town in southern Oregon, just north of the California border, was traveling through Juniper and stopped by the hotel; he told Grant a strange story. On Saturday, May 5, 1945, five children and a minister's wife on a fishing trip had been killed by a Japanese device that appeared to be a balloon bomb. The exploded bomb had gouged out a hole about three feet across and a foot deep.

After the explosion Forest Service employees had found Japanese paper, string, shrapnel, an unexploded incendiary bomb, and various metal rings and pieces to set off the bomb.

Because of the fear of panic, and because the government didn't want the Japanese to know that at least one of their hundreds of balloon bombs had been successful, the deaths were known only locally. The traveler confided in Grant as though it were a secret, speaking in a low voice, and furtively eyeing the other patrons.

Pacific Coast residents had long heard reports of Japanese submarines in the nearby waters. In fact, extensive watches were in practice all along both coasts. But despite several false alarms and constant patrols by the Coast Guard, those six people were the only victims of enemy bombing in the United States.

Grant read nothing in the papers about the deaths, and he mentioned it to no one in Juniper. The balloon bomb must have been one of the last tactics of a defeated nation. No sense causing a panic. The Japanese couldn't be much of a threat while they were constantly attacked by the Allies

* * *

On Sundays, Gloria and Alice entertained the entire family for dinner. Food held an enhanced fascination for Alice since her days as a prisoner of war. Gloria willingly gave her free reign in the kitchen, which now contained an electric range and a refrigerator.

Grant, enjoying the family event, said in a teasing voice, "You realize that Alice stole this lasagna recipe from my cook, don't you?"

"Pay no attention to Grant." Alice piled the plates high and passed them around the table. "He told me that I could finagle the recipe."

John kept them up on the war news, which he followed assiduously.

"The Russians are at the outskirts of Berlin. Why don't the Germans surrender?" he lamented, accepting his plate with relish. "Seems a useless defense of their homeland at this stage. I wonder why the British and the Americans aren't in on the liberation of Berlin."

"Maybe General Eisenhower doesn't think Berlin is worth the trouble and the loss of life," David said, helping himself to fresh rolls.

"But it's a propaganda victory for the Russians, isn't it, capturing the capital?"

"Maybe the Russians think they should have the honor," Grant said. "After all, the Germans betrayed them, attacked their country, and burned and slashed and killed as they left."

"Does it really matter who takes Berlin?" Gloria could think of no reason.

"Another thing," John persisted. "According to the papers, the Russians have managed to put communist regimes in every country they have occupied: Poland, Romania, Bulgaria, Hungary, and Yugoslavia."

Gloria said, "Kate, I want to show you the new dresses I'm making for Linda and Marie from feed and flour sacks. The white sack I'll use for collar and cuffs. I've made the skirts a little longer. When the war is over material will be more plentiful and dresses will be longer."

"You think so?" Emma was thoughtful. "I better hold off on new dresses until we find out for sure."

"Just allow more fabric for the hems. Then you can take them out if I'm right."

"Thank God, Helmut was in the section liberated by the Americans," John said.

"I'm so eager to hear from my POW patients," Alice said. "Billy and Joel must be recovering if they survived."

* * *

And at last it came. V-E Day. After more than five long years, victory in Europe. On May 7 the news leaked out in Britain. And that day two hundred bombers flew back to Britain carrying more than thirteen thousand just-liberated prisoners of war from camps in Italy and Germany. The news of victory quickly spread to New York, where the city celebrated a day early.

On May 8 President Truman announced the news to an ecstatic nation. All over the country people hugged and danced in the streets.

Grant urged the Bauer family to watch the celebration in downtown Juniper from his hotel food counter. Linda and Marie danced in front of the hotel with their friends while loudspeakers blasted lively music.

Perhaps fearing too much celebrating, the commander of the local air base had ordered the bars on base closed until further notice, which might have accounted for all the airmen in town.

Cars full of happy young people cruised through Main Street. Nobody worried about conserving gasoline. The war was over. Well, yes, there was still fighting in the Pacific, but it would soon be over there too.

The enthusiastic joy was dampened by the tears of many people over those killed and left behind—and those left to fight in the Pacific. For on V-E Day, American boys on Okinawa still fought against the Japanese, who tenaciously held their line in the hills. Seldom surrendering, they fought to the death and took many Allies with them.

Mrs. Mayfield fretted about Steve, her older son. The Bauers thought about Freda, still nursing in the Pacific theater. There was still a war to win, but fewer young men would be required to kill other young men who were required to kill them. And the bombing would stop in Europe. Civilians would no longer be at risk of death from the air.

Alice immediately applied for discharge. Since she had so many points, granted to veterans on the basis of length of service, she expected to be released soon.

Marjorie mailed her the few possessions that she'd left in England and informed her that the nurses with fewer points would be transported to the Pacific War. They were packing up and preparing to leave. She suggested that when the terrible war was over, the nurses get together periodically to visit and reminisce.

By the end of May, men and women with sufficient points began to make their way back to the States. The others, war weary, no matter where they happened to be at the time—Europe, Asia, Africa, Australia, even at home on leave—dreaded the final war with Japan.

Chapter 39

Tom Hansen, Jennie's friend from the Portland shipyard, wrote that he was returning to the fruit orchards of Hood River and asked to see her sometime. He had served his country as an aerial engineer and a top-turret gunner in bombers.

She answered that she would like to see him when he returned, but she would be off at college. And she thought he was foolish not to take advantage of the GI Bill by going himself.

Recent legislation allowed servicemen to go to college with financial help from the US government. After all, Jennie wrote, someday Tom may want to try another line of work. Besides, there were things to learn about growing fruit. He wrote that she had given him something to think about.

* * *

A few weeks after V-E Day, Emma and David lunched on sandwiches at the hotel counter between their Saturday banking and shopping errands. A young, sandy-haired soldier, carrying a small duffel bag, entered and sat down at the counter. He ordered coffee and then asked the waitress if a blond girl still worked there. Emma and David exchanged glances.

"Maybe you mean me," Emma said. "I used to work here."

The soldier looked at Emma closely. He noted the faint birthmark on her jaw, almost covered by makeup. "Holy mackerel, it's you. I sure hoped I'd find you. I owe you money. You fed me when I was starving a few years back."

"I remember you. You were searching for work. Did you find any?"

"I worked in an orchard in Hood River for a Japanese fellow. He was good to me—let me stay in a little shack on his property. I worked for him until I was old enough to join the army. After I left, he wrote to me from camp Minidoka in Idaho. He and other Japanese were interned there, even though they'd lived in Hood River for years."

"Oh, that's sad."

"Later he joined the service. His wife wrote that he had died in battle."

"How ironic. I'm sorry. But it's good you had work. I worried about you. My name is Emma Walker, and this is my husband, David."

"I'm Kenneth Payne." He shook hands with David. "Call me Ken. I'm just back from action in Germany."

"Well, you needn't pay me anything. My boss was glad to hear that I'd given you food. He's the owner of this place." Emma signaled to Grant across the room, and he joined the group.

"Grant, meet Ken Payne, home from service in Germany. You provided food for him during the Depression when I was working here. Remember, I took it from the kitchen?"

"Well, hello, soldier." Grant extended his hand. "It's always good to meet one of our fighting men."

"I can pay for the food now. I remember she gave me some sandwiches, apples, and a bottle of milk. It all tasted so good. I hadn't eaten much of anything for days. Otherwise, I would never have come in begging."

"Forget it." Grant waved a hand in dismissal. "We're the ones who owe you for your service to the country. In fact, have a meal today on me. Don't even try to pay for anything."

"Well, thank you, Mr. Hunter." Ken beamed. "I'll have a liberty steak."

"A hamburger? Of course not. You'll have a real steak." He ordered a large steak dinner for Ken.

"How are your parents?" Emma asked.

"They both died while I was overseas. My younger brother's in the army too, and my sister is a WAC."

"I'm sorry to hear about your parents. What are you doing now?"

The soldier grinned. "I'm looking for work again. Anything around here?"

The young man impressed David. Imagine coming back to pay a debt that didn't amount to more than a few sandwiches. He broke in, "Know anything about animals?"

"I sure do. I was raised on a farm in the South."

"You don't say." Emma smiled. As if they hadn't noticed his drawl.

David looked at Emma tentatively, observed her slight nod. "Would you like to try ranch work? We own a ranch about ten miles from town."

Ken's eyes widened. "Would I. You're not joshing me, are you?"

David laughed. "We can always use an honest worker. If you're willing, you could ride out to the ranch with us, look around, and see what you think. We'll be coming in tomorrow if you decide you don't want to stay."

"Got a place to sleep?"

"We have a bunkhouse, but it hasn't been used in years. We'll have to get it cleaned up for you."

"Sure, I want to go. How soon do we leave? Everything I own is in this duffel bag."

"You'll have to ride fence. And we don't get into town much."

"Who cares about town? I'm a country boy."

David picked up Ken's bag and headed toward the door. "I'll put this in the truck for you. We'll finish our errands while you finish your meal. Then we'll be back by to pick you up. We'll be proud to have a serviceman at our place."

* * *

In Portland, Naomi still missed Roy. War provided no time to grieve. There was nothing else to do but keep working at the shipyard.

At first she had functioned as though in a bad dream. Then slowly her sociable nature took over. She accepted dates to help quell the loneliness and forget her sorrow. Servicemen on leave were good company. She pitied them because she knew many would never return. Roy didn't.

She sought to give them pleasure while they lived. For a time she made love with all of them, drinking heavily in order to quiet her inhibitions.

But with the fighting over in Europe, she began to think about her own future. Did she want to spend her life in this way? For years she'd been a one-man woman. It was time to start making her plans for the end of the war.

* * *

Grant joined Alice on her lunch break at the hotel food counter. "How's it going?"

"Fine. I'm glad you talked me into taking this job with Dr. Weber, even though I find the day's work pretty much wears me out."

"Is it too much for you so soon?"

"No, an eight-hour day is fine with me. We didn't often get those in the army or at the POW camp. I'm also glad I don't have to hop on a bus after work. That's probably what I would have to do in Portland."

"We're only two blocks away from Dr. Weber's office. Stay over with us if the walk after work is too much for you. Kate would love to have you. Jennie's overnight visits please her. And she likes to have Linda and Marie too."

"It's only a mile or so, but thanks. I might take you up on it sometime."

"Or you could use my car."

Alice smiled. "That won't be necessary. I'm sure you have better uses for it. Is Kate enjoying her summer here, now that she has no college classes to take?"

"She's like a student with time off. It's the first summer she's had free in years. She's decided to do some redecorating and landscaping in the garden."

"That will be something to see. Unlike you, she knows the difference between a weed and a desirable plant." Grant's yard was badly in need of a loving hand.

He gave her a sheepish grin and then changed the subject. "I got a strange letter from Brad a few days ago from Bowman Field."

"Did you? Does he write to you often?" Alice examined her nails.

"He's never written to me before. But he's wondering why you don't write."

"I didn't know the two of you were that close."

"He stopped by here while he was home on leave."

"So what's he doing?" *Probably dating some woman nearby.*

"Well, he's wondering why you don't write to him. He was relieved to hear that you were safe."

Alice fussed with her empty coffee cup. *Oh, sure. Probably so relieved that he called some woman that night.* "And I'm relieved to hear that he's safe. I've got to get back to work. Don't forget Sunday dinner. Aunt Dorothy and Russ will be joining us. I'm trying out a new recipe for soy chicken."

"Wouldn't miss it. Let's have Sunday dinner at our house sometime."

"Sure." She bolted out, her eyes clouded.

* * *

"What's going on between Brad and Alice?" Grant asked Kate that evening. She sat on the sofa with a book of decorating tips in her lap.

"Is something going on?"

"She quit writing to him. And he's upset about it."

"Oh, that. Gloria told me that she's angry because he dated Odette Glass when he was home on furlough."

"I don't think he exactly dated her. He just drove her to The Dalles to shop."

"Some people would call that a date."

"Well, I wouldn't. And it's not right. The poor guy was devastated while she was gone."

"Perhaps. But they'll have to straighten it out themselves."

"How can they straighten it out when she won't even write to him?"

"Then I guess it will have to wait until he comes back. It won't be a long wait. He should be coming home soon."

"I suppose you're right. After all, I waited over twenty-five years for you."

She reached for his hand. Sinking down on the sofa, he put his arms around her and kissed her face and then her lips. "But it was worth it."

After a time he stood. "I want to talk to you about Alice and our will. Now that we've put all our assets in both our names, we need to provide for the possibility of our dying together."

"Don't you have some cousins?"

"Second cousins. I barely know them. I have a few charities in mind. Do you want to leave everything else to Alice?"

"I've been thinking about that, Grant. It wouldn't really be fair since John's children shared the same life as she did."

"Can't we leave something for them too?"

"I have a few personal items I'd like Alice to have—my rings, a necklace from my mother, a picture she's always admired. Otherwise, it might be best to divide the estate evenly among Alice and all my surviving nieces and nephews, the same amount for all. I'm sure Alice would not find that unfair. She's always been generous and protective of the others. Perhaps we could reserve a portion for each of my surviving sisters and brothers. What do you think?"

"I think you are a very sensible woman, as well as a beautiful one. I'll give you a list of the charities I want included. You talk to the lawyer and get it all written up the way you want. Then we'll sign."

Kate sighed with contentment. "I'll do it. What woman can resist a man who calls her beautiful every day?"

He kissed her again. "I just hope Alice and Brad straighten things out. I want them to be as happy as we are."

Chapter 40

For Sunday dinner Alice served her relatives a new dish—chicken in a soy sauce served over rice. John grinned in delight. "Alice picked up some good recipes in the service."

To which Alice laughed. "I certainly didn't pick them up in the service or in the POW camp. But the army did have a way of making me appreciate good food."

David tasted the dish. "She's almost as good a cook as Emma." His wife flashed him a big smile.

Gloria burst into laughter. "What a diplomatic man you are."

Grant savored the food. "If Alice wasn't trained as a nurse, we'd sure be able to use such a gourmet chef in the restaurant."

"Have you heard from Jennie or Fred lately?" Kate asked Gloria.

"Fred will be coming home soon. He's walking, able to travel. Jennie says she is dropping her tools the minute the war is over in Japan. She wants to come home for a time. Then she might go to college. How about Edith?"

"She's thinking of marriage to a marine."

"Another one?"

"Yes, Paul was a good friend of Oliver's before he died. They've become very close. Now, with Paul in the Pacific, I'm worried about her facing another death."

"And with good reason."

John nodded. "The fatality rate in the Pacific theater is extremely high. General McArthur has a tough job there."

Aunt Dorothy and Russ Turner told them about their daughter, Doris, serving as a WAC in Washington State, waiting impatiently for the end of hostilities, and about James, on his way home from Europe. Both were eager to get on with their lives.

"We're hoping they'll both go to college," Russ said.

"But Doris has been writing to a young man. Who knows where that will lead? These are very good green beans you've raised, Gloria."

"Thank you. You've no idea how I've scrounged water to raise them."

"Yes," Linda said. "We have to save our bath water and our dishwater. But they're worth it."

"And it's patriotic," Marie chipped in.

They all laughed merrily at that. Already patriotism seemed a bit dated.

* * *

On August 6, an American plane dropped a terrible atomic bomb over Hiroshima, Japan, annihilating the city. When the Japanese failed to surrender, another plane dropped an atomic bomb on Nagasaki on August 9. The atomic bomb was said to be a thousand times more powerful than the largest ordinary bomb the Americans had ever dropped.

On August 15, the war was over. Emperor Hirohito made a surrender speech on the radio to his people in Japan. Over twenty nations had fought against the Axis powers. Their people, and those in neutral nations as well, rejoiced.

In the United States, President Truman announced over the radio that the war was won. American servicemen and servicewomen, stationed all over the world, destined for the Pacific War, breathed sighs of relief. They would not have to face death. They could make plans for their lives. They could go home.

Now the real celebration in the country began. Church bells rang, sirens wailed, car horns honked. People gathered in the streets, screamed, and hugged one another with joy.

Munitions plants around the country stopped production. In Portland the news blasted over the loudspeakers in the shipyards. Jennie, Naomi, and Tess joined the crowds milling about the streets in Portland, laughing and dancing. In celebration, people threw toilet tissue, previously rationed, out of upper-floor windows. Cars drove up and down, with people waving flags out of car windows.

Late that night Jennie packed her bag. Though she worked as an electrician now, she knew her skills would not be needed in the shipyards. The yard would probably not even operate. The next day she caught a bus for Juniper.

Portland had been good for her. She was proud of her long days in the shipyard where ten-thousand-ton Liberty ships were launched every few days. She had gained work experience and maturity.

She had no clear idea what would come next. She just wanted to get home and forget that there had ever been a war or a shipyard. She was as war weary as any soldier.

John and Gloria spent quiet time with Dorothy and Russ. They shared the relief felt by the whole nation, but still grieved for the boy they had lost in the war. John thought about his younger brother, Ernst, who had lost his parents as a teenager, and then his own life in the fighting.

"A super bomb," John mused, responding to the news of the Japanese bombings. "What kind of wars will we have in the future with such weapons available?"

Exuberant as they were by the end of hostilities, people were shocked to learn about the tremendous power of atomic energy.

"Perhaps now the new United Nations will help countries solve their differences by talking," Russ said.

"Imagine," Gloria said, "Eleanor Roosevelt served as a delegate when the nations wrote the UN charter at the April conference in San Francisco. And it was only a short time after her husband died."

"Will the country go back into a depression now?" Dorothy asked.

"Not if the government doesn't put new tariffs on goods as they did in Hoover's time," John said.

"Not with a Democrat in the White House." Gloria patched one of John's shirts. "Let's keep President Truman there."

"But the debt," Russ said with a moan. "The country has gone deeply into debt paying for this war. Can we afford the things President Roosevelt did for the economy back in the thirties?"

Though it was not obvious at the time, people in Poland and other eastern European countries soon learned that they had merely exchanged one dictator for another with the end of the war. Instead of Hitler's dictatorship, they now had Stalin and his puppet governments.

Later Alice learned that Billy, Joel, and other American POWs had been sent to Camp Lucky Strike in France for treatment of various ailments. Suffering from malnutrition, they were fed an eggnog-type liquid to soothe their tender stomachs until they could handle soup. Billy wrote:

> We were euphoric when the Yanks liberated us; the prisoners yelled and danced and sang, even those of us who'd been in the hospital. As we filled out forms and happily wrote letters home, the camp loudspeakers played the song, "Don't Fence Me In."
>
> We showered in the guard barracks, munched on doughnuts and coffee, and got treated by doctors and medics. Of course, Joel and I were almost well, except for losing weight for lack of adequate food. But you know how the Hungarian doctor hated to send anyone back to the POW barracks, so we avoided that completely. Joel often talked about how you saved his life.
>
> My girlfriend waited for me. We're getting married. I hope your boyfriend waited for you.

Alice cried when she read the letter. *No, Billy, Brad did not wait the few months I was missing.*

Much later she heard from Butch that he and the crew of their downed plane had been taken much farther east to a POW camp after they left her. When the Russians moved close, they were marched off with hundreds of other prisoners to the west. Most of them were badly malnourished by then, and those who lagged behind were simply shot by the guards.

As the Russians kept coming west, the prisoners were marched off to other camps over and over again to keep them away from their possible liberators.

As it happened, the Russians, Ukrainians, and other POWS who had been forced into the Russian army were not especially eager for liberation by the Russians. They were expected to fight to the death. Those who had surrendered feared repercussions from their own army.

Eventually the Allies liberated Butch's camp. Emaciated and exhausted, he was sent to Camp Lucky Strike.

With the end of the war, all rationing in the United States immediately stopped. People could buy anything if they had the money and the stores had the products. Alice went right out and bought some previously rationed canned pineapple for a fruit-and-cabbage salad.

Within days the Bauer family learned that Fred was on his way home. As he limped toward them in the Portland train station, John and Gloria wondered if the limp would stay with him. He was thinner and still rather pale after some surgeries, but otherwise seemed recovered. The three spent the night with Naomi and Tess, who served a roast beef dinner, a rare treat after the rationing of wartime. The young women discussed their futures with the others.

"I'm going back to Juniper to see my folks, maybe take some courses at the training school there," Naomi told them at the dinner table. "We gals aren't needed in the shipyards. Women are being discharged all over Portland since the men are dribbling home to take over the work. We're going to have a tough time with millions of servicemen looking for jobs."

Meanwhile Aunt Tess had signed up for a secretarial course. "Office work is still available to women although it pays much less than the factory jobs. But if I can continue making my home mortgage payments, I can get by with my widow's pension."

John nodded. "With munitions and shipbuilding and aircraft building stopped, it's hard to imagine what will happen with the economy."

"We'd better prepare for the worst." Gloria got up to start clearing the table. "Remember the Great Depression."

Fred pushed back his chair. "Say, Naomi, why don't you ride to Juniper with us?"

"Why that's kind of you. I could pack up this evening. Are you sure you don't mind?"

"Certainly not. I only have one small bag. We should have room for all your things."

"We'll be in time for the big Juniper victory dance they're holding at the air base," Naomi said, with a sparkle in her eyes.

Chapter 41

When Fred limped into the Bauer home in Juniper, his sisters and his niece and nephew were waiting to greet him. They hugged him and hovered around, asking about his health and the war. The children stared at him, awed by his uniform. Jennie happily vacated his room and moved back in with the girls.

Alice told Fred she was ready to help with college expenses, but Fred chortled and told her, thank you, her help was not necessary. He would have support from the GI Bill of Rights.

Linda and Marie, out of school for the summer, took over the nursing, bringing him everything his heart desired. Having missed years of his life, they were eager to become acquainted. They thought of him as a hero as did the rest of the townspeople.

He was surprised to learn of the marriage of his aunt Kate Bauer. On top of that, Grant and Kate invited him for a lavish dinner at their new restaurant. Later, over dessert at their house, they explained their early relationship and Alice's birth. It sounded like a dime-store novel.

After they had made the matter clear, Kate poured him more coffee. "Do you have any idea what you want to do now?"

"It's strange to have the war over. It's all we've thought about for four years. I never looked ahead. But I have some ideas now."

"And they are?"

"I'm going to finish my schooling on the GI Bill. I might eventually become a commercial airline pilot, but there are other avenues to explore too. I could make extra money flying small planes on the weekends or in the summer. I'll need to see about licensing requirements."

"That's wonderful. A good choice. Where do you want to go?"

"Where else? Oregon State University in Corvallis, if I can gain admittance by the fall. I'll try to share an apartment with someone to cut expenses. Do you know anyone else going there?"

"Well, maybe Jennie or even Alice. We haven't heard what either of them is planning. Dr. Weber's regular nurse is expected back at work soon."

"Jennie and Alice needed to rest before making any decisions," Grant said. "They've both been under stress. Imagine, over eight million servicemen and women are overseas waiting to go home. Their families want them back, but the ships can only carry so many."

"I expect many will be flown home. But some will stay for occupation duty."

Kate said, with a sad face, "I hope we can send relief right away for all the millions of refugees in those suffering countries."

"Have you heard from Aunt Edith?" Fred, relaxed, sipped his coffee.

She brightened. "Edith left for San Francisco to marry Paul, her marine. She's looking for work nearby. Freda is back in California too. The war uprooted our family, Fred—my brothers in the army and navy, you and Alice in England, Jennie in the Portland shipyards, Freda nursing in the Pacific. You all took off because of the needs of the country. How will you all ever settle down again?"

"How ya gonna keep 'em down on the farm after they've seen Paree?" After quoting the song title, Fred laughed. "Believe me, most of us have had all we want of the world for a long time."

Chapter 42

In the backyard, Alice hung clothes on the line one Saturday in late August. The clear morning air felt like a warm caress, making it a joy to work outside. Gloria's delight in her electric washing machine amused Alice. How had Gloria ever managed without it?

In the distance, coming from town, she watched a man in uniform walking toward her, following her family's worn path through the sagebrush. Her heart began to beat faster.

As she waited, fascinated, she made out his face. Brad. Looking fit and tanned and determined. She would never forget the Adonis who steadily walked her way.

She thought of the many times they had walked together over that path long ago in the dark after work—close because it was narrow. Without moving, she watched until he stood in front of her. Her heart ached as she stared at his even features and his tall, straight frame.

Almost hypnotized, she said, "Hello, Brad."

He examined her shapely form and her symmetrical face, thinner than he remembered. Perhaps she suffered more than Grant had told him.

"Why didn't you write, Alice?"

She turned away. "I thought you might be busy."

"Busy!" he lashed out. "Oh, I was busy. Busy waiting for a letter from you. I need an explanation."

Her cold eyes stared at him. "Didn't you get letters from Odette Glass? Answering her must have kept you busy. And surely there were women around Bowman Field."

His brows furrowed. "Odette?"

"I heard about your dates with her. Don't try to deny it. Everyone in town knows about it. She's waiting for you to get back."

He stared at her in disbelief. "I drove her to The Dalles."

So it was true.

He saw the quick pain in her eyes. "Look, Alice, we were together once. Just once. She asked if I would drive her to The Dalles if she provided the gas and the car. I wasn't busy, and I wanted to buy a gift for my mother, so I did. That's all."

There was a long silence. Alice ran her fingers through her hair. Finally she said, "I'm not sure I believe you."

"You've got to believe me. Look, ask Grant, ask my mother. Heck, ask Odette. I repeat, we only made that one trip to The Dalles. I was worried about you, and Mother told me to get out and quit moping around. Anyway, you rejected me. I can't understand your anger."

"Rejected you? Rejected you? How can you say such a thing?"

"You wouldn't marry me."

"Oh, Brad, I didn't reject you. I just didn't see any sense in marrying in the middle of a war."

"Then you don't reject me?" Brad asked quickly.

Gloria called to Alice from the house. "Another basket."

"I've got to go, Brad."

"Well, will you think about it? I want to see you. When can we get together?"

"I don't know. I don't know what to do. I'm working for Dr. Weber now."

"I heard about that. Are you sure you're well enough? You've lost weight."

"And I'm moving away. Good-bye, Brad. I'll see you around town, I suppose." She turned and sprinted toward the house. He watched her disappear inside. Then he turned around and retraced his steps, a heavy pain in his gut. She was moving? Where?

* * *

Gloria looked curiously at Alice when she entered the house. "I wouldn't have called if I'd noticed Brad Mayfield was with you. Is he out of the service for good now?"

"I suppose he is. He didn't really say." Alice busied herself with clothespins.

"Well, what did he say?"

"Nothing much. He said he drove Odette to The Dalles only once while he was here on furlough."

"Well, that's something. It sounds as though they weren't seeing each other at all."

"I don't know what to think. The women at the coffee assumed they were dating." Alice picked up the basket of wet clothes and headed outdoors again. In the distance she could see Brad walking slowly toward town, his shoulders slightly slumped.

* * *

That day John received a letter from Helmut Bauer. He was translating English-written material (some by Ernest Hemingway and William Saroyan) into German for the use of prisoners throughout the United States at a special POW camp in Rhode Island. He wrote:

> I was never a Nazi. I deplored their actions. My comrades and I were horrified to learn of the grisly Gestapo abuses at concentration camps. How can Germany live down the massacres? We'll have to try. I want to do my part to help Germans learn American ideals of democracy and freedom. All of us German officers here have renounced our ranks. We want to practice democratic ideals.
>
> We are well treated. We eat better than we ever did. Nevertheless, I look forward to the day when I can join my wife and child again. I know they must be suffering. I read in the papers that food is very scarce even now in Germany. But they

live with my wife's parents. Perhaps they have things they can barter for food. Her father was a successful businessman. At one time the family had a comfortable house. It was a pleasure for me to meet your wonderful daughter Alice in Germany. I wish we had met under better circumstances. She was a brave nurse to the prisoners in her care. She worked hard for them, and they all loved her.

John showed the letter to Alice. "I'm glad he's all right. He's a good man," she told him.

"Do you suppose he knew what was going on in those concentration camps? I read that most Germans are saying now that they were not Nazis, that they were living in ignorance."

"I just don't know. Of course, the POW camp was different. There was some mistreatment—of Joel, for instance—but Helmut's assignment was just the hospital. Still he had to know how little they were feeding the working prisoners. But what could he do, even if he wanted to? There was no more food available. The ports were blockaded. The army got whatever food there was."

Alice had thought about it a lot, ever since the atrocities in Germany were made public. She remembered her numbing fear that the guards would discover her role in hiding Joel. She had known she faced death. Surely German citizens had felt the same fear. Had she the right to judge?

John said, "Helmut complained about the treatment of the Jews for many years in his letters. He and other professors even signed a letter of disagreement about it. As a result, some of his colleagues were picked up as dissidents. Luckily, he escaped that roundup by the storm troopers through powerful political connections—his father-in-law, I believe. But you can imagine what effect the arrests could have on dissent of any kind."

"I admired the fact that he did not abandon the patients, as so many others were doing," Alice said. "He expected to be killed by the Russians."

"Maybe as time goes by, we'll learn more about that kind of bravery."

John carefully folded the letter and put it away in his desk drawer. He decided to see if he could help Helmut's wife and her family. If Helmut sent him an address, he would send packages or money.

He thought about all that had happened since he and Helmut had corresponded in the old days before the war. What a grim time it had been. How could the world recover from the worst war its people had ever lived through?

* * *

In the afternoon Jennie returned from morning errands with exciting news. "Let's go to the victory dance they're holding in an empty building at the air base tonight, Alice. Musicians are coming down from Portland. Now that we can drive, we'll get Dad's car and spin out there for the dance."

"Oh, I don't know..." Alice said. "I've got some mending to do."

"Oh, go on, Alice," Gloria said. "You need to get out and see some of your old friends."

"What old friends? Most of them have moved away or been killed."

"Then make new ones, Grumpy. The war's over. There are things to do. You've got a whole new life now."

Surprised at Gloria's insistence, Alice laughed. "Are you going to push me out the door?"

"I might, if you don't quit being so stubborn."

"All right, Jennie. Seems I must go."

"Good. Now let's go upstairs and pick out something to wear."

"Hardly a problem since Mother keeps churning out new clothes for me, when I haven't even worn out the old ones. Shall we ask Fred?"

"He and Peter have other plans. I think they're seeing that war movie downtown."

"Heavens. You'd think he would have had enough of that."

"He says he wants to see what Hollywood has done with it. Did I mention that I applied for work at Grant's restaurant?

"No. Do you think he'll hire you?"

Jennie grinned. "Well, I am his niece now. I should think that would count for something, unless he doesn't like his new relatives. Maybe you could put in a good word for me, being as he's your father."

Alice laughed. "I doubt that you need my help."

"Truth is, I think I have the job. I heard that one of the waitresses is getting married and doesn't plan to return. Of course, I can only work a few weeks before college."

"Who wouldn't hire you? You're beautiful, healthy, and hardy. Good luck."

Alice pulled out some ivory-colored, open-toed pumps for the evening—the first she'd worn in years. She had bought them in Portland with some of her first real wages after she had finished her training. As she dressed for the dance in a full-skirted red-and-white-striped cotton frock, she wondered if Brad would be there.

Should she believe what he had said that morning? Jennie told her that she had questioned some friends about him dating Odette. None of them had seen the two together anywhere. And Grant had verified that. Perhaps Iris was misinformed when she announced that the two were dating.

Jennie, always direct, scolded her for listening to gossip about Brad. Alice, amused at her younger sister's romantic advice, but convinced by the body of evidence from her and others, regretted her abrupt dismissal of Brad that morning. Now she might never see him again.

* * *

At the air base, the dance hall rocked with loud music, laughter, and stamping feet. The end of the war had spawned an exuberance that could not be contained. A new era dawned.

Townspeople crowded around the returning veterans. Alice's ordeal had been written up in local newspapers. Almost the entire town greeted her and wished her well. She looked for Brad, but she didn't see him among the crowd.

She danced with several old classmates, pleased to be back in a place where she felt she belonged. Once she observed Chet Southwick talking at the side of the dance floor. He turned and watched her.

What a good time to get back at Alice. I've been waiting for this chance for a long time.

When he saw Jennie leave the dance hall with some friends, Chet moved in. He quickly approached Alice and told her in an urgent voice, "Your sister needs help. She asked me to fetch you."

"What?"

"This way." Chet took her arm. "She's outside."

He pulled her rapidly along, beyond the lights, beyond the dancers out getting a breath of air, a drink from the bottle, or a kiss in the moonlight.

"What is it? Where is she?" Alice kept asking as he hurried her along.

Chapter 43

Grant worked late in his hotel office, going over the books. The new restaurant was booming. They ran through inventory faster than he could refill it. He needed to order napkins, aprons, and new tablecloths.

Was there a way to purchase these locally? Would someone in Juniper be able to make them? He decided to talk to Gloria about it. Maybe she would be interested or knew someone who would.

When he saw Brad enter the restaurant, he stopped to talk. "Hello, Captain Mayfield. It's great to see you back. Let me treat you to dinner on the house in appreciation for your service to the country."

Brad smiled. "That's very good of you, but I've eaten. I was hoping Alice might be here. No one's at home at the Bauer house."

"They're probably visiting. Or…have you tried the dance hall at the air base? Half the town's out there tonight."

"That's an idea. I'll go out there. I tried to talk to Alice earlier, but she didn't believe me. She thinks I dated Odette."

"Well, give her some time. She's been under a mistaken impression for weeks now. She'll need time to get over it."

"I never really dated Odette. I don't know where she got that idea."

"I know that."

"It's silly to think I could forget her in just a few months."

"Of course."

"I don't know why she wouldn't listen to me."

Grant shook his head in sympathy.

"I'll see you later. I've got to get out to the air base." Brad rushed out the door as Grant stared after him.

At the dance hall, Brad waved to his brother, Steve, just home from service in Okinawa, who had come with friends. Odette, in a low-cut rose dress, which set off her long wavy black hair, smiled invitingly. Just as he decided that Alice wasn't there, he saw Jennie enter the hall with several others.

"Is Alice with you, Jennie?"

"Hi, Brad. Yes, Alice is here." She looked around. "But I don't see her."

Odette, standing nearby, broke in, "I just saw her walk out with Chet Southwick."

"What?" Brad recoiled. Having seen him that morning, would Alice have left with Chet?

"She went out with—"

"I heard you. Where did they go?"

"I saw them head to the back of the field, where Chet parked his car." Odette tried to steer him back toward the dance hall.

"Which way?"

Odette pointed. Steve touched his shoulder. "She probably wanted to leave with him. Maybe you should come back inside."

"Oh no, she didn't. She wouldn't have gone with him. He tried to molest her in the past."

He raced through the cars with Jennie on his heels. Near the end of the parking lot, Brad saw them. Chet was almost dragging her by the arm, and she kept saying, "Where is she?"

Brad stepped in front of Chet. "What's going on?"

Alice put out her hand. "Oh, Brad, it's Jennie."

"Jennie's right behind me. Did he tell you that she was hurt or something?"

Alice stared at him and then looked at Chet in amazement. "You made that up."

"No, I didn't."

Brad stepped close. "Get out of here. And don't ever bother Alice again or you'll hear from me."

"Who the hell do you think you are? Go away." Chet started to pull a revolver on them. Before he had a chance to point it, Brad, fit from army training, knocked it out of his hand and gave him a blow on the jaw that sent him sprawling.

"Jennie," he cried, "get Officer Carson out here. He's standing at the entrance."

Jennie ran off as Brad watched Chet, and Alice scrambled for the gun.

After hearing from the witnesses, Officer Carson led Chet away. "Menacing, threatening, pointing a gun…," he said.

Alice collapsed against Brad. "Oh, what a fool I am. He said Jennie needed me."

"It's all right, Alice." He put his arms around her. "He's a danger to society."

With his arm still around her shoulders, they strolled toward the dancing.

"Do you feel up to a spin around the floor? I'd hate for anyone to think you'd actually left with Chet."

Her heart lifted. As he swept her onto the floor, the tar-paper barrack became a grand ballroom, the lights gleaming chandeliers, and the music a symphony. When the dance ended, he escorted her to her chair, his arm about her waist, gently, intimately.

He asked her to dance again and again. They talked about the people they knew and the changes they had found in Juniper. At last he asked to see her home, and she agreed, stopping to tell Jennie as they left the celebration.

Alice was quiet on the way. "I apologize, Brad, for this morning," she finally said.

"OK, I accept your apology for treating me so badly this morning. Now when are you going to marry me?"

"Well, we have some things to talk about."

"So let's talk." Brad parked the car in front of her house.

She bit her lower lip. "I've found out some things about myself that I didn't know until I got home."

"And they are?"

"Well…" She gave him a pained look. "My parents are not my parents."

"What?"

"I mean they raised me, but my aunt Kate is really my mother."

"What?"

"And Grant Hunter is my father."

"What?"

She gestured helplessly. "It was a shock to me too. But it's something you have to know. I'm illegitimate."

Brad burst into laughter. "Oh, Alice. Do you really think it matters to me who your parents are?" He put his arms around her.

"And another thing," she said, leaning against him with relief and pleasure. "I want to go back to school and take some classes on the GI Bill."

"But so do I," Brad said with pleasure. "We can do it together."

"All right then." She snuggled against him. "Let's get married."

"I'm certainly willing. I don't have a ring yet, but I have a bracelet that I bought for you that day I went to The Dalles with Odette. I was thinking of you."

He pulled out a narrow, silver wristband inlaid with emerald-colored stones. "It's your color."

"It's beautiful." She clasped it around her wrist and admired it. "For this, I forgive you for shopping with Odette."

He chuckled. "Thank God. Now what's all this about Grant and your aunt?"

She held the bracelet up to observe it in the porch light. "People now know that I'm their daughter, but they think Grant and Kate were secretly married before Kate left for Wyoming. The story is they divorced, and he married another woman. He later divorced that woman when she moved to California."

"Do all his women leave him?" Brad deadpanned.

"Don't be funny. Now, as a potential member of my family, you've got to uphold the fiction for the sake of the younger girls as well as for Grant and Kate. The truth could taint all my family for life."

"I doubt that, but you can fill me in on the details of this later. Now I want to know how soon we can be married so that we can light out for college."

"I've already been admitted to college in Eugene."

He smiled with delight. "I applied from Bowman and was accepted too. So the last detail is the wedding. Can we go for a license Monday?"

She threw him a smile. "You are impatient, aren't you?"

"I don't see any other way in Juniper to get you into bed with me." He gave her a lustful look.

"Meet me Monday at Dr. Weber's office at noon, and we can go get a license at the courthouse."

"Perfect. Do you want to visit our relatives tomorrow? I'd like to have us see my folks, and your family if you like."

When he walked Alice to the door, Brad couldn't remember a more beautiful evening. As he gently kissed her good night, the silver moon smiled down at them, the summer sky studded with glittering stars.

* * *

The next morning, Brad went to see Grant at the food counter. "I guess I have you to thank for sending me off to the dance looking for Alice. We're applying for a marriage license Monday."

"Well, congratulations." Grant extended his hand.

Brad took it with enthusiasm, smiling. "I know it's customary to ask for the father's permission."

"She told you, I see." Grant gave him a steady look.

"Yes, as if it would make any difference to me. But I would have heard about it eventually anyway. My mother gave her version this morning at breakfast."

"Well…we want to save face if we can. As for permission, I don't think anyone gives a damn about such niceties these days. But, for the record, I couldn't have chosen a finer man myself. You might want to talk to John Bauer since he and Gloria raised her. I'm sure he thinks of her as his daughter."

"I plan to talk to him today."

Chapter 44

Alice and Brad visited Brad's parents to announce their engagement. The Mayfield family, including Steve, was pleased. Things could not be better, thought Mrs. Mayfield. Both boys are home and now a fine marriage with that lovely Alice Bauer.

Later Alice and Brad joined the Bauer family for dinner at Grant and Kate's house. This time, Jennie, taking a leaf from Alice, as well as her cafeteria training, prepared the meal: Hungarian goulash, summer vegetables, and apple cobbler.

Fred sniffed the air as he arrived—onions, mushrooms, and cinnamon. He headed for the kitchen. "I've been looking forward to seeing you all day," he said as he lifted the pot lid on the stove.

Jennie stared at him. "Are you talking to me or to the goulash?"

"Yes, I was." He playfully pulled her apron string loose as he left the room.

Brad pulled John aside to talk on the front porch. He asked the man if he had any objections to his marrying Alice. John smiled broadly and assured Brad that he did not. He'd be pleased to see them marry. Had Alice told him about her true parentage? What were their plans?

"We want to get married this week. We need to get to Eugene and find an apartment. I'll have to look for a part-time job."

Fred joined them, and the two airmen talked of planes and ignition systems and carburetors and instruments and maneuvers and flying missions.

John guessed that returning veterans would be swapping stories about the war for decades to come. Some horrors they would never discuss. He wandered into the house.

Gloria sat with Alice on the couch, examining the dresses in the Sears catalog. She would want to make Alice a new one. Linda and Marie lingered near, glancing at the pictures, excited about all the commotion.

Alice, flushed, seemed healthier than she had in some time. Jennie, along with Kate, bustled to and from the kitchen, getting steaming food on the table; Jennie seemed particularly happy this afternoon. John had no way of knowing that she had heard from Tom Hansen, who had decided to try college in Corvallis and hoped to see her there.

Emma and David Walker settled Davy and Nancy in their special high chairs for the meal. Did Emma's face look filled out, prettier than ever? John guessed a third child was on the way.

Grant, happy to be part of a family at last, played genial host, rounding up extra chairs and pulling out books for the little girls to look at.

John felt a great wave of happiness and contentment. His grown children, home after service to the country amid considerable danger, were preparing to leave the nest again. But this time they would be investing in their own futures. It was almost more than he could have wished for; they had survived the war intact and hopeful.

Excited about the news of the wedding, Kate served the meal with pleasure. "What college course are you planning?" she asked Alice.

"I want my four-year degree. Otherwise, I haven't decided. My nursing courses will fulfill some science requirements."

Grant said, "If you need a car to locate, please take mine."

"That's very good of you. We want to live near campus so we can walk."

"Still, you need to drive around to look at housing and get settled."

"We want to buy a car as soon as more of them come on the market," Brad said. This led to an animated discussion regarding the merits of the Ford versus the Chevrolet.

Fred crossed his arms. "Hope that Chevy doesn't give out on you. They're known more for looks than reliability."

"Who says?" Grant moved around the table, pouring coffee.

"Why, it's a well-known fact. That old flivver might not make it to Eugene at all."

"We'll chance it," Brad said. "How about you, Jennie? What are you studying?"

"I'm not sure yet, but Dad is lending us his Ford to move. I'm going to share an apartment with Fred, so long as he promises to keep his clothes picked up, does his share of the cooking, and cleans his own room. I'm not going to work around those model airplanes again."

Fred smiled good-naturedly as everyone laughed. "I don't make model airplanes anymore. I fly them."

"I can still work for a few weeks," Jennie told Grant.

"Good. We can use you. Yes, you young people get your degrees, and then get back here and look after the hotel and restaurant while Katherine and I visit Europe. By that time they might be ready for tourists over there."

"Won't that be wonderful, Kate?" Gloria asked.

Kate smiled. "It's something I've always dreamed about."

"But how am I going to finish the dresses for the wedding? There's no time." Gloria wrung her hands.

"Don't despair. The rest of us can do the cutting and the hemming."

"I'll make the wedding cake," Jennie said, passing the green beans. She considered herself an expert after her cafeteria experience.

"What do I get to do?" Linda asked.

"As a matter of fact, Linda, you're my best seamstress on the sewing machine. You'll be a big help with the dresses," Gloria told her. "I think she enjoys sewing more than any of the other girls," she said to the group.

"What about me?" asked Marie, the youngest.

"You get the best job of all," Alice said, slightly embarrassed by all the attention to her wedding. "You can serve the wedding cake."

"How about getting married in this house?" Grant asked. "It's bigger, and we would both be pleased."

"I could rig up some kind of an altar," John said.

"I'd like that." Alice smiled and sipped her coffee. She was a lucky woman. "And I'd like both my fathers to walk me to the altar."

Complete silence followed her remark. When they had all given it some thought, Gloria said, "That would be very appropriate." She took John's hand under the table and squeezed it. He squeezed it back to tell her that he was all right.

Grant's voice was hoarse. "I'm truly honored."

* * *

Author's Note

The towns of Juniper and Springdale are fictional as are all of the characters in this book, except for historical figures.

The events of World War II are well known, but I have taken some liberties with the training of flight nurses. They were trained at air bases in the United States, generally stayed together, and were stationed at special bases in England.

In order to keep my four nurses together, I have allowed my flight nurse to stay with her three friends.

Made in the USA
San Bernardino, CA
05 April 2014